Praise for
The Satin Sash

"Five stars! . . . [A] realistic love story a cut above the rest and well worth keeping on your bookshelf."
—Night Owl Romance

"Four and a half stars! There is plenty of sex in this book—hot, steaming, mouthwatering sex—but that is not all that keeps this book together. If you are looking for a well-written love story, then do not pass this one up."
—The Romance Readers Connection

"Plenty to like in this well-written book, including a sympathetic heroine and smokin'-hot sex!"
—*Romantic Times*

"The emotional impact the threesome has on their respective relationships brings a nice balance to the sizzling eroticism, making *The Satin Sash* an engaging tale you won't want to miss."   —Romance Reviews Today

The Feather

RED GARNIER

HEAT

HEAT

Published by New American Library,
a division of Penguin Group (USA) Inc.,
375 Hudson Street, New York, New York 10014, USA
Penguin Group (Canada), 90 Eglinton Avenue East, Suite 700, Toronto,
Ontario M4P 2Y3, Canada (a division of Pearson Penguin Canada Inc.)
Penguin Books Ltd., 80 Strand, London WC2R 0RL, England
Penguin Ireland, 25 St. Stephen's Green, Dublin 2,
Ireland (a division of Penguin Books Ltd.)
Penguin Group (Australia), 250 Camberwell Road, Camberwell,
Victoria 3124, Australia (a division of Pearson Australia Group Pty. Ltd.)
Penguin Books India Pvt. Ltd., 11 Community Centre,
Panchsheel Park, New Delhi - 110 017, India
Penguin Group (NZ), 67 Apollo Drive, Rosedale, North Shore 0632,
New Zealand (a division of Pearson New Zealand Ltd.)
Penguin Books (South Africa) (Pty.) Ltd., 24 Sturdee Avenue,
Rosebank, Johannesburg 2196, South Africa

Penguin Books Ltd., Registered Offices:
80 Strand, London WC2R 0RL, England

First published by Heat, an imprint of New American Library,
a division of Penguin Group (USA) Inc.

First Printing, June 2010
1   3   5   7   9   10   8   6   4   2

Copyright © Red Garnier, 2010
All rights reserved

HEAT is a trademark of Penguin Group (USA) Inc.

LIBRARY OF CONGRESS CATALOGING-IN-PUBLICATION DATA:
Garnier, Red.
The feather/Red Garnier.
p. cm.
ISBN 978-0-451-23006-5
I. Title
PS3607.A7655F43   2010
813'.6—dc22   2010006112

Printed in the United States of America

If destiny had wings, then—as lord of my own—

wouldn't I be entitled to its feathers?

Acknowledgments

A huge, heartfelt thank-you to Tracy Bernstein, who, as always, makes my books shine; to her assistant, Talia Platz, who gives new meaning to "fabulous"; and to the talented minds at New American Library, who made this book happen.

This book is dedicated to my TTS—all three of you know how much I love you.

The Feather

Chapter One

This had to stop.

As soon as she found herself, for the sixth night in a row, riding a cab toward Columbus Circle, Meredith knew this had to stop.

And yet here she was. Heart pounding. Hands fiddling with her hair, then sneaking under her cashmere coat to smooth out her skirt, her blouse. The day had dragged on—it had seemed interminable. She'd had to review some notes from accounting and go over her company's intellectual property rights and licensing to stay clear on what the big guys were offering. As an in-house counsel for E-Doll, the largest electronic doll software supplier, Meredith needed to understand every nuance of Inctel's acquisition offer.

For three weeks, she had been meeting with Inctel's team of corporate lawyers—the biggest sharks in the business—to write and revise the legal documents that would eventually bind the companies together. The deal was moving forward, though not at the speed Meredith would have liked, as three weeks was all it had taken to make her a little cuckoo over the unfairly gorgeous, infamous head of Inctel's team, James Hamilton.

Honest to god, that man was . . . *pow!* Just . . . *wham.* Out. Of. This. Universe. He was so attractive, so damned smart, it was just . . . wowing.

Meredith had *never* worked with someone so savvy. James knew the law inside and out. He was smart; he was calm; he was focused. He led the team to where he wanted it to go. He considered all possibilities, weighed the pros and cons of each, made sure both parties were happy, and the deal closed. James was . . . a genius. One day working with James Hamilton and Meredith remembered why, exactly, she loved corporate law so much.

Every day, their teams would meet to revise the contracts, jot down the required amendments, and discuss the tax and securities laws and how they would affect both corporations if and when they merged. During which time James would lean back in his chair, listen, smile that devastatingly slow smile of his, and ask questions in a voice that sent shivers to her toes. It took all her concentration to keep from fumbling around him— he was that good-looking, that *overpowering.* And late one evening, when James had finally dispatched everyone, Meredith jumped up to gather her things. But being one of only two women, and the one with more items scattered across the table, she'd been left behind. With James.

Who made her pulse race.

She'd been babbling nervously about the contract when James said, "Meredith?" She'd looked up to find him alarmingly close, his eyes smiling down at her. "Shut up." He'd said it softly, almost tenderly, before he slid a hand up the back of her head and kissed her. A knee-buckling, out-of-this-world kiss that was as shocking, as indescribable, as James.

And Meredith, who'd never, ever invited a man to her apartment, invited James. She knew what would happen. And she wanted what would happen with every ounce of her lonely, overworked being. They'd had such amazing sex; she'd done things with him she'd never seen even in movies. But when she'd woken up, he was gone. With no note, no farewell, no nothing. Her only consolation was that he couldn't—literally *could not*—take his eyes off her the following day. He'd rubbed his face, apologized to his colleagues—"I'm sorry. My concentration's shit today"—and then had dismissed them early when he couldn't seem to regain it. "Not you, Meredith." And Meredith had cocked an eyebrow, intending to act nonchalant—because maybe it was not too late to play hard to get?—but he said, "I'm sorry I left early."

"No, no, no, that's fine. I totally understand."

He'd nodded, clearly not very happy about something.

"I *am* sorry. This isn't a line."

"That's all right, James. I do mean that, too."

But that did not mean she wasn't hurt the next morning not to find him in her bed. What did he want from her? What did she want from *him*?

It was two a.m. by the time the other lawyers left the following day. Meredith seriously did not know why she hung back. Maybe because his shirt had been rumpled. His black hair with that hint of silver had been rumpled, too. He'd looked as tired as Meredith had felt. And she'd wanted to wrap her arms around him and cuddle. The fool. But when she'd forced her feet to move and was finally about to leave, he caught her hand and reeled her toward him, slow and easy, like a pro—until she ended up flush against him and inside the circle of his arms. "Stay."

"Oh no, James. I can't—"

His finger came up to quiet her. "You can stay." Then he slipped his elegant, long-fingered hands into her hair. "You can kiss me." He took her lips, then murmured, "You can suck me."

She smiled as he nibbled. "Suck what?"

And when he showed her the yummy thing he wanted her to suck, something started that she didn't quite know how to name. An affair? Because surely that was all she could hope for. God, who was she kidding?

She was hoping for so much more. She wanted more of that decadent, wild-animal sex they'd had that night, more of James telling her what to do and when to do it. . . . God, the way he'd made her drink him up and then ordered her to sit on it and ride it . . . Damn, why wasn't the line of cars moving?

Gathering her purse, she pushed open the back door. "I'll get out here," she told the cab driver, quickly slipping him a bill. Traffic was slow moving today; it seemed everything was conspiring to keep her from James—the new exhibit at the Museum of Natural History, which had all the streets nearby in a jam; her boss, who'd kept her in his office, interrogating her about the latest on the deal.

Instantly hit by the chilly March air, Meredith tucked her purse under her arm, stuck her hands in her pockets, burrowed deeper into her coat, and took off down the sidewalk. The park was quiet except for noises from the skaters in Wollman Rink and the occasional conversations of those who passed. Her eyes were on the building looming ahead. The top floor was illuminated. He was home.

She wanted to fling off her heels and run. She wanted to charge in there and have him tear off her panties like he had yesterday and—oh, god, she was obsessed. *Obsessed*. It might not have been worrisome if she were a besotted girl just out of high school, but Meredith was no virgin teenager. Passion and love and all that bull was not . . . *real.* . . . Was not . . . not for people like *her.* This thing with James . . .

There seemed to be a way around every law in the book. Even gravity got a decent fight from the plastic surgeons. But the law of attraction—there was no going around that one. There was no stopping the loud, anxious thundering of her heart when James stepped into a room. No controlling the wave of heat that almost swallowed her like a tide whenever his eyes sought hers across a room. There was no helping herself, no lifesaver, no hope—*nothing* to keep her from crazily, stupidly wanting to take that plunge, that lethal free fall, that reckless ticket to a place where nothing mattered but James's mouth on hers, James's hands on her, James's hungry body taking and taking and *taking* hers. . . .

She stepped into the marble lobby, greeting the men behind the granite counter with a tremulous smile. The attendant waved her into an open elevator, as though she was expected now. As though she were James's . . . something. James's someone.

Which she was not.

She was just a one-night stand. More precisely, a series of one-night stands.

She felt the elevator's slow ascent; watched the LED numbers climbing. And her nerves sang inside her, jumping with the knowledge that it would be minutes, *seconds,* to see James. Hamilton. God.

The elevator doors rolled open on the penthouse,

revealing James—six foot two inches of tall, dark, and devastating—walking straight toward her, speaking into a headset. Meredith took three steps inside, offering him an apologetic smile, like, *Hey, sorry for interrupting*, and her stomach moved when he smiled back. His hands squeezed her shoulders in a somewhat proprietary way as he helped her take off her coat. And he did all this without missing a beat in conversation. James worked like he *loved* his work, and for the past three weeks, Meredith had watched him work with a combination of awe and amazement. James Hamilton's passion for the law would inspire even the most jaded lawyer.

Meredith let him guide her toward the modern sitting area by the limestone fireplace, slowly taking a seat while he paced around and went on with his call. He was in sleek black slacks and a button-down shirt, undone at the top, rolled up to his elbows, wrinkled at the small of his back just above his belt. He was so sexy.

And Meredith had the perfect excuse prepared. *Oops, I'm such a case, I left my scarf here last night.* Okay, it wasn't the perfect excuse, but at least it was better than *James, I'm a little bit in love with you, and please, oh, please can you touch me like you did last night? Just have sex with me and I'll be out the door before you even realize!*

He poured her a drink from the wood-and-chrome bar, then brought it to her, his silver gray eyes sparkling down at her as he continued speaking. " . . . Statutory law, we could . . ." He turned away to finish and, after taking an absentminded sip, Meredith stared down at the glass. Vodka, soda, and ice, with a lime wedge on top.

He remembered.

Meredith dared not dwell on what that meant. Hamilton was an intelligent man, self-possessed, in control. He would remember *anything*, even the most inconsequential fact, such as what Meredith had drunk the last time he'd offered.

He commanded the space around him—and it was a large space. He had an entire wall of Warhols next to an entire wall made of glass overlooking the park. Both were mesmerizing. One was dotted with city lights; the other with artwork. He had two Maos. A large Elizabeth Taylor. He had a flying Mickey Mouse—for some childish reason, Meredith liked that one. And James moved around the polished marble floors with the ease of an animal of prey. He was so striking. The combination of his every feature was virile in a dark, forbidden way. He had the thoughtful brow, the bronze skin, and stubborn jaw of a bad boy, but his eyes were dark silver rather than brown. Then there was that rumbling voice and the crooked smile that crinkled his eyes, and the presence that exuded sophistication and male appeal. When he slid a hand into his pocket, braced his feet apart, and smiled at you, you could just *die* from lust.

As she distractedly flipped through an art book from the stack atop the coffee table, James, from a few feet away, covered the headset and said, "Meredith?" His eyes were so beautiful to look at. "You hungry?"

A deep tightening inside her belly brutally reminded her of her craving. She could still feel his mouth on her. Plump, pink, pliant lips that hardened when his eyes did and were hot and relentless when they loved her. She was hungry for that mouth, the way he'd dragged it all over her body last night, the way he'd buried it—

Tearing her eyes off his tanned, chiseled face, she took a deep inhalation, set the book back with the rest, and shook her head. If James noticed her nerves, he didn't show it. He continued moving, speaking, winding around the stainless-steel kitchen. Occasionally he popped an almond or something similar into his mouth, giving her the impression that he usually had dinner while pacing and on the telephone. While he did this, Meredith began to fidget with the buttons of her jacket. The pearls on her neck. Pull her left earring.

Then, when he said, "All right, once I've got this," in a dismissive way that told her he was wrapping up, he paused and covered the headset microphone once more. "Meredith?" He cocked an eyebrow like he did when he was being dead serious. "Get in my bed, sweetheart. I'm almost through."

She was so shocked that her reasons for being here were so obvious that she was about to blurt out something like, "Oh, no, James. I'm just here for my scarf. Thank you," but she bit the inside of her cheek to keep from speaking. She was thirty, and he was thirty-six. They were two consenting adults and . . . they wanted each other. Meredith assumed James had wanted many women in his life, but Meredith had never even dreamed of wanting a man the way she wanted James Hamilton.

James Hamilton—who took off his Armani and had hard, loud sex with her while he whispered soft, wicked words to her.

His room was down the hall—a room for a male, with sparse furniture, dark wood, and walls done in an earthy sand color. A black-and-white photograph of a lonely, crooked tree hung above his bed. A black silk duvet stretched over the mattress; the bed was always perfectly made when she came. Sometimes she wondered whether James didn't bother to pull the covers back when he slept alone.

Meredith set her shoes down on the left side of the bed, folded the duvet to the foot of the bed, and, while listening to the deep, resonant timbre of his voice coming from the living room, began to undress.

Once she'd placed her jacket, skirt, and blouse atop the chair, she wondered whether to leave on her panties for him to tear, her bra for him to nibble; then she was so wet, she just wanted James Hamilton not to do anything but hold her still and plunge inside her. She stripped completely.

Goose bumps rose along her naked flesh as she slipped into the bed and pulled the covers up to her shoulders. His sheets were stark white and deliciously soft, a blend of cotton and silk. They felt cool against her skin, and they shimmered when she moved restlessly within them.

She'd been marveling over their texture when she realized the penthouse had fallen silent. He'd hung up.

Resting her head on a pillow, she tried to appear lazy or even sleepy while she kept her eyes fixed on the door. *Oh, James, James, what am I doing here?* She was lava under the sheets, had an urge to squirm and move and rock herself. The way he'd taken her last night . . . Meredith had never felt so sexy. So desired. He'd pushed inside her and groaned as he started coming. The thought that she could make him so hot as to come within seconds had proved to be all she needed to follow him.

When he filled the doorway with his broad shoulders and paused, his hands in his pockets, his lips slowly curled into a dazzling smile. "Hello," he said quietly.

Meredith's body was screaming. But she kept it from showing, even managed to sit up slightly and clutch the sheet to her chin, her manner aloof. "Hi, James."

He stared, and it seemed unholy that there could be such awareness, such consciousness, in one gaze. The black of his enlarged pupils almost swallowed the metal-colored gray, and lust lurked like a prowling panther in their depths.

Her heart thundered. "James?"

He flicked open a shirt button.

Aching need.

It tightened her throat . . . her tummy . . . her sex.

"Yes, Meredith?"

Her pussy clenched. Her smile shook. Her voice dropped to a puny whisper. "I'm utterly naked in your bed."

He parted his shirt and shrugged the fabric off his broad shoulders. Flat, hard inches of bronzed, rippling muscles were revealed. His voice was a terse murmur, thick as the shaft unapologetically straining his slacks. "As you should be, Meredith."

Flutters. "Was this what you had in mind"—she shrugged—"when you told me to climb in here?"

His belt and slacks dropped to the floor, and her heart almost popped with excitement.

"Part of it," he said. "Yes."

God, what a body. Mean. Delicious. Shamelessly addictive. This was what she wanted from him. *This.*

Muscles stretched taut across his torso. Snug white cotton briefs rode low over his narrow hips, and the fabric seemed ready to be ripped open by his erection. A long, pink, beautiful cock. Instrument of pleasure. Of her obsession. His legs were thick and long, and the thighs bulged as he kicked off his pants.

In silence, he seduced her eyes. The breasts God gave her throbbed for this man. Her nipples burned for his mouth. He made her feel as if a powerful cyclone were sweeping her off the ground, and she both feared and loved him for it. This would have to end soon. Nothing this good lasted long. Nothing real could possibly be this good.

"What was the other part about?" she mused, attempting to veer back into the conversation.

"This," he said as he freed himself, cock slapping against his stomach, his voice plunging deeper, "inside you."

Smiling at this, she bit her lip and surveyed his erection, the lance thrusting out prominently, the sac underneath heavy.

No wonder. No wonder she felt so full when he was in her. No wonder she was achingly empty when he wasn't.

"James," she said, because that was all she could think, all she could say.

He came forward, gray eyes hot, proprietary, *intense*. "Meredith."

Chapter Two

~~~

$\mathcal{S}$he fascinated him.

Exhilarated, infatuated, excited him.

At the sight of her tucked under his sheets, every cell, atom, fiber, nerve, and muscle in his body vibrated. With need. With heat. With urgency.

For thirty-six years, James Hamilton had been known as a restrained, self-possessed man, but when it came to Meredith, his rioting emotions were as tamable as a deadly tornado.

Tracking his every move, Meredith sighed when he joined her in bed. He was ready to worship her, craved her spirited cries of ecstasy as his hands craved touching her.

He needed her *now*. Had to have his hands on her in the next minute. Wanted her nipples in his mouth this instant.

In a voice so low it sounded unnatural, he met her

sparkling blue gaze and murmured, "I can't stop thinking about you."

She sucked in a breath.

He wanted to be closer. The mattress squeaked under his weight as he slid to the center. His dick ached when she, too, squirmed closer, her body so warm, so female. "I think of you, too," she said.

Her hair spread across his pillow, and her eyes, shining with lust, were barely open when they fixed on his face.

His gut clenched, a feeling that came when he saw her. Had anyone ever gazed at him the way she was doing right now? This minute, in his bed?

He set a lingering kiss on her smooth forehead. "I know."

He could not resist ducking his head, opening his mouth, and suckling her smooth, bare shoulder. Hungry, he licked her skin, then swirled a path up her throat and gave the sheets a tug.

"If you want me to give you what you came for, you're going to have to let me see." His words were muffled against her skin as he uncovered her. "God, look at you, Sinclair. . . ."

Her breasts were two perfect globes, with large, beautifully pink areoles, puckered up by the time his eyes reached them.

He lifted his free hand and scraped a thumb across a taut pink peak. "Your nipples are hard. Do they hurt?"

Her chest rose and fell with each breath. "Yes."

His thumb made another slow pass. Her nipple sprang up, longer and darker after he'd stroked it. "Do they want my mouth? My tongue? My teeth?"

She swallowed thickly and cupped the lush globes in her little hands. "They ache. For you."

The words were like a fist around his cum-laden balls. "Squeeze them."

She did. Her teeth came down on her lower lip as she bit back a sharp cry. He almost barked out from the pleasure that gave him.

His blood roared in his ears. His voice plunged even deeper. "Do they still ache, Meredith?"

Her eyes were heavy lidded, fluttering to stay open. "Yes."

"Squeeze them again. Harder. Tell me why they still ache."

"They ache because . . ." Her hips rolled instinctively. Her fingers clenched her flesh. Her breath seemed to tear past her quivering lips. "Your hands are bigger and stronger. I just know it's not you."

He stared into her hazy blue eyes, seized her wrists, and forced her hands down at her sides. "Stop."

"Touch me, James."

He gazed down at her lovely, upturned face, the lustrous fair skin, the red-tipped lashes resting against her high cheekbones. His chest cramped, and he ran the back of his fingers down her cheek. "I will lick you,

Meredith. I will suck you hard into my mouth and I will kiss you, your lips, your breasts . . . your sweet little cunt."

He kissed one breast tip, then engulfed the nipple with his entire mouth. He used his tongue, his teeth, giving strong, greedy pulls that had her bucking up to his mouth, while his hands fondled and squeezed beneath him.

The other breast followed. Sweet. Hard, tight nipple. Getting a good, hard fuck from his tongue and teeth. Her hands flew to clasp the back of his head and hold him to her, but there was no need. He could suck her breasts all day, by god. He loved the stab and bump of those aroused little beads.

Her gasps rang in his ear. When he drew back, chest heaving, he could barely hear his voice through the roar of his drumming pulse. "Open your legs."

She lifted her arm and stroked a shaky finger along his jaw, dazed. "James."

The muscles of his face bunched. He was as close to desperation as he'd ever been. "Open your legs. Now."

In the quiet of the room, he could hear her start to breathe faster. She was panting violently by the time she spread her thighs apart. So was he.

Jesus Christ, it hurt to look at her.

His eyes watered as he stared at the valley of curls between her legs, the glistening pink flesh he wanted to nibble. He groaned and went searching for something to lick. "What a sexy pussy." He squeezed the firm flesh of her breasts with his hands and suckled her neck. "Wet. Delicious. Pussy." He sank into the urge to gently bite the skin at the base of her throat, and tugged with his teeth. "I want to bite that sweet little pussy like this."

She shuddered. He shuddered, too, felt dizzied with her scent, the sounds she made, the way she tasted. His cock throbbed, demanding satisfaction.

They'd been engaged in foreplay all day. All. Day.

Meredith, I'm very interested in your suggestion on the . . .

James, this clause is brilliant; you really dotted all the i's here. . . .

Of course, working with someone like you, Meredith, it's naturally easy to . . .

James, your observations on the proposed stock offering are absolutely spot-on. I really love how you . . .

He'd compliment; she'd compliment. They would smile. And James's guts would be twisted in a knot, his balls in a painful throb. For what James really wanted to say, as he bent over her shoulder and took those impulsive whiffs of her hair, was *I want you. . . . I count the hours until I can be buried balls deep inside of you. . . . I need to hear you screaming my name, feel you creaming all around my cock and clawing my back again. . . .*

He'd spent the afternoon in pain. Now the luscious feel of her was torment. Agony. Nirvana.

Inhaling her fragrance, he nuzzled her face with his

and curled his hands to get two handfuls of soft, silky auburn hair. He forced her to meet his burning gaze.

"There isn't a word," he murmured, "not one word to describe what I want to do to you, Meredith." He ducked and dragged his tongue across her lips until she parted them on a gasp. "No word dirty enough, wild enough, for what I want to do to you."

"James," she moaned softly, and the way she uttered his name catapulted his need to alarming levels.

"Tell me." He brushed her lips with his, and the sudden stroke of her velvety tongue tore a groan from his throat. "God, tell me you want me."

"I want you."

He slanted his head with a strangled sound. He took her mouth, roughly cupping her tight, round bottom and dragging her closer, letting her feel the painful length of his erection. He pushed his tongue into her mouth and they moaned in unison.

She looped her arms around his neck and played with his hair, meeting his every thrust, every bite, every harsh tug.

"I want you, too, Meredith. I want you, too."

"Oh, god, I need this," she gasped as her mouth trailed down his neck and bare torso, quick and hungry. No, voracious. James felt dizzy as she peppered warm, moist kisses on his heated flesh and stroked her fingers down his abdomen. He felt . . .

Don't think about it, Hamilton.

He yanked her back up before he lost it, then groaned against her neck. "All those revisions you asked for today," he muttered, and fondled her soft breast, kneading it with his fingers. "Just you planning to keep me around for a while, hmm?"

"No, no, I'm looking out for . . ."

He nuzzled her neck and tweaked a tightened nipple, making her vault up for more. "Admit it." His tongue swirled over her delicate throat. "You want me longer; you want to play with me. So let's play now, hmm? Let's play . . . who comes first." He nipped her ear, and through a damp, long flick of his tongue, whispered, "I vote Meredith."

Her fingers slid to tantalize his sac, cupping his testicles. Jolts of pleasure speared up his straining cock.

"Hmm. God, no, baby. No. Ladies first." His voice became guttural, barely intelligible even to his own ears as he stilled her hand. "Lie back for me."

When she hesitated, he urged her down.

"Lie back, Meredith."

She obeyed, her hair spreading out across the pillow. Her hands made fists over the sheets. "What are you . . . what are you doing?"

He stroked the creamy mounds of her breasts. "Shh."

She hissed through her teeth. Invigorated, he flicked his tongue over and over the taut peak of one breast, felt it tighten and rise for him. His blood stormed inside him as he stroked her entry until her hot, slick arousal coated the length of his fingers.

He felt starved. As though he'd never again get to taste her.

Wanted to do a thousand things to her. Had already proven to himself he could not stay away from this, from her. Was beginning to believe these breasts . . . beautiful, soft breasts . . . these nipples, Christ, so puckered and sweet . . . this pussy . . . god, *yes* . . . had been made for his mouth, this very woman made for *his* pleasure . . .

Watching her face, he circled his thumb over the hard nub of her clit and plunged two fingers into her wet pussy, screwing them in with such force, her head fell back on a strangled sob. "Ohh," she said, a breathless exclamation, "this is too much. I can't. . . . This is . . . ."

"You're a river, Meredith. A river. Just for me."

She moaned in delirium, her hips instinctively dancing to his hand. He reached under her and enveloped one plump buttock in his grasp. He rubbed, kneaded, palmed her. And, fuck, her skin was so fevered, it singed him. Stroking her luscious cheek with his hand, he brought his mouth to her heat. She smelled so damned good. He'd never eaten her climax before. He was shaking, wanting—hell, *starving*.

Her hips pitched upward and a sound tore from her chest as he gave a deep, satiny lick of his tongue at the very seam of her pussy lips. "Come in my mouth." Her back rose off the bed, her pelvis rubbing against his feasting mouth. She sobbed out his name, and he trembled. She was made for a man. For sex. For James.

He speared his tongue into her scorching channel, lapping the tangy nectar of her juices with the realization that he'd never wanted to devour a sweet little pussy like this. "Come. I'm very hungry for you."

He hadn't predicted how exhilarating tasting her orgasm would be, but the moment she started coming, a pool of her heat gushed down his throat, and his gut twisted. His eyes rolled back in his head, and he shuddered as he licked, kissed, ate her, fucking her cunt with his tongue. Meredith convulsed under him, her body shimmying on the bed. Her cries were so sexy; when they faded, his ears rang for more.

Aftershocks feathered through her. Settling above her, James snagged her wrists and pinned her arms over her head, nestling his aching cock in the cradle of her thighs. He gazed down at her, her awesome blue eyes barely open. A soft, dazed smile appeared on her face. The thought of someone seeing her like this . . . no. It bothered him, but it shouldn't. Shouldn't.

He took her lips in a possessive kiss and wedged his knee between her legs, forcing her thighs apart. "You want me," he rasped, reaching between their bodies.

"Yes."

He played with her moistened sex, but suddenly he needed to hear more—more than her gasps. More. "Say this pussy wants me. It wants my cock. All of it."

"Please. Now. Do it, James."

Pleasure whipped through him at the evidence of her urgency, and on impulse he pulled her knees apart and buried his face between her legs and stabbed his tongue into her cunt for one last taste.

She screamed, and he was so worked up and sweaty that he wanted to yell, as well. But he held back and came up to stick that same tongue down her throat. "Taste that—how sweet you are, how hard you came for me."

She framed his face between her hands and rubbed her breasts against his chest, her mouth moving across his lips, his jaw, his chin. Ecstasy surged through him, clenching his muscles, whipping him into a firestorm of need.

He clutched her face more wildly than she did. "I want your pussy." He flattened his tongue against her jaw and dragged it all across her cheek. "I want it all around me, gripping my cock until we pass out from fucking."

His words brought a slight rotation of her hips and a string of moisture to her turgid pussy lips, and Meredith—hot, sweaty, wanton Meredith—watched with heavy lashes as he grabbed a condom from the nightstand and rolled it on the cock. And it was *the* cock; he'd never been so fucking fat, ten fucking inches long. He wanted all of that inside her.

As he spread his body over hers, she reached out and

wrapped herself around him, trembling, supple, sliding her tongue into his ear as her limbs coiled around his body. "Fuck me."

Past gentleness, past thinking, he pulled her arms up over her head and held them in one hand, working his hips between her legs, opening her up as she rocked in welcome. His heart beat so hard, he thought he'd crack a rib, and his pulse skyrocketed when he found her center, laced his fingers through hers, and thrust. He barked with pleasure. *Christ Jesus God.* Christ Jesus God!

"Yes," he said through gritted teeth, and dropped his head to scrape his jaw across her shoulders, her neck, languidly dragging his mouth along the tendons of her throat as he started a slow, torturous rhythm. She was so slick, tight as a fist around his driving dick, her nails biting into the backs of his hands as he pumped.

Sweat beaded his forehead; he could feel it as her breath gushed across the side of his face.

"Can you work your legs higher?" he asked.

She pulled them up to the small of his back and locked her ankles, and when he plunged into her sheath again, she pitched her hips upward. He buried himself up to the balls.

His muscles—his biceps, his abdomen, his ass— spasmed. "Yes, Christ, yes."

Her brilliant half-mast eyes clawed into his soul, and if possible, she went even wilder with his hands pinioning hers. "Harder," she gasped, surging up to get that little mouth on him anywhere she could. "Fuck me like you mean it."

He laughed darkly. "Oh, I mean it."

He loosed her hands, grabbed her hair in one fist, and yanked her head back until her neck arched. She hissed a breath, but he kept her pinned there so he could nip her throat as he rode her, her fevered body writhing under his as he fucked and fucked and fucked her. Like he meant it. Hell, did he ever.

She was teeth-grindingly snug and so damned hot, whipping him into a firestorm with the whimpers that tore out of her at each plunge of his cock. Her choppy sounds turned into drawn-out moans that pulsed inside his balls as they clapped against her body.

"That's it." He tongued her ear, diving sloppily into the crevice, his cock buried to the hilt again and again. "That's it. Go for it. Go for it, or I will."

She raked her nails down his back so hard, he was sure she'd scraped off skin. And when she grabbed his ass and her fingertips bit into his flexing muscles, yanking him closer, swallowing more of his cock, his eyes rolled to the back of his head.

The pace mounted into a frenzy of slapping flesh, groans, and the slick, wet sounds of sliding flesh. He felt every clench of her walls, every inch of him sliding inside her. Longing, desire, heat, completion. He felt that in spades as he penetrated. "Too." He thrust with a groan. "Damned." Harder. Deeper. His ass clenched in her hands. "Good."

She shattered. She just shattered. Clawing at the bunched-up muscles on his back, tucking her head under his chin, and gasping against his neck as she came *apart* for him.

He shut his eyes and groaned at the hot moistness of her mouth on his skin, her teeth biting the top of his shoulder. He'd never been held on to so hard, or had his name whispered in such a prayerlike way. Or maybe he hadn't bothered to notice things like these before.

He encircled her waist with his arms and cradled her body as dozens of tremors racked through her. Her explosion lasted for minutes, it seemed, and through the tight little clenches her cunt gave, James dropped his head to her cushiony chest, rammed his hips upward, and in a guttural sound of pleasure, said her name.

His orgasm barreled through his being, tearing a yell from his throat as his body bucked with pleasure over hers.

Minutes later, propped on his elbows, James surveyed the pink-cheeked face gazing up at his in wonder, feeling awed, humbled, so damned content.

Beneath him, Meredith looked like he wanted her to look always: supple, well loved, happy, and . . . with those sultry blue eyes staring at him as if he'd cut hundreds of pieces from a single diamond and hung them up in the sky for her.

He had an urge to wipe the sweat from her brow. He wanted to kiss places he hadn't thought to kiss before—

the back of her ear, the tiny pulse at her temple, the shadowed dent at her collarbone. But Meredith ducked her head and untangled her body from his.

He could tell she was blushing.

"All right, Meredith?"

"Wonderful." She would not look at him, her hands flying over her head to comb down her hair.

James wanted to help her smooth out the knots at its tips, but instead watched her fidget in the puzzled, admiring way a man watches a woman fix herself.

A few minutes later, he strode into the bathroom to clean up, and emerged to find her dressed in one of those business suits she wore: skirt to her knees, fitted jacket, plain blouse underneath.

Had she been any other woman, James would have thanked her for leaving before her stay became unwelcome. But the fact that she wanted to leave before her stay became even *remotely* unwelcome made him frown.

He wanted her, sated and sleepy-eyed, curling at his side and telling him things, as she had the first night at her apartment. She hadn't volunteered anything else about herself since. Not about Christmases with her family in Atlanta or about the hell of law school. She'd slapped shut that part of herself to him, and he cursed himself for not explaining his reasons for leaving her that first night. *Fuck.*

"It's late," he said, gently taking her elbow and steering her back to his bed. "Stay here until morning."

But there was no trace—not even a hint—of the siren he'd just had in bed as Meredith pried her arm free and tucked her hair behind her ear. "I'm fine. I really must get going. I've got an eight o'clock, and I need to go over my notes."

His frown deepened. Meredith denying him something he wanted pricked at him big time. "You have an eight o'clock?"

She flicked some invisible speck of dust off the collar of her jacket, her smile crooked. "You're not the only one with eight o'clocks, James."

James clamped his lips together, noting the slant of her chin and the I'm-a-modern-woman-and-I'll-do-what-I-want set to her shoulders. In fact, *come to think of it*, her expression sort of said *Screw you. I'm getting my way no matter what you do.* He sighed. "Give me a minute, all right? I'll see you home."

Was it strange that he would want the cuddling part after the sex? That he, rather than she, felt robbed of it now that she wanted to go?

The more he touched her, the more it became difficult for him to leave—or to let her go. Every inch of him, every instinct, screamed at him to *get. The. Woman.*

While he rummaged in his closet and fumbled for a clear idea of how, exactly, to handle an affair with a woman like Meredith, James plunged his legs into the first slacks he could find and shoved his arms into the shirt he'd tossed aside earlier. But when he came back into his bedroom, Meredith was gone.

She was late.

Little could compare to the total awkwardness of stumbling into a room packed with lawyers—all in their seats, all staring at you. Unwittingly, Meredith's eyes just sort of found those striking gray ones she'd dreamed about—and her breath left her in one swoop.

James was totally, royally pissed.

Meredith's knees almost buckled as she forced her legs to carry her to her seat. The look in his eyes was sharp as an ice pick. And as a calm, confident man who clearly did *not* like to be pissed, he greeted her with silence.

But in her mind—in her traitorous, besotted mind— she heard his voice, felt him move inside her, remembered him urging her on, his body strained above hers, his words. *Say this pussy wants me.*

Pulling herself together before her blush became reason to blush even more, she smiled brightly as she opened the leather folder with her name on it. "James," she told the first page, then lifted her head and smiled in general. "Everyone. Good morning. Sorry I'm late."

Some nodded; others returned the greeting. They all went back to their reading. She might have done the same if James's chair hadn't given an alarming creak. His footsteps were muffled by the carpet, but she still sensed them going around behind her, and her heart contracted in dread.

He planted a hand over the new contract stipulations, his musky, intoxicating cologne seeping into her lungs as he bent to whisper, "Don't ever, ever, walk out on me again."

His voice went through her like a bolt of lightning. His dominant tone brought out the most shameful reaction: her blood heated, her nipples poked up beneath her bra, and her pussy felt a jolt.

Angry sex.

Oh god, *angry sex* with James. Right here in the boardroom. She could tell him where he could shove his stupid, arrogant orders, and he could furiously stick his tongue down her throat to quiet her and— No.

Really. No.

She swallowed.

With his breath coming from somewhere close, so close, behind her, she could feel eyes on the top of her head. Not James's. But prying eyes. Wary eyes. Eyes of people who would later talk at the copy machines, in the restrooms, in the garage. She said, very softly, "I understand, James."

Inch by inch, and as though it was painful to move, he straightened, and out loud said, "We've got a hundred-twenty-page contract in our hands, Meredith. Hope-fully, if you like what you read, we'll close."

Her stomach pulled in all kinds of directions, but Meredith smiled tightly and skipped the index. "Of course."

James took his seat across from hers, steepled his fingers before his face, and watched her.

She had no idea how he did that.

How he had her in a mass of aching, throbbing, painful sexual awareness with that single heated look. A look so sharp and intense, it fairly tweaked her sensitive nipples, made every moist part of her ping and clench and *remember.*

God, and he expected her to read? Giving up on the words, she rose to fix herself coffee. Unable to stifle the impulse to taunt him, she said, "I like your tie, James. It's very . . . black."

Elbow resting on the armrest, he twirled a pen between his fingers. "Thank you, Meredith."

Obviously, a compliment from him would not be forthcoming.

Hiding her disappointment with a smile, she puttered around at the small coffee-service cart and reached for a plastic spoon.

"That's not sugar, Meredith."

She glanced at Gregory Spears, one of the youngest lawyers on the team. "Pardon?"

He gestured at the container in her hand. "That's

salt." Meredith stared down at her coffee, noted the amused twitch of James's lips, and promptly set down the salt. And took a sip.

She'd rather they think she liked her coffee with salt—*eww*—than that she'd been absentminded because some dark-haired, silver-eyed lawyer was staring at her.

When all six people continued to stare, rather dubiously, too, she stalked across the carpeted space. "If you'll give me a few hours to go over this in the privacy of my office . . . Meet me here after lunch?" she asked in her most businesslike tone. She gathered her files and tucked them under her arm. "James? Is that all right?"

He slapped his copy shut. "As you wish, Meredith."

"I appreciate it." She shoved the glass doors with her hips, and added brightly, "I'll see you after lunch, then."

Only when she was safely ensconced in her office did Meredith plop down behind her desk, put her face in her hands, and groan.

Her life was falling apart at the seams. Her nerves had been on high alert from just knowing a certain Hamilton was in the same zip code. And she'd had zero rest the previous night.

The sex had been so intense—his mouth hot, his hands hot, his words so damned hot—she'd freaked out afterward; she just couldn't leave soon enough.

What in the hell was she doing? How healthy could

this obsession with him be? Meredith was usually so cautious; she didn't know this alien nympho who'd taken over her body. This constant state of arousal was infuriating and not very conducive to work. And yet a tiny part of her—the reckless part, not the sensible one—painfully pointed out, *Who cares about self-preservation if you'll never again get to feel* this?

This whopping, toe-curling, nerve-racking, mind-boggling wanting that made her feel so . . . alive!

James Hamilton and all the suppressed feelings he made flourish had toppled down all of her erected walls, and, god, he made her want to feel so much. Feel everything. Her heart was suddenly out of its trap and was fairly screaming *yes* to the dark, sinful invitation to disaster that was James Hamilton.

Even when he was pissed with her, her tummy was knotted with wanting him. She knew she might have acted childish in his eyes, storming in there for a fuck and leaving him without a good-bye. *That is so not done, Meredith.*

She kept running to him and then away before he could reject her. *Why?*

"May I come in?"

The sudden question was preceded by two taps on the door and followed by the appearance of James Hamilton. Black suit, black tie, no smile. All perfect. Her office shrunk two sizes on the spot.

Meredith stiffened in her chair, then frowned at her

computer as though she'd been riveted by some e-mail or file on it. "James. What a surprise."

He shut the door behind him with a *click*. And her heart went *thud. Thud, thud, thud.*

Suddenly, his bold, sophisticated presence made her inhumanly aware of everything *un*sophisticated about her office: the corkboard haphazardly hung on the wall behind her, the silk roses in the glass vase on the corner of her desk—roses that had never seemed so fake before.

He could have been Bond—*James* Bond—and she the silly Miss Moneypenny.

Unaware of her distress, James stuck his fingers into the pockets of his pants and crossed the small space to stare thoughtfully out the window. Meredith's tenth-floor office had a very uninteresting view of the back alley. No one had ever stared so long at it before.

When silence had reigned for minutes, Meredith brought her hands up to the keyboard, so that if he turned, she could busily type something. He didn't glance at her, though. He braced a hand on the window frame above him, while the other stretched the material of his pants as he fisted it in his pocket.

"You didn't let me drive you home."

His voice throbbed, so thick and so unlike him that a ball of regret plummeted to her stomach.

She swallowed painfully, feeling foolish. Like the coward she was.

"Meredith . . . I don't say anything I don't mean—"

He cut himself off. His thumb tapped in his pocket in what had to be the first sign of restlessness she'd ever seen from him. "When I asked you to stay, I wanted you to."

Meredith hadn't noticed she was twirling the phone cord until she had to untangle her finger. "I'm sorry. I belatedly realized how inappropriate it was of me to stop by uninvited."

"Did I give you the impression you weren't welcome?" he asked quietly.

The bed creaked in her ears. Her moans echoed, his soul-melting voice uttering sexual commands in her ear. She shivered.

"No. No, you didn't," she admitted, noting he seemed to have forced his thumb to be still. "But I considered how neither of us wants any complications, and I thought it best to leave. I hate to inconvenience you."

"Christ." He laughed—not a happy laugh—and shook his head. "You don't. Inconvenience." He came over in three determined strides. "Haven't you read between the lines yet?"

"I'd need a loupe to read one of yours," she said, smiling. She fell solemn when he bent over the desk, his expression serious.

His nostrils flared. Silver eyes that were gripping in their intensity coasted across her features, making her breath quicken. With one tanned hand flat on the leather-topped surface, the other reached out and . . . and . . . felt so good as it glided . . . over her cheekbones . . . her lips. His voice, when he spoke, was deep and thick, and the most erotic thing she'd ever heard. "Spend the night with me."

Her womb constricted, gripping tight with need. While muscles that needed him rippled with awareness, Meredith tucked her face into his warm, dry palm, unconsciously seeking his caresses. With his thumb, he brushed her skin up to her cheekbone, then ran his knuckles up and down before his thumb returned.

"Will you come to me tonight?"

What kind of things did a woman wear and buy and say and do to drive James Hamilton crazy? Meredith would like to know. Because inside, her mind was a whirl, her body not even hers anymore, and she felt so alone. . . . She feared only *she* was in this turmoil and he was just calm, confident, sexy. . . .

They were enclosed in her office, but they were whispering like misbehaving children hiding in a closet so they wouldn't be caught. Meredith could feel their hot, intimate whispers running over her bones like ribbons. Her voice was breathy and soft, and her head fell forward as she asked, "Do you want me to?"

His thumbs took ages to trace the contour of her lips, to slide sinuously between them. "I'm asking you to."

She ached. Felt void without it. Him. Thrusting and thrusting and thrusting.

Her breasts prickled, demanding she take him up on his offer and beg him to rub her with his palms and fingers.

He was asking her for a night, an entire night, and she did not want to think of the dangers. Only of the pleasure.

Relaxing in her seat as he fondled her lips, Meredith allowed her tongue to slip out to lick him, and she closed her eyes when he pushed his thumb in for the delectation of her senses. She softly suckled, tasted skin and salt and him. He murmured, "Come to me tonight."

"Why?"

"So I can kiss you."

"Everywhere."

"Make love to you."

"All night."

She buried her face deeper into his hand and nuzzled him as she pressed a kiss to the center of his palm.

"Do you know what else I'm going to do to you?"

She was breathless with anticipation, susceptible to anything he'd say he'd do. And if he said, *I'll hurt you, Meredith. I'll break your heart and make you regret every word and sigh you ever gave me*, she would still succumb.

He came around the desk with agonizing slowness, then behind her chair, to tug the backrest down with his hands as he bent to whisper in her ear. "I'm going to restrain you," he said, his voice like velvet flowing into her veins. "I'm going to tie you up from the top of your head down to your two little feet, so the only part of you that can move will be your mouth as you cry out my name."

Oh, god. His arms came around; one hand slipped under her jacket and the other delved into her skirt. Meredith's body arched to accept both of them, and his amused chuckle made the little hairs on her arms rise to attention.

"You like restraints, don't you? They excite you." He fondled the sex, the breast, the taut, beaded nipple. His fingers burned her through her clothes. "You're a sassy little lawyer; you like power, but you like feeling helpless, too. You want to feel trapped, to wiggle your way around the free area. . . . You like limits, knowing there's something bigger than you out there, and messing with it. You like messing with me." Her soaked silken panties were glued to her flesh as he stroked his finger up and down the material, tracing the entry of her sex. "Guess what." Her nipple pinged when he grasped and pulled. "I want to take you there. I want to take you high and low, touch and lick you until you're so hot, so fucking aroused, you'd come at the touch of a feather."

"Oh, god, James."

"Say yes, Meredith. Come to me tonight. Come play with me."

"Meredith?"

When her assistant's voice outside her office registered in Meredith's lust-fogged mind, she started in her seat, pushing James's hands away. By the time the young blonde opened the door and peeked inside, Meredith sat calmly in her chair while reviewing the contract, with

James looming behind her, his head bent as though he were reading, too.

"I'm sorry. Did I interrupt anything?" Kylie asked, and Meredith looked up and blinked.

Come at the touch of a feather . . .

She set the contract aside and waved a hand in the air. "Kylie. Oh, no. Mr. Hamilton and I were just . . ."

"Actually, Kylie, you are," James said, propping a hip on the corner of Meredith's desk and gazing at her with the confidence of one who is used to being obeyed. "Do you mind giving me a minute with Ms. Sinclair?"

Kylie's smile faltered as she scrutinized James first, then Meredith.

Come at the touch of a feather . . .

Meredith felt such hot, blazing color creep up her neck and cheeks, it took all her effort to keep from ducking under her desk.

"Julian wants to see you," Kylie finally told her.

Meredith rose from her chair, her thighs still weak from the desire pumping through her veins. But Julian was, after all, the owner of the company, and her boss. "I'll be right there."

When Kylie nodded and shut the door behind her, James's presence became a Herculean force inside the room. Pulling at her. Weakening her. Every atom inside of her, every cell, seemed entirely focused on him, on his steady breath, his virile scent, his size and frame and the entire space surrounding him.

He caught her elbow as she tried to pass. His fingers around her bone formed a steel-like bracelet as he flicked his wrist and spun her around. His eyes burned his question into her. Stamped his *desire* into her. "And my answer?" he prodded, the silver orbs of his eyes almost engulfed by the growing black of his pupils.

Desire crashed through her like a frenzied stampede that abolished doubt and reason. Lava inundated her veins.

Inwardly trembling with anticipation, afraid of everything he made her want and feel and crave so potently, she pulled her elbow free.

With the cacophony of her heartbeat echoing in her ears, Meredith strode across the room and set her hand on the doorknob. And without meeting his gaze, before even trying to continue to rationalize all the feelings he stirred in her, she whispered, "Yes."

Chapter Three

_T_here are moments when time altogether stops. Then there are other moments—the worst, in James's opinion—when time only slows.

Slows to convert a simple second into a torturously long minute or more.

Slows to make you aware of yourself, your feelings, your hidden needs, as you wait.

For the woman who's gotten under your skin.

"I have to say, this is taking longer than it should. Is there anything I should be concerned about?"

Clamping his jaw in response to his boss's tone, James gazed out at the orange skyline of Manhattan and held his cell phone to his ear. "No," he told his boss quietly. "There's not."

A fire crackled in the living room. Another fire—quieter, hotter, worse—tormented his groin, his mind, his heart. For the dozenth time this day, his thoughts ran to where he and Meredith would go tonight—somewhere deep and dark and wild—and his dick got so hard it threatened to rip through his slacks. Christ, what was this?

"Are you meeting with resistance, then?" J. T. Myers demanded on the other end of the line. "Is their in-house lawyer—what's her name?—being troublesome?"

"Sinclair." James scraped his hand down his face. "Meredith Sinclair." *My every adolescent fantasy come to life.*

"That's right. Sinclair. A rookie, I understand."

James smiled tightly, forcing himself to silence. He could almost touch his partnership. Thirteen years with Myers, and he could almost taste it. He wasn't compromising this now. He shifted his weight on his feet. "Rest assured, J.T. We're almost there. It'll be a week. Two at most."

"Two? She's that competent?"

Hell, yeah. And if James could only screw his head on straight for a minute, he might actually stand a chance against her.

"She's passionate," James admitted. So damned *passionate.*

Anticipation sprinted through him as he surveyed the city, the park, the pedestrians below. Meredith. Tied up like a present, her pussy wet, writhing in her binds. Meredith.

Meredith, Meredith, Meredith.

A desert-dry laugh came over the line. "No room in

law for passionate people," Myers said. "You must be cold. Hard-hearted. She could take a lesson from you—not that I'm suggesting you give it, mind you."

Hard-hearted.

That had always been James. Business first; pleasure later.

No chink in his emotional armor.

No chick ever worth it.

But after endless consideration, puzzling over Meredith's effects on him and trying to resist the wild impulses she stirred, James was, as of today, determined to pursue this. *Her.*

There was no point fighting it anymore. Hell, he'd *surrendered*.

He wanted this, whatever it was. Would gobble it up like a starved man.

His life had been dedicated to law. But now there was lust, now there was . . . Fuck, it was *more*.

He had feelings for her—more than desire, more than wanting and lust. Yeah, she was the hottest, sweetest, most wanton sex goddess he'd ever encountered. Who had his balls in a tight little vise. But he had eyes for no one else, not the barest thought of anyone other than Meredith. Christ, he burned with jealousy when she smiled at the other lawyers, craved to be the reason for that smile, wished to know her every thought, her every *desire*.

But he'd put a price on her head if he ever admitted this to Myers—and that he was not willing to risk.

"If it's all right with you, I'll drop by tomorrow to apprise you of the requested revisions."

The forcefulness in the prickly man's voice eased some. "You do that. You do that, then. And as soon as we take over, we're restructuring. You understand? No point in keeping our legal departments separate, and I'm confident you can handle it on your own. The first thing we're doing is clean out the old, bring in the new."

He froze. Icicles of dread pricked his back. "With all due respect, J.T., Meredith is a great asset. She knows the workings of the company, and her insight—"

"You and your team can handle it," the man bluntly interjected, then paused. "You're saying you want her in your department? Or is this something more personal I should be aware of? Well? Should I? I wouldn't take kindly to a mucked-up deal. Gregory said you're impressed with her in . . . all respects. Are you?"

Damn Gregory. Damn impertinent, infuriating little fool. "I . . . respect her," he said carefully.

"Do what you must to get her under your heel—understand? And I want the details ironed out *now*. I'm not a patient man. Crap! I missed."

James imagined the restless old man putting in his office again. How easily he played his games. How easily James had helped him before. But to take away Meredith's job . . .

"Hamilton!" he said, snapping him back.

James exhaled. "I'm here, J.T."

"So you are. Good, good. You're not very focused, but then it's the end of the week, so I guess it's forgivable. I'm having a dinner tonight. Just a few business acquaintances. Me, my wife, and my daughter. I'd like you to be there."

Gritting his teeth, James thought of all the times he'd said yes, of all the things he'd never done because he'd been appeasing a volatile, hot-tempered boss. And Myers's efforts to match James with his daughter, Cordelia.

He leaned a folded arm against the window, moderating his timbre. "I'm afraid I have a prior engagement," he said. "But please send my regards to Olivia and Cordelia."

"James," the old man said, a warning. "Don't fail me."

Don't play with me, or I'll win, the old man meant. James stared at the phone a moment, then hung up. His mind whirled.

Myers's possessiveness of his people was surpassed only by the man's pride and vanity, both of which James had wounded. And although James and Cordelia had remained friendly after their fumbled attempts to please the autocratic man, Myers still would not give up his hopes of a match.

James had unwittingly put Meredith in a precarious position, and now the urge to protect her overwhelmed him. But . . . to give her up?

Anger churned inside him. The thought of once again sacrificing his needs for a stubborn old puppeteer made his blood boil. But for Meredith's sake, should he cancel his evening with her?

Pondering, he glanced over at the credenza by the entrance. A medium brown box sat there, unmarked except for James's name. Could he pretend the contents urgently required attention? Could he pretend whatever lay hidden there was more important than a night with Meredith?

James lifted the package; it weighed nothing. He carried it to the kitchen and sliced a knife through the tape. One eyebrow came up in surprise as he spotted the contents.

Whatever he'd expected, it wasn't what lay inside. And his reaction to the sight shocked him. His heart twisted so tight, he had to drag in a breath to calm himself. Who'd sent this to him?

He flipped the box around.

No return address, no markings. *Meredith? Meredith. Christ.*

The thought of her giving him something, giving him this loud, beautiful, tantalizing *yes* to their evening, set his blood on fire.

His hand trembled as he reached inside, his fingers running through the smooth, silky strands before he extracted the long white object and held it in the air. A feather.

"Okay, friend, you have officially lost your mind."

"Cherry, I'm walking down Central Park West, barefoot, with a *fishbowl* in my hand. Of course I've lost a screw."

"What happened to your Manolos?"

Shivering from the cold, Meredith picked up her pace. The pavement could've been an ice rink under her feet. So where were her shoes? Excellent question. "They're in my briefcase. I just wanted to . . . you know. Interact more with nature."

"Then pet something furry, for heaven's sake! Why walk barefoot down those filthy sidewalks? You really are having a brain crack, Mer. And did I hear things, or did you just say you're staying the night?"

"Yes, for the tenth time. Yes, I'm spending the night!" A telling giddiness crept into her voice, but Cherry's groan on the other end of the line seemed the opposite of excited.

"Oh, sweetheart. Sweetie, no, no, no. You've got . . . well, shit, you've got a packed twelfth house. Your house of karma and dreams and secrets. It's packed, Meredith. This makes the encounter somehow fateful and yet full of secrecy, and then there's an eclipse tonight—eclipses are life-altering moments. Life altering. This one is powerful, baby. This one is— Mer, stay home."

"Of course there's secrecy. We're closing a deal!" Meredith hissed, bumping a passerby's shoulder. She mumbled "Sorry" and verified that the little fish, Max, hadn't flown out of his bowl. "We can't openly date. Not right now."

Brisk shuffles on the other end. Worry in the air. Cherry seemed not to have heard her. "And then you've got Mars. Mars in your eighth house of sex. The sex could be dangerous. Oh, god, Mer, it could be dark. Did you not say two weeks ago that you were steering clear of James Hamilton?"

"There is no steering clear of him, Cherry. I'm sucked in. I'm going tonight. I'm *staying* the night."

"Mer—"

"Cherry, I want him." Meredith stopped midstride and clutched the phone so tight, her knuckles hurt. "With all my life, I want him." She glanced at her bare feet and bright, newly painted toes. *Raspberry Love.* Perfect for . . . well, love. She wiggled them thoughtfully. "Look, he's not married. I'm not married. Please just put the chart aside and be my friend."

There was a moment, brief but somehow eternal. Then a sigh. "What am I supposed to say?"

"What you've been telling me for years. To do something crazy—to *go* for it!"

"But you already have. You're plunging into an affair, and I can see here, I'm afraid . . . Mer, there are too many violent energies. Your house of sex and obsession is so damned loaded I can't even begin. Saturn's there, Mars is there, then Uranus, the planet of the unexpected, is in your sign. Pluto, that little bugger packs a real punch, baby, and he's in your sign, too. None of these are the friendlier planets, Mer. They're not Jupiter."

"Don't. Just don't, please." Resolved, she started walking again. Her eyes settled on the gleaming fifty-story modern masterpiece of James's building, and her heart galloped toward it. "Look, I've got to go."

"Wait. Just wait a sec. Let me draw up his chart, okay? Do you have his birth date and time?"

"Cherry."

"Fine! I'll Google it. Don't go until I've called back."

Meredith opened her mouth to reply. Oh, god, *James*. Through the people bustling down the sidewalk across the avenue, she could see a dark, still figure standing at the foot of the building. He leaned against the shiny, smooth glass, his arms crossed, his black coat flapping at his calves.

Her blood bubbled with excitement.

Pushing himself upright, James came toward her, his strides long and purposeful.

"Mer?" Cherry murmured.

The earth. Was it moving? Cars rumbled past as Meredith struggled to come to her senses.

"Fine, yes, okay," she lied, flapping the phone shut and tucking it into her purse. *God.*

There was nothing—nothing—Cherry could do or say to keep Meredith away.

From James.

And the feather . . .

Did he know what his wicked proposal did to her?

Know that she dreamed of a long, silky white feather, whispering across her skin, over her eyelids, her nose, her chin . . . ?

With a quickening heartbeat, Meredith hurried to the corner, but, like James, she was stopped helplessly by the rush of cars down the avenue. It felt as if it took ages for the white WALK light to pop up. And then what Meredith covered in seven steps, James covered with three. He swept around and gently tucked her into his coat, engulfing her frame with the thick fabric as they both headed for the building.

A rush of inner warmth spread through her legs and tummy, causing the air to feel colder along her jaw.

"What are you doing out here?" Good god, she was grinning like a fool.

He flashed her a smile, his teeth beautiful and white. He squeezed the breath out of her. "You know what."

Her grin stretched, and she pressed closer. "Maybe I just want to hear you say you were waiting for me."

"I was waiting for you." He crammed both of them into the revolving doors. "Seems pretty cold for a walk, Meredith."

"I picked up a bag at Bergdorf's—just a couple of blocks."

"Barefoot?"

"I . . ." Fire rose up her neck and cheeks. *Everyone* in the lobby seemed to have heard that. "Please don't ask."

"OK, I won't."

Damn. Now he'll think I'm a loon. "Well. Suddenly I wanted to experience things more hands-on—you know, achieve some physical . . . connection . . . with . . . things." They reached the elevator bank, and James looked at her with a steady, somber gaze.

"I know what you mean."

God, don't say these things. Don't be so wonderful.

He guided her into the elevator and jerked his chin in the direction of her shopping bag. "So, are your shoes in there somewhere?"

As James knelt at her feet and pulled out her pointy Manolos, an older woman with a small Chihuahua nestled in her arms bustled into the elevator before the doors could close.

She had the bemused expression of someone deep in her cups, or perhaps of someone who lived in an alternate reality, blissfully happy, blissfully ignorant of the war in Iraq and of plane crashes, parasites, and death in the world.

"Jimmy! Jimmy, how are you?"

It was odd that while he drolly answered, "That Chihuahua's bigger than a mastiff, Mrs. T. What are you feeding it?" he was gently slipping on Meredith's shoes, holding her ankles with long, stroking fingers, making her want to melt.

"Oh, just a little of what I eat," the woman replied, petting behind the dog's perky ears.

He chuckled. Oh, god, definitely. *Melt.*

"Lucky pup," James murmured.

He rose and used his hand, curled appropriately around her nape, to pin her to his side.

At E-Doll, they couldn't do this. At E-Doll, he was a lawyer and she was another, seated across the table from him. And yet here he held her like a lover. And it was all just too wonderful.

He smiled indulgently at the older woman, whose attention became riveted on Meredith. "Meredith Sinclair, Mrs. T.," James introduced. "Meredith, Mrs. Susan Trent."

The woman tapped her thinning lips, quite concentrated all of a sudden. "Sinclair . . . Sinclair . . ." She seemed hard-pressed to think of a Sinclair she knew.

"My parents live in Atlanta," Meredith offered.

"Oh. That explains it." And to James, she smiled and said, "She's pretty, Jimmy. Prettier than"—she snapped her fingers several times, and the dog's ears pricked at attention—"what was her name?"

Meredith's spine stiffened as if a rod had been shoved down her throat.

"Lora? Cora?" the woman mused. "You never did get engaged, did you?"

"Cordelia."

The sound of James's voice quietly saying a woman's name made Meredith's stomach lurch. She became wood in his arms—not wooden; wood. Rotting wood, actually. Wood being eaten by termites.

"Ah yes." The elevator pinged, and Mrs. T. waved a hand in the air. "Well, here we are."

Wow. Just like in the movies. An old lady with too big a mouth discloses something that makes one of the lovers want to barf.

Meredith stared down at Max, cradled against her chest, swimming and swimming and going nowhere.

He wasn't much of a pet, really. He did nothing. Just swam, his nature demanding he be left pretty much alone. The only time he exhibited feelings was when she approached to feed, and he began swimming round and round in excitement. But he was so fragile, you could kill him in a few seconds by pulling him out of the water or even by crushing him in your hand. And suddenly Meredith felt just as fragile as that silly, lonely little fish.

James peered down at her through lowered brows.

Mrs. T. had, of course, provided Meredith with the perfect excuse to stop, just halt, this insanity. Cordelia. She glanced down at the tote at her feet, the shopping bag with her briefcase rammed inside, and, underneath it, her sexy new purchases meant to drive a certain man crazy. Now all she wanted was to hide that bag somewhere. Evidence of the stupid things she'd been letting herself hope for.

She hesitated as the doors opened on the penthouse, but James swept her shopping bag up with one hand and pried her fishbowl away with the other. "Didn't figure you for a pet person." He weaved into his apartment, lifting the fishbowl and peering inside. "Does he do anything besides float there?"

"He eats."

"That so?"

Her smile was as tight as a size zero on her size-six frame. "He'll kill another betta if you slip it in the bowl with him."

"Ahhhh." He seemed impressed by her quiet viciousness, and set her pet on the speckled black granite kitchen counter.

"I just got him," Meredith said, for lack of anything else to say. But James didn't seem a man to like either tails or scales, she reflected. He seemed like a man who liked to win.

Had he proposed to her? Had he wanted to marry this *Cordelia*? And why did Meredith suddenly want to *hate* her?

"Sinclair." The crisp word cut through her musings.

Her heart stuttered. The daylight caused shadows across his face—virile, weary, beautiful.

"What?"

He set down her shopping bag, shrugged off his coat, and pulled out a hanger from the coat closet. "If you want to talk about her, just say it."

"No. I don't. I don't want to talk about her." Stiffly, Meredith lowered herself onto the sofa. When James only stood there, towering and staring, her hackles raised. "Do *you* want to talk about her?"

He crossed his arms and shot her a look of incredulity. "Meredith, the last thing I want to talk with you about is her."

He stared. Her lips tingled when his gaze had strayed there, and she felt an uncomfortable fluttering in the pit of her belly.

With a shrug he added, "She wanted more, and I couldn't give it to her."

"I really don't want to talk about her."

"She found me emotionally inaccessible."

She lifted her brows, a halfhearted attempt at humor. "And that was a surprise?"

He crossed the carpet with measured steps, scrutinizing her thoroughly. "If I'm spilling my guts out, you might as well share the joy."

She shook her head, dropping her gaze to her lap. "There's been no one serious."

He leaned over, arms stretched out on the couch. "No one. Hmm." Her head spun when his familiar scent tickled her nostrils. "Why no one, Sinclair?"

A wealth of satisfaction echoed in his words. He *liked* that there had been no one. Meredith liked the fiery branding of his gaze.

He curled a finger under her chin and tipped her head so she could not avoid his scrutiny.

"Why is that, Meredith?"

God, his eyes. There was such depth there, such intensity. She could not look into them, and at the same time she could not look away.

"Cherry says I'm looking for perfect. And that perfect is not . . . not achievable."

"Uh-huh." His eyes darkened and he bent his silky head. A moist, fluttery lick of his tongue at the seam of her lips made her breath catch. "Define *perfect*."

Three words popped into her mind.

This! You! Us!

Again, the tip of his tongue stroked between her lips, leaving them moist. And tingly and parting for more. "Define it, Meredith," he murmured against her mouth.

She ached—oh, god, he made her ache from head to toe. "I can't define *perfect*," she breathed, craning her head back.

He cradled her nape and drew her closer. "Is it a feeling?" Her lower lip became trapped between his lips, and he gently sank his teeth into her flesh. "Is it a sight?"

He released her bruised lip, and, trembling inside, Meredith ran her tongue across the stinging flesh. "I've always thought I'd know in my heart."

"Hmm." His breath fanned across her face. He licked and licked her lips. "That sounds corny, Sinclair."

Corny or not, his voice had thickened with need.

The room smelled of her arousal. His arousal. Now he followed the path her tongue took on its retreat, and he plunged deftly inside. "Tell me. Your first time was with . . . ?"

"Robbie Nelson." *He tastes of brandy*, she thought, and leisurely slanted her head to taste more of his mouth. He'd been drinking before she arrived? "The moment it started," she said, nibbling in return, "I wanted it to end."

"You didn't enjoy it?"

She'd somehow gotten her hands into his hair and she couldn't seem to stop stroking, stop nibbling, stop kissing. "I cried all night. Does that answer your question?"

He paused. "Sex made you cry?"

The directness of his stare made her insides jell. "I wanted fireworks. I wanted . . . the movie stuff. It took me years to get around to having sex again."

"Making up for lost time with me?"

He stroked her breasts with the backs of his hands, casually, and Meredith arched for more. But he stepped back, straightening. "I seem to forget I have all night for this," he said, and set loose that oh-so-sexy smile.

He headed over to the kitchen and began to mess with the impressive appliances. A silence fell, making Meredith aware of her heartbeat, of her crying pussy—everything.

"Music?" he queried.

Before she could answer, he flicked on background

music. Music for seduction. Damn it, he'd had her on the sidewalk before WALK lit up.

"I find music relaxing. Do you?" Was he actually making salad? Yes, he was. And when he sliced through the lettuce, the image was too domestic to ignore. A pang struck her between the ribs.

"Yes," she said, shifting in her seat.

She watched him putter for minutes. She hadn't noticed the darkening in his eyes—those gunmetal eyes—until now. She also noticed the tautness of his shoulders, stretching the fabric of the crisp topaz blue shirt he wore.

He's tense. Like me.

Tapping her fingers together, she surveyed the table gracing the dining room, adorned with candles and a half dozen lucky bamboos. While the city outside darkened, the sound of soft, humming music wafted in the background.

He'd done this—the music, dinner—for her?

"You cook, James?"

"It appears that I do."

She came around. Something wild surged in her as she watched his hands move. She loved his hands, felt flutters just watching them, remembered where they'd been, how those long, thick fingers had stroked and pleased her. He'd rolled up his sleeves, and his hair was mussed from her fingers. As she stood behind him, she dragged in his scent.

She wanted to wrap her arms around his waist, press her cheek to his back, and slide her hands in to squeeze his cock in her grip. God, she was so doomed.

"I'm not all that hungry."

He continued chopping the tomatoes, frowning slightly at her words. "You won't deny me the pleasure of having dinner with you, will you?"

"No, it's just that . . ." She wound around the kitchen island, searching for an explanation.

She did not know why she felt so desperate. It seemed as though her entire life she'd been waiting for a spark, to feel something like this, and now she was afraid it might be a fantasy, an illusion, something fleeting. She did not know why she felt so frantic, as though their hours were counted, as though she'd never again have his hands on her, his mouth on her. The urgency made her not hungry, not thirsty, for anything but what he'd promised. *When are you going to tie me?*

"You don't have to do all this," she said at last.

He set the knife down with painstaking slowness. His eyes blazed into hers. "Meredith, if the fact that I left that first night made you think I wasn't interested . . . I am."

She hadn't expected to ever touch this topic, and she fought not to squirm. "It's okay. I like to know where we stand."

Did she? Did she really?

"If I could do it again, I'd stay." He searched her

face, his expression somber. "You blew me away that night, and that's the honest-to-god truth, Meredith."

She ducked her head and walked around him, hiding her face so he wouldn't notice the exhilarating effect those words had on her.

"Look, I'm not Cordelia," she said, one hundred percent nonchalance. "Sex is fine with me. I want to keep my expectations in line with that. We'll be . . . fuck buddies. For a while."

The silence that spread between them was the most oppressive and awkward to date. "Fuck buddies," he repeated. Then another pause. "Like kids?"

"James! Kids do *not* have fuck buddies."

His pale eyes regarded her as he hauled her toward the dining table, his lips thinning as though he were displeased. "I'm not your fucking fuck buddy, Meredith. Now sit."

Sit.

He liked ordering her around—didn't he?

He reached around her to remove her coat, but she wrapped her arms tightly to her chest. "No! I'd like to leave it on. Please."

He cocked a brow. Said nothing.

If he only knew she'd been freezing her buns off. That under her coat, she was wearing practically nothing but skin and a lacy blue thing that cost almost as much as her coat and shoes had. But she was spending the night. . . . She was sleeping with James Hamilton . . .

and all would be wonderful until tomorrow, when she would awaken and realize she had nothing to put on but a coat.

He stared at her lips with a distinctly brooding expression and slowly began pulling out her chair. A ripple of need fanned out of her womb at the primal, sexy air he produced.

"Still cold?" he asked nonchalantly. Of course he was never ruffled.

He was stroking her nape, and an image of his cock and the way it looked, all swollen and needy every time he freed it, made her flush.

She tried a smile. Sat. Wondered, *How to go about this seduction? How to drive him out of his* mind?

Her nipples felt hard as diamonds, and they throbbed when they grazed the edge of the table. They ached for his mouth. His lips. His tongue.

His eyes traveled to her breasts as if bidden, his expression bleak and famished, propelling her heartbeat to new, alarming levels. She could've sworn he saw through her coat.

His roughened voice scraped over her skin. "I changed my mind. Get up." He snaked one arm around her waist and pulled her up to her toes, the napkin falling from her grasp.

His hands slid languorously down her back; then he greedily palmed her ass and flattened her against his lithe, muscular body. "You smell like a cupcake, Meredith."

The perfectly formed stalk of his penis was large and evident under his slacks, and Meredith had to bite back a sound of surprise as that delicious bulge bit into her stomach.

His eyes flicked to her breasts, crushed wantonly against his chest, and his wolfish smile struck her like a lightning bolt. "You're naked, aren't you?" He dipped a finger under her coat button, trailed it down her cleavage, stroking the snug passage between her breasts. "Show me what you got here."

A melting sensation spread down her thighs. "Have a look." Her words were throaty with arousal; her entire body began to shake.

Before she knew it, he was ducking his head and delivering a whopping, out-of-this-world kiss. At the electrifying contact, Meredith gasped in surprise, joy, and something unnamable. "Ooh" was all she could say before his tongue plowed into her mouth. *Yes.* Yes, yes, yes, this was it—what she wanted; *all* she wanted.

"I'll have you for dinner," he murmured against her lips, his mouth moving against hers as she fumbled with his shirt buttons.

"Yes." She got stuck on the second button.

"Let's go to my bed."

"Yes." *Damn that button!*

He cupped the back of her head, firmly locked his lips to hers, and his passion spilled into her like a bright, burning light. "I want you," he growled.

Flaring up like a bonfire, intoxicated by the burning feel of his body heat against hers, the spicy scent of him around her, she looped her arms firmly around his neck as his tongue tangled heatedly with hers. "I want you, too."

"You do. And I want you to be a good, good girl and do exactly as I say. Exactly. Understand?"

He dragged her to his bedroom before she agreed, and Meredith could smell herself, how shamelessly she'd moistened. Her pussy felt swollen, the lips bloated between her legs. Ready and aching for James.

James had grown so stiff, so large, with their foreplay, his pants could barely contain him. And oh, she thought she'd *come* with one look from him.

He let go of her as they entered, and headed to a set of drawers. *Come with the touch of a feather*, she thought with a bevy of butterflies in her stomach.

Exhaling a breath in search of calm, she gazed out the window at the flickering city lights and strained to hear him advance behind her. But instead of him walking toward her, she heard a whisper from the foot of the bed, hoarse and coated with arousal. "Look at me, Meredith."

She bit her trembling lower lip and turned her head.

Her heart stopped. He was fully naked. His skin gleamed under the lamplight, his beautiful body perfectly defined; it was a body one could show without a stitch of clothing, and with pride, to the world. His cock jutted out so tall and long and thick that her eyes almost popped out of their sockets.

Letting go of a shuddering breath, she found herself walking to the foot of the bed and gripping his shoulders. "Oh, god, James. Touch me."

She rubbed her body against his, almost crying out at the seductive feel of his big cock against her belly.

But rather than touch, James stared at her, his pupils dilated, his breath a hot rasp on her face. "How hungry are you for me?"

God. Hunger of the worst, most horrible kind.

Meredith didn't understand it, didn't understand anything. How she could be in awe of someone, why she felt unworthy of his eyes when they touched her, and felt almost grateful that they did, that he'd want to be with her. She'd never experienced such insecurity before, of wanting to please him, say the right things, touch the right places. Her childhood had been a happy one. Loving, living parents, many friends, many male admirers. With being a lawyer came a satisfying sense of power, of control. She had never felt fragile, breakable, as she did with James.

She loved it.

She hated it.

James fingered the collar of her coat. Then he tugged it aside. "Much as I like the sight of you in your fancy black coat, I want you writhing, so *strip.*"

Strip.

She felt cold when she eased it off her shoulders, letting it fall in a pool at her feet. His eyes flashed at what he saw. She wore a lacy corset, tight around her waist, that made her breasts spill over. She wore no panties, just lacy white garters and stockings, the curls of her sex bright and moist and exposed to him.

"Are these mine?" He pinched her nipples. "Hmm? All mine?"

Her *yes* came out a gasp.

Moving like a whip, he drew her up against his body. Skin to skin was the most delicious thing.

Her palms fell over that chest she adored, the taut, rigid muscles flexing under her fingers. Her insides rioted and she began rubbing like crazy.

Making a sound in his throat, he lowered her onto the bed and came down with her. Her wrists ended up above her head, pinioned as her sex cradled the hot hardness of him against her. She was ready. Wanting. Willing.

One hand secured both her wrists as he dragged his mouth down her throat, his head slanting, lips grazing, while his tongue poked at her skin. Licking over and over. Down her neck. Between her breasts.

His nose traced circles around her navel, and her head fell back on a moan as his fingers glided across her rib cage. Hot, possessive hands covered her breasts, and the relief she felt when he squeezed overwhelmed her.

Low in her throat, a purr. She arched and moaned, "James."

The sound he made was deeper, coming from his stomach, muffled by the valley between her breasts as he buried his face between them. He rubbed one nipple with his thumb, and she opened her eyes and watched as he took his mouth there. She trembled when he swiped his tongue across the tip, swirled it around and around, and then caressed her thighs with his fingers and grazed his knuckles across her pussy.

She whimpered, twisting her face to the side as she admitted, "I've thought of this all day."

"It makes you wet."

"Yes."

"You wanted to touch yourself."

"Yes."

He pulled her breasts high and watched with a look of raw ecstasy as she wiggled restlessly, feeling close to delirium as her nipples beaded from the cool air.

His mouth clamped onto a reddened nipple. He sucked so hard, her back lifted from the bed, the suckles filling her pussy with spasms. When he slid his knee between her thighs and let it ride up to her burning sex, she rolled her hips, whimpering as her movements created the most delicious friction.

His utter control against her utter lack of it made her weak; she wanted him to lose it, wanted him to take everything, take without asking, possess her until she felt she was a part of him rather than a part of her quaking, wanting self.

His eyes flashed as she cried out, her hands on his shoulders, and he pulled away and just stared at her, aroused, somehow wild looking.

She panted. She was going to come lying here.

She didn't know who moved first, but it took three seconds, three heartbeats, to smash together again. He pulled her up by the hair, took her mouth swiftly and possessively.

She clawed at his torso. "Fuck me."

He smacked her butt. "Get on your knees."

She rolled. Got on her knees and closed her eyes, her face pained in a tight, lust-filled grimace.

His mouth clamped on her ass.

Hot mouth, *hot* body, *hot* man.

Gently he caressed her thighs, her knees, used a hand to graze his knuckles across her pussy.

She whimpered, agonized by the touch. Her face was distorted as she said, "I'm so wet."

"Soaked." He stroked outside her labia; then he was licking both his fingers, draining them. He thrust them in her again. "And spicy."

His lips fastened to her sex. He sucked so hard, her body strained upward, muscles taut. And then he was sticking his fingers into her channel, then her mouth, telling her to taste herself. She tasted.

Something soft and silky fluttered against her back.

"Close your eyes." A ghost of a touch ran across her face.

"What is it?" she asked, doing as she was told.

"It's a feather."

Pleasure rocketed through her. "Oh."

Come at the touch of a feather . . .

Trembling, she rolled to face him and stared into those worn-silver eyes, glazing now, the pupils engulfing the irises. "It's unique." He trailed the delicate tip along her nose. "Like you."

"It's beautiful." But she was looking at James's hard-boned, handsome face. Impulsively, she reached out to cup his clean-shaven jaw. "You're beautiful."

She could've bitten her tongue for that. It was something you didn't tell a man, much less one like James. But he didn't seem to hear; he was too busy stroking the feather down her neck to circle the globes of her breasts.

"I want to give you so much pleasure, you won't tell it apart from pain."

She felt the feather flutter downward, and she bucked as electricity bolted to her head. Her breasts jerked as she sobbed, "James!"

She fell back on the mattress, and she panted as he slid his middle finger in and out.

"I ought to turn you around and slap my hands across your ass for wiggling it at me all day. Driving me fucking crazy."

The phone rang three times, four. It was Meredith's.

James growled, "If you get that, I'm going to spank
you so hard, you won't be able to sit tomorrow."

And something, something unholy and bad, made
her dive for her purse and answer.

"Mer! Your charts are . . . You need to see this. You
need to see this *now.*"

James put his finger back in her, and she creamed all
around his hand. His gaze bored into her while his finger moved inside her, pressed hard and high in the gripping channel.

"I . . . not now. Tomorrow, Cherry."

"I've never seen anything like this. Your suns are
inverted. Your moons are inverted. You have his and he
has yours. . . ."

And his finger was up her pussy. Stroking. Taking
her to heaven.

"And yet there's a square here—bad times, difficult
times. Mer, he'll *hurt* you. You'll hurt him. You'll hurt
each other. I think you have shared pasts—not happy
ones. There's death and destruction and—"

"Cherry, I can't now!"

She hung up and tossed the phone to the floor.

He'll hurt you. You'll hurt him.

She gazed into his dark, dangerous eyes, breathless
with anticipation.

With a dire shake of his head, James pulled her across his lap and whacked her ass so fast and hard, she yelped. "You're a bad girl, and now you're going to have to suck my cock."

She moaned at the moist, warm stroke of his thumb between her ass cheeks. Her pussy watered. "Make me."

He hesitated.

The moment was charged with need.

"What did you just say?"

She trembled, waiting for his next hit. Wanting it.

"Did you just say, 'Make me'?"

"God, yes, I said that." She went wild, writhed on his lap, jiggling her ass up higher so he'd please, please do it again. "Please make me suck cock."

He chuckled. "You *are* a bad girl." He grabbed her hair and pulled her head back—arching her body and holding it there as he slapped her ass three consecutive times. *Thwack. Thwack. Thwack.*

She hissed, "Yes, yes, yes."

He reached around and grabbed her corset. The fabric resisted, but when he pulled harder, it tore. Her breasts jerked from the violence of the move, and she scrambled back on the bed, panting, desperate, wanting to be taken not only physically, but in every way. He was night, and everything that prowled in it, everything that went on in it, good and bad, poignant and illicit.

He would hurt her.

She would like it.

Oh, god, his eyes looked black now, his pupils so dilated.

"What did we agree on, Meredith? What did I just say?"

"To . . . to suck your cock."

"Well, then." He stroked the lengthened shaft once as though to tempt her. And he did tempt her. With his commands, his authority over her body. She'd never realized sex could be like this.

Out of breath, she shifted to her knees, reaching for his cock with trembling hands. He held the back of her head, preventing her from taking it, forcing her to stare into his face as he murmured, "Suck it. Nice and slow."

Tendrils of excitement rippled deep in her belly. She opened up, and her throat closed from hunger as the mushroom-shaped head urged her lips apart.

"Take it in." He secured a fistful of hair in his hand and pulled her to him with a sultry growl. "Do you like to suck?"

"Yes," she gasped.

"How do I taste?"

"Salty."

"You like salty cock?"

"Yes."

He held her head still and thrust. Her scream was muffled by his invading flesh. His member filled her mouth, and she found his musk arousing beyond her senses. She was dripping, could feel a drop of moisture on the inside of her thigh. She massaged one testicle with her hand, then reached to cup the immense, hard muscle of his ass.

He bucked into her, the tip of his penis massaging her throat, flattening her tongue with each demanding slide. His hold didn't loosen on the back of her head, but pinned her for his hips as he began fucking.

She made a gurgling sound deep in her throat when his cock jerked, filling her mouth with his creamy, musky cum. His need vibrated in his voice as he continued pumping.

"You're going to eat it all. . . ."

She could swallow him again and again, would lick and suck for more. When he hauled her up, he was hard against her belly.

"And then you're going to fuck it when I say so," he growled.

"Anything."

He spread-eagled her on the bed, arms over her head, legs open, pussy exposed. She closed her eyes tight and felt the silk of a tie around each wrist, binding her. She began to quake so hard.

"Can you move?"

She couldn't move; could hardly speak. "Can't move." James brought the feather to the bed and stroked the tip up her left thigh. Tingles raced through her, tingles of fire.

"Oh, god, don't stop!"

His lips formed a wicked smile, his eyes tracking the feather. "Beg for it, hmm? Beg for your orgasm."

Her pussy contracted. Her nipples beaded. "I . . . please."

Still not pleased enough to give her release, he stroked the feather over her navel, and she closed her eyes, spasming as it trailed delicately across her fevered skin. She was lost, out of control, needed him to seize her passion and rein it, steer it, ease it.

The feather's touch was like nothing she'd ever felt before. Magical. Dizzying. Sending her into a spiral. "Please make me come. I'm begging you, please. . . ."

On impulse, James lifted a long, silky strand of hair to his nose and inhaled, as if letting her scent travel the length of his body. "That's better, much better."

She was so engorged, so swollen, it almost hurt when he positioned himself between her legs and authoritatively slid his penis inside her.

"Oh, god!"

The penetration, it felt amazing.

His cock filled her—glorious, hard, burning. And he watched with blazing, half-closed eyes as he impaled.

Meredith exclaimed and surged upward, aware of every scrape of him, pressing her breasts to him as she moved her hips. Desire pooled around him. She squeezed tight and gripped, saw the tendons pop out in his neck as he rocked inside her.

She wanted to rake her hands over his chest, bite his lip. She moaned when he touched no part of her except for her sex. Slowly pounded by his cock.

James. James. James.

He squeezed her breasts, pinched the nipples, roared as he thrust in and out, in and out, sliding that long, hard cock up and down, up and down.

It seemed like she'd been waiting all day for this. Years for this. Lifetimes. His head twisted to the side and he formed her name in a guttural sound.

"Meredith."

She couldn't keep her eyes open; she was breathless. She began to quake, her orgasm building.

"You want to come already."

She couldn't nod; she felt the shudders poised and ready to take her.

He buried his mouth against her nipple and sucked so strongly, she came off the bed with a cry, twisting her head back. His hand smacked her ass as he withdrew.

"Not yet. Not until I say so."

Where she'd felt full of him, now she felt empty. She thought she'd sob when he drew back, was ready to beg for his cock, her orgasm, but instead she arched like a bow when he touched the tip of the feather to her moistened breast. "Oh, god, that feels amazing."

"Does it?" He tipped his head to study her, all of her indecently exposed, and her own gaze kept straying to watch the marvelous length of his penis, pushing out of that mat of dark hair, jerking every time she made a sound of pleasure.

Her mouth watered when a drop of semen leaked. She fought her binds, writhing in desperation. *Fuck me*, she thought. *Fuck me, please!* Was so breathless she couldn't speak it.

"Let's see if you're hot enough . . . to come like this." He grabbed one of her ankles and lifted her leg, then stroked the feather across her open pussy. The sound she made was harsh and tearing, unlike the delicacy of the touch.

"Now. Come."

Her orgasm ripped through her, vicious, deadly, and he immediately mounted her, feeding her his shaft. "Come harder!"

Meredith sobbed as he started riding her, the tremors heightening at each demanding shove of his hips to hers.

Who's your lord, your master. Who do you belong to?

The words blasted into her mind. Was it James speaking? It was his voice, but not his accent. . . .

She could feel him, his strong, stiffened penis driving mercilessly into her, taking her to new heights of pleasure, thrusting and thrusting until . . .

Beg your lord. Beg him to make you come. Beg him to love you—tell him *you love him.*

She cried out in alarm, shivering uncontrollably. "James!"

"Meredith?"

For the first time there was concern in his voice, and she felt herself slipping, his voice sounding faraway, far, faraway. She could hear James saying something, but she could not make out what. She felt heavy, then lost, pulled somewhere. A park . . . swirling with fog . . . a man. James. He was there—yes, of course he would be there, and she . . .

Meredith . . . can you hear me?

She was there, too.

Meredith!

Yes, she was there. She was looking for him. Always. Looking. For him. Did he know her? Did he want her? He was a stranger, and yet he was not. He never would be. . . .

Meredith!

Chapter Four

London, England, 1844

"The thing is, Margaret, you gotta look at 'em pricks like they're food; otherwise, you cannot go through with it."

Her friend Nuri, a bona fide coquette, twined a strand of loose hair around one finger and smiled her most charming smile at the passing elderly gentleman who tipped his hat to her.

"That's what I always do, you know." Her eyes settled on the next oncoming gentleman, this one a tad younger. Nuri added in a conspiratorial murmur, "Look at it this way: You want some real food? Eat 'em pricks and you'll get it. Pie and sugarplums and meat."

Margaret did not reply, her thoughts on the last prick she'd had in her hands. Eating it hadn't left her with much of an appetite.

Hyde Park was swamped with ladies of pleasure this chilly winter night. Between the hours of five and ten, before the gates closed, these fallen women were as abundant as the fog. *Fallen women*; how Margaret hated that term. As if there was hope still. As if someone would pick her up from where she'd fallen and erase all she'd done and allow her to forget all the pricks she'd eaten.

Yes, Margaret was among those who performed the Social Evil. Yes. She was fallen. Yes. She was corrupt. Yes. Now she gazed across the lawn, looking for her next customer. She must live. Yes. Yes. Yes.

"Well! Whaddaya know? Young lords right over there."

A group of four men lingered by the canopy of a tree. Nuri rearranged her hair. "Good tippers, they are. Such a pity they weren't here last month. They'da paid for that hymen o' yours. Like Lord Claymore right there. Lord, that man likes his pleasures."

"Who—who is Lord Claymore?"

"Who do ya think? Dark as the devil, that one. Magic hands."

Margaret's eyes fell on the dark-haired lord who slapped his gloves on his thigh as though impatient. Bored, he studied the gardens, his eyes sliding across the lawns and benches, passing her, then sharply returning to her. The walls of her stomach caved in.

His face was dark and gaunt, haunting in its peculiar beauty. It was strong and hard-boned. Arresting eyes that from afar looked black held hers trapped as the wind whipped through his hair. He was tall and lean, broad shoulders swathed in a dark, billowing cloak.

The heavens were closing in, flashes of lightning illuminating him like a dark phantom, fading fast. Nuri's voice rose over the seething sound of the incoming storm. "Flap your mouth shut, Margaret, and go flaunt yourself before one of them girls pounces. You come one more night without a man and Mrs. T. will think the better of housing you. Earn your wages, girl."

Indeed not one, but several girls were pouncing. All female eyes were on him, and Margaret's skin prickled when his eyes remained solely on *her*.

"Stars, but I burn to see the man in action." Nuri nudged her in encouragement. "He takes his goddamned time. He's an explorer, that one is. Shameless when he wants it. Been a while since he came over."

"Have you . . . ?"

"Had him? In my dreams. One of the other girls, the one who married the regular, Mr. Brown? She had him a few times. Truth be told, she's never looked so glowy."

Margaret adjusted her dress, taking in the strong nose, the slanted eyebrows, the wide forehead and jaw. One night with such a man and she'd glow like a star above, too.

His lips were curled sardonically as he listened to one lady's proposal. "Now that I think on it, 'e might be a little too rough for you, that one," Nuri continued. "Look! Sir March. 'E'll do. You need to use your beauty, Margaret, and find one man to get you out of here. One's all you need, you see."

Sir March was not yet senile. He had a comfortable face, gold and leathery. Still, Margaret looked longingly at the dark stranger, the one touched with the majesty of a god. A woman would follow him like a sleepwalker.

"But I want *him*," Margaret said. The man, the stranger who wore his tension like a suit of armor.

A huge clap of thunder followed her words, and the first heavy drops of rain began to fall. Nuri shoved her forward. "You're too shy to be a gay woman. You must be bolder. Let 'em know you're willing to let 'em fuck you; otherwise, there are those of us who *will*."

"Nuri, do you think it is him?" Margaret whispered, a feeling unlike any other making her light-headed. Raindrops fell on her hair, her shoulders.

Nuri pondered the question, and Margaret had to shake her hard. "When you read my tea leaves this morning and said something momentous would occur," she said, reminding herself Nuri never used big words like *momentous* before. Her heart began to pound at the sight of this man, thrilling and alluring, calling to her femininity so that her legs quaked with the urge to run to him. "Maybe it is him. No?"

"Maybe he is," Nuri said, softly smiling. *These shapes near the rim of the cup . . . Something momentous is about to* happen. *You will meet someone, someone who will be very important. . . .*

Nuri was half Gypsy, but she did not travel with her tribe, as they were treated worse than whores were, and Nuri had fallen in love with a sailor. She had taught Margaret how to trail a scarf over her arms and twirl and dance to entice a man.

Her extensive knowledge of cards and tea leaves had been taught to her by her mother before she passed. Her name wasn't even really Nuri. Some Englishman told her the name meant "Gypsy" in Egyptian, and Nuri had wanted a brand-new name to go with her brand-new future and dropped her former one, whatever that had been. *Nuri! Beloved Nuri!* she said her sailor wrote to her, and sometimes she still read those letters out loud to Margaret. *Pray tell me your heart is constant, for mine has been entirely stolen by an angel!*

Nuri had assured him of her love time and again— she said this. But in the end, it was he who became inconstant.

"Go, Margaret," she urged, pushing none too gently. "Sir March has his roving eye on me, and your stranger will find himself being ridden till daylight by that foul Minnie if you don't get your arse moving."

Minnie! That woman spit on the sidewalks, and the thought of her riding a beauty like him was all Margaret needed to charge forward.

She approached the dark-headed stranger, close enough

to hear the proposition Minnie and her friend were making to him. "Pleasure you . . . together . . ."

Why! She gaped at Minnie, her heart accelerating. How did one seduce a man like him? He was so incredibly . . . large. No. Not large. Formidable.

She felt woefully unprepared. All the things she was instructed to say, seductive words and promises, seemed to have left her at this inopportune time. She tried to smile sultrily, telling herself that it was him. Someone important. *Momentous*. Perhaps it was; perhaps it wasn't. It didn't matter. Right now, tonight, it was him.

Without further thought, Margaret made a little sound of distress, as if she were a bird squashed under a carriage wheel, and promptly fainted.

She fell. Landed with an uncomfortable thud.

But no. This was all wrong. He wasn't coming to her rescue.

This was so alarming, she began feeling faint for real. Then she was being scooped up in the strongest, biggest arms she'd ever had the pleasure of experiencing. "Is she dead?"

Minnie!

The provoking little reptile. Margaret felt infuriated that the lowliest women were being favored with his attention.

But then—then he spoke. And what a lovely voice he had, a devilish rumbling in her ear. "You're pretending, aren't you, you little minx?"

Her heart stopped, and she let her weight sag even more, for how embarrassing to be caught this way.

Is she dead?

Margaret wanted to slap Minnie, but then a chuckle came, and ooh, it was delicious. Delicious.

She grinned against his chest, thinking, hoping, praying, her Mr. Momentous had arrived.

His carriage was brought up with full speed, and within seconds Lord Gavin Claymore, Earl of Claymore and future Duke of Hartfield, had settled his package across the seat from his.

He was not considered an imbecile. Radical, sometimes. Curious by nature, and a lucky bastard at the gambling tables, but never an imbecile.

He knew who the little chit was, or more exactly, what she was. No lady.

He also knew what she had done. Vaguely, he wondered if she pretended to climax for a man as she did that little faint. Not her best performance, surely.

And yet still enthralling. Why, yes, very much so.

He struggled to control his curiosity, riding in silence as he surveyed her. She was a young, fragile little thing. He couldn't wait to fuck her.

"You may drop the act now. We're alone."

The beauty blinked and sat up. "I . . . well." Her hands fluttered over her hair, worn loose, delectable, without a cap, without modesty. She was an invitation to delight.

He frowned to himself over her fumblings, taking in her delicate features, the straight shoulders, the graceful neck exposed on one side as her hair tumbled over the other. A beauty with her chest near bursting out of her dress.

"My friend told me I'd meet someone important tonight," she said.

He didn't know what to make of her. "Did she." The words held no inflection.

She shrugged. "Instead I met you."

He felt himself smile. A real smile, not practiced or learned.

"Gavin Claymore," he said plainly, skipping all formalities.

She merely stared. He returned her stare, aware that his carriage was beginning to smell like her; then he leaned forward impatiently. "Do you have a name, or do I call you whatever I please?"

"You can call me anything you'd like, my lord. But for me to answer, you might have to spend a farthing or two."

He threw back his head and laughed, her wit both delightful and unexpected. "The day I pay a woman to talk to me is the day I'm institutionalized." He narrowed his eyes. "French, are you?"

"Not for a while." She smiled, and her smile disarmed him. His cock stirred. His balls tightened under his breeches. *Well.* He had to admit . . . he'd *noticed* her.

From afar, he'd noticed her. And what she offered, Gavin wanted to take. For his father's sake, he'd been restrained this week, polite, but inside he was seething. Inside he craved sin and darkness. Not batting eyelashes. Not innuendoes. Not gloved hands clutching his arm. A forthright woman. To get blissfully foxed, blissfully fucked.

"Why do you look at me like that?" his little visitor questioned.

His lips curved sardonically. His brows rose minutely. "The dress moves me to look at you," he said. It was a nice blue color, but frilly, cheap, and displaying a most succulent amount of pink, smooth flesh that he would gladly pay to possess.

She beamed at his words and colored prettily. "Does it? Move you to look?"

He made a low, noncommittal sound: "Hmm."

It moved him to do that and more. His gaze lifted of its own volition, tracing the curvy fall of her hair. It gleamed, as silky as a spiderweb, and invited his touch. "And that hair." He did not recognize his voice; it was very husky. "An interesting shade, I'll give you that."

She touched a silken strand and curled the tip around her finger, genuinely blushing. "It is merely brown."

He had seen it across the park, and though its rich color was concealed in shadows now, he could remember the light in it. "It has streaks of red in it. Very fetching."

The carriage rocked soothingly. Her scent became more powerful in the close confinement. She smelled clean. She was full-lipped. Big-eyed. Quite an interesting little thing. Her eyes were clear and bluish gray; disturbing to look at, for they looked old on her young face. He glanced outside, trying not to think of the pleasure it would give him to draw her over his lap. But when it was no use, he turned his attention to her.

"Most of all, your mouth."

She blinked. "We are still talking about me?"

"I am, at least."

Awareness of his interest stole into her eyes, teased up the corners of her lips again. She smoothed her hands along her dress, and he watched with fascination as the long, slender fingers unwrinkled the damp spots.

He desired that touch on his person, those fingers over his distended flesh.

He scraped his chin with his gloved hand, puzzled by his reactions to her. "I find it distracting. Your mouth." What did she do with it? Where had that mouth been? What ventures had it taken, tasted, enjoyed?

She seemed unnerved by his praise. She jumped when the carriage hit a rock, and tugged her skirts low, fingers fidgeting, feet tapping on the ground. "Your carriage is very nice."

She mustn't have been in many of them before. His carriage was plain black, and it suited his mood sometimes. "Black is simple. I appreciate the color."

Her eyes ventured along his hair, his eyes, his clothes. "I appreciate the color, as well, sir . . . my lord." She studied him closely. "Are you in the city before the season begins?"

"Tell me," he interrupted, his thoughts of what she was, what she would *do*, what she would allow him to do making him impatient. "Were you looking for a man tonight?"

She met his level gaze unflinchingly, with a raw hunger that stirred his loins. She did not bother to conceal it. She was a woman who enjoyed sex, and he relished women who possessed no shame of it.

His appetite clawed inside his body—a beast straining to get out.

"For five shillings, I will let you feel," she announced.

"You will let me feel," he repeated as the thought twirled and twirled in his mind. His eyes raked her in a way that his hands itched to. Her curves were not very pronounced, and yet he longed to grab them.

"Yes. And for ten shillings, I will let you both feel"—brazenly, she lifted her skirt a bit to reveal her ankles, stockinged and creamy and delicate—"and *see*."

His eyes went to her ankle. He was feeling generous. No. He was feeling devilish. "How far will twenty pounds get me?"

She gasped at the amount, her eyes widening in excitement. Her head nodded and nodded. "Very far. My lord."

Slowly, he gestured at her lovely and illicit little

person, his smile meant to disarm. "Will it get me under those skirts?"

His question, remarkably, made her turn a nice color, made her voice drop a notch. She could hardly speak. Her breasts quivered under her dress, she seemed so excited. "Deep under these skirts." *Deep in me*, she could have said.

Silence.

His britches were strained, and a fire seemed to be spreading to his lungs. She was entirely too good. . . . The way she stared at him . . . the way she breathed . . . the way her body seemed both open and closed to him . . .

A mystery, no matter how many times he'd traced a woman's cunt with his fingers. Their minds. *Mysteries.*

His lust ran fiercer than ever, his thirst strong for her pale skin, the sight of a nipple, the gaping slit of her sex. He wanted passion and submission, sin and liberation, all of it tonight, all of it from her. Tonight. He shifted in his seat, closer to her—not as close as he would like, but close. He inhaled her scent. Lavender, was it?

"I could use a woman's touch tonight," he said, fingering her wrist with one lone fingertip. Soft and delicate. His heart pounded, and her scent made him slightly dizzy. It had to be lavender. "Would you take me to your bed? Ms. . . . ?"

"I . . ." she said, glancing down at his fingers, stroking her wrist. "Margaret."

He cocked a brow, seized her chin. "Yes, Margaret?"

She stared at his mouth with ill-concealed hunger. He had to have this woman. He would pay anything. He wanted her fiercely, imagined her rimming his cock with her pink mouth, gathering the weight of his testicles in her palm.

"Answer me," he commanded.

She licked her lips. "I . . . forgot." Her eyes searched his. "I forgot the question."

He slid his hand up her arm. "Will you take me tonight? I am never rough unless the woman welcomes it." The covetousness of her gaze was so stark, he struggled with the impulse to take her dress in his hands and tear it. "I've had a long day today. All I want is a long, slow fuck."

"A long, slow fuck you shall get."

His cock jolted at her brazenness, the admission of a woman indeed wanting this part of him—to enjoy it, take it, relish it—making his head spin. He'd had whores. He'd used them to satisfy a need, a curiosity, sometimes even an experiment. He was older now. He had duties he would need to see to. He had a thousand questions in his mind and a thousand unhappinesses. He had a cock, and she had a cunt. He was hard, and if her voice was any indication, she was wet. And suddenly, he had never in his life wanted anything so much as to bury himself inside that wet cunt.

His voice dropped dramatically. "Where shall I instruct the driver to take us, little Margaret?"

Margaret told him where, and within minutes, they

pulled up to the modest residence. A fresh wind blew and spread rain on her face. Margaret did not recall ever being this excited. She gathered her skirts and stormed inside, making sure he followed.

Claymore looked impassively at the men and women groping each other in the parlor on the first floor. Her woman parts began to burn. Her cunny was on fire— oh, goodness, he was so direct, a little insolent, very much handsome, and so very, very fine. *Magic hands . . .*

Her corset seemed suddenly too tight for breathing.

"I shall get us a room," she announced, and signaled for him to wait before she climbed the steps. The first room was occupied by a fucking couple. The second with another. Margaret's room was occupied by Nuri, who seemed to have managed to snare Sir March. She opened the last door to find one of the girls stroking herself while a man watched, frigging himself, too. Drat, if this wasn't just Margaret's luck.

Back downstairs, Lord Gavin was leaning against the wall and had taken off his gloves and held them in one hand at his side. Her heart tripped at the sight of him.

She gathered her courage and began to walk forward. Through the boisterous, bawdy sounds of men laughing and harlots entertaining, she approached him.

"The rooms are occupied," she said.

"Ahhh," he drew out the word, infusing it with a wealth of meaning. He stared at her, her bosom quivering, her cheeks pink, and softly, almost sadly, slapped his

gloves on his hand. He stared at her for another moment, and his lips were so pink, so mobile when he
spoke. "Perhaps I will drop by another time. Margaret."

Her rising hope took a steep decline, until she could
hear it splat at her feet like a drunken sailor. She seized
his wrist. "For ten pounds, I will pleasure you here.
With my mouth. I will find a good little corner, and I
will make it worth your while."

Curling a finger under her chin, he tilted her head
back and met her gaze. It was dark and hot inside his eyes,
sunless as night, somehow secret, and it made her want to
lose herself. "Perhaps it is more than your mouth I want."

The possibility of him departing her life as suddenly
as he'd entered it made her press on. "Would you like to
play, my lord?" she asked breathlessly, feeling him harden
against her. "I will be any woman for you tonight, any
thing at all, in fact."

"Is that so?"

"Yes."

Margaret held her breath until he brought her closer,
hunger dilating his pupils as he gazed at her mouth. He
wore an avid look, as if no one had ever fed him in his
life.

She thought he wanted something from her, sensed
something essential and primal in him calling her in a
language she could instinctively understand. He then
seemed to compose himself, and eased back. "I suppose
I could wait a few minutes."

She went loose with relief, and then urged him into a shadowed corner with an empty lounge chair. He fell into a seat. He set his gloves aside.

Margaret eyed his lap, imagining herself on it, purring to him like a kitten. "Have you ever played Poor Pussy, my lord?"

"Poor Pussy?"

Her eyes widened at his bewilderment. "You had a childhood and never played Poor Pussy?" She laughed. "Well. One of us is to be a kitten, you see? And you sit right there just as you are, and the kitten—I make a lovely kitten—meows and purrs and acts pitiful. And she sits on your lap and asks you to take her home. The kitten must beg, and you must sit with a straight face, and three times pet me and say, 'Poor pussy.'"

"Indeed, you'd make a lovely pussy," he said wryly.

Margaret sat on his lap with a sly seductress's smile.

"Will you take me home, sir?" she said, playfully squirming to discomfit him. "I will be a good pussy."

Motionless in his seat, Gavin gazed into her eyes, visibly struggling to hide an emotion she thought resembled her own cyclone of need.

Slowly, so slowly, he drew her deeper onto his lap, his eyes fastened on her mouth.

"You must say, 'Poor pussy,'" Margaret murmured, this contact, this closeness, beyond anything she'd ever experienced before.

His eyes were uncharacteristically warm, and crinkled at the corners as he brushed the little hairs back from her forehead. "Poor pussy cat," he murmured.

Grinning, she made a sound, the closest she could to a purr. "My lord, take me home, pretty please. I shall be such a good kitty, such a good pussy to you!"

She was attempting to make him laugh, but his face remained sober, spectacularly concentrated on her. He bent his head and placed a close-lipped kiss on the corner of her mouth. "Poor pussy."

Her heart leapt to her throat. "I . . . M-my lord." Suddenly, her mind was as empty as a worm's, but she plunged on. "I seek a home, am a sad little pussy in search of company, and—"

He yanked her head down with a swift pull, his lips fastening to hers with searing force. Something exploded inside her at the sizzling touch of their tongues.

His hands came to her hair, fingers tangling the loose strands as he slanted her face. *"Say you will fuck me, little Margaret."* He speared her with a damp, scorching tongue.

The prominent bulge stretched upward, biting into her buttocks.

Margaret's entire being seemed to be pulled to opposite ends. Her breasts grew heavy and a needy pulse fluttered in her womb as he thrust in his tongue over and over.

Her palms slid up the fabric of his coat and around his taut shoulders. "I will do anything you wish of me."

"Make room for me between your legs."

She parted her thighs, straddling his hips. His knuckles grazed her nipples over her dress. Waves of anticipation arrowed from her nipples to her aching pussy. The muscles of his face relaxed with arousal as he covered the flesh and massaged the mounds.

"Breasts drive me mad." He managed to draw one out of her corset and growled and nipped at the nipple. The stimulation was almost too much for her to stand, her muscles stiffening at the sensations rippling through her. "I'm going to suck your nipples so hard, you're going to feel my mouth on them tomorrow."

Pleasure whipped through her as his hands curved around her ass, grinding her against his erection as his tongue shot into her, plunging inside over and over again, drawing out her moans. The heat, the friction—it was astounding. When he pulled back, she was a burning flame, and trembling head to toe. He cupped her sex between their bodies. His eyes were wild, possessive, drinking in with greed the sight of her reddened lips. His voice was a deep, frightening growl. "Get on your knees, take my prick, and put it in your mouth. All the way in."

She was panting, because when he spoke like that, with such power, she throbbed to be filled up to her throat.

Before she knew it, she slid down his hard thighs, falling between his legs.

He watched with hot eyes, and when he pulled out

his shaft, an electric current shot through her. Its flesh was reddened, the crown bloated and shiny. It made her head spin.

He was incredibly large. And beautiful. And suddenly, it struck her that no matter how many pricks she had licked—which were not many, really; only a handful—she was not prepared for this one.

The skin was stretched and gleaming, so thick, lustrous—yes, as Nuri had said, she could weep.

"You stare," he said, grabbing his shaft with one hand.

She knelt and stroked a fingertip from the silky, dark hairs at the base of the stalk up to the shiny, stretched head. "Yes."

Then she studied the lines of his face, liking all that she saw. His dark, virile face, those heavy-lidded eyes, the thick neck and broad shoulders, the mouth that spoke of sinning. "And you, my lord, seem to grow larger with my stare," she said, noting his face tighten with arousal at her words.

His grin was the devil's.

"Poor pussy. Now you will have to eat it."

She smiled wickedly. "Meow." Oh, truth be told, sometimes she wanted to be a lady. But at this spectacular moment, she wanted to be Margaret Bigler, eating this man's cock.

His thick flesh filled her mouth, and tendrils of excitement rippled deep in her belly.

Sitting back on her heels, she grasped the stalk with one hand and began to move her head like she'd learned to. She could not help peering up at him through her lashes—and found him gazing down at her with eyes that smoldered with black heat.

"You are . . ." he murmured, lifting his hands to the back of her head. He did not finish the sentence, leaving her longing to hear what he'd planned to say. She was what? Wonderful, she hoped. Exquisite. Glorious.

His fingers delved into her hair, massaging her scalp, and the gentle way he did this made her crave more of him than his cock—more of that touch and more of the words he groaned as he began to rotate his hips. "Is every part of you as hot as your mouth, Margaret?" His raw, descriptive language felt like a coil tightening around her womanhood. Each word caused a spasm in her, made her sex burn. She was dripping, could feel a drop of moisture on the inside of her thigh.

He bucked into her, the tip of his penis massaging her throat, flattening her tongue with each slide. His hold didn't loosen on the back of her head, but pinned her for his hips as he began fucking.

She made a gurgling sound deep in her throat when his cock jerked, filling her mouth with his creamy, musky liquid.

She swallowed him again and again, licked and sucked for more. And surprisingly, she felt a shudder go through her. She whimpered, clinging to his still-erect cock, licking as another spasm took her, and then she closed her eyes and stifled the orgasm that threatened her inside. She was so aroused, she would do him for free. She would pay what he owed her to feel him. She would jump to his bidding to feel that cock driving into her aching pussy.

When she recovered, she licked his taste from her lips and quickly fetched a wet cloth to clean him up. She did so lovingly, aware that he watched.

"How long," he asked softly, "must I wait for a room?"

Hope flourished inside her. "Give me a moment, please." She rushed upstairs again and flung open the door to her room.

Nuri was engaged in lively lovemaking with Sir March. Suddenly, Margaret wanted to see exactly how to move her hips, how to drive a man mad, what to say so that next time Claymore wanted pleasure, he would think of no one but Margaret.

"Sir March! Oooh! You are an animal, a beast. Give it to me!" Sir March seemed pleased by the comparison.

"Let me come in you, my darling!" he gasped.

"Yes, yes! Oh, Sir March, I have spent years and years, and now I finally feel like a woman in your arms."

"Then take me! Take me in your woman's fortress, my darling. Let me come in you!"

My darling, Margaret thought with a pang. They said

this, the men. All the time, they said this. When they were fucking you, it was as if they loved you. They called you *darling* and *precious* and *sweet*, and they spilled some unknown yearning or pain or wanting inside you. What sort would Lord Claymore spill into her?

Her blood bubbled with anticipation. She wanted it—would embrace it. She felt fluttery, like a fool, waiting for his lips to say a word so she could do as they bid, waiting for his eyes to touch her so she could come alive.

In one month and dozens and dozens of men, she had never experienced such an overwhelming ardor. On the occasion of losing her hymen, she had done practically nothing but lie there. Her second time had been better, with a middle-aged bookseller who did it slowly and allowed her to gradually come into the pleasure. But with most of the rest, Margaret had done it in such a businesslike manner that she'd promptly forgotten them the instant she was paid.

Claymore came behind her so slowly, she did not feel him until he was reaching over her shoulder, sliding a hand over her bosom.

"You like watching," he murmured in her ear, his voice so rich and thick it made her pores sing.

"No," she breathed, "I was merely thinking of ways to captivate you."

Sir March finished with his grunts and straightened. "Lord Claymore, fancy seeing you here."

"Hmm. Fancy." Claymore sounded distracted, and suddenly his lips were on her bare shoulder, tracing.

He was the first man she'd ever known to realize women like her had shoulders. Not just tits and a cunny.

"You know 'im?" Nuri asked, pushing herself back into her gown.

Sir March busily tucked himself into his trousers. "The question is, Who doesn't in this city?" Chuckling, he patted Nuri's rump and filled her hand with money, then gave Margaret a sly look. "Truth be told, Claymore is the most debauched man I've ever known."

Nuri shoved the money under her skirts and turned her attention to Margaret. "Do you want me to leave you with . . . 'im?"

Debauched. Exactly what did that mean? The tone was in jest, and yet the sparkle of warning in his eyes was unmistakable.

"Leave us." This from him. Claymore. Debauched, gorgeous Claymore.

Margaret heard the door close behind them. The oil lamp trembled on the nightstand as though the darkness of him was too much for one little light.

Margaret did not know where to start. Kiss him? Stroke his cock? Perhaps debauched men were more into biting—

"We have become shy," he said huskily, and he turned her around, hands trailing languorously down her body.

His touch sparked a rush of heat as she struggled for an answer. "I was wondering . . . how to please you. If you would tell me what you like . . ." Her thoughts scattered when he drew off his jacket, then flicked open a shirt button. His lips quirked in such a manner that her breathing altogether stopped.

"I don't seem like an easy man to please?" he asked.

She doubted that he was. An easy man. He would be satisfied with nothing. Certainly not with Margaret.

He chucked her chin. "Just do as I tell you to," he said.

Her cunny burned at the words. *Obey him. Please him. Service him.*

Yes. Oh yes, yes to all.

As he discarded his shirt, his gleaming, bronzed skin beckoned like a sugarplum, and she wanted to lick. Lust coursed through her, so potent it frightened her.

Bare chested, he strode to the bed with the slow majesty of a winged angel ascended from hell. "Come pet me."

He stretched out a hand to her, and the gesture pulsed with force.

Dizzied with anticipation, she moved forward, her body frenzied, no longer hers. Swiftly rising in her was a tide of desire so great, she could not breathe. She was aware she needed to speak, was known to have a word for any moment and any man, but all she could utter was, "My lord."

And he said two modulated words "Pet me."

He was instructing her, the tone almost command-ing, and never had she seen such self-possession in a man. Never had she felt so exhilarated. She forced her hands to move, allowed them to tremulously stroke the smooth, bronzed skin. She swallowed. "I have waited years and years, and now I feel like a woman."

His eyes glinted in amusement. They were so dark they could be black, but in the light of the oil lamp, Margaret noticed they were rimmed with silver.

Holding her breath, biting her lips against the tem-pestuous need coursing through her, she pulled at the ribbons of her bodice with shaky fingers.

He went still, but his body radiated energy, as though he were ready to spring. She held her breath as she tugged down her corset and bared her breast like an of-fering. His eyes devoured her risen nipple.

Margaret felt her breast heave, and something in her squeezed tight at the rapture in his eyes. He did not touch, did not do anything at first. But then he lifted his hand and pinched her with two fingers. He pulled her nipple slowly but hard, and did not release her until a pleasurable pain speared through her system, her head rolled back, and she arched in helplessness.

"This pleases me," he said, his voice a rumble.

He enclosed the exposed breast in his hand, lowered his mouth, and bit her.

Her knees buckled and her hands flew to the back of

his head as she cried out. He growled and suckled and nibbled. He bit so hard, she swallowed back a scream.

His head came up and he stared at her as he tweaked the nipple he'd just sucked. "Very good," he cooed. "Let's see if you can remain quiet while I do this. . . ."

Her nerves jumped with anticipation when he eased his fingers under her skirts, into her drawers. He paused before sliding between her legs, tickling the hairs, testing her moisture. "I don't think I've ever made a prostitute so wet."

"I . . . my lord, I'm frantic for you."

"Then touch my hard prick."

She stroked his impossibly hard prick and savored the feeling. He dipped his head, and she groaned when his mouth covered the peak and sucked her into a hot, scorching vortex.

"Yes."

He sucked her in so deep, she thought he'd swallow her entirely. He loosened the pressure, and the nipple sprang loose. His breath on the wet pearl had her sobbing. He answered with a brush of his lips against it before capturing it again. His voice was thick against the swollen globe as he cupped the bottom and pushed it higher. "I could drink your milk."

When an arm snaked out to smash her against his muscled chest, she made a moan much like the one Nuri had done, and felt his cock stab into her thigh. "Oooh. You are an animal, a beast. You make me . . . you make me . . ."

His eyebrows furrowed. "I make you?"

What the devil had Nuri said? She stared blankly, and then lost all thought as his finger went in so deep that she made a long, starved sound.

"I make you wet," he growled.

"Oh yes."

What was she doing? This was her livelihood. Her only means of survival. But . . . to enjoy it so thoroughly? To wail for one touch? One wild moment?

She could smell herself, how shamelessly she'd moistened. Her pussy felt like a river of fire, the lips bloated between her legs. Claymore petted the curls once, twice. "Good girl. You'd fuck the devil if it pleased me, wouldn't you?"

Margaret parted her thighs and watched him, entranced by his power. "Yes."

He straightened all of a sudden, scowling, and flung her skirts back to her. "Get rid of your skirts if you don't want me to tear them."

Margaret did as she was told and watched him step out of his britches. His cock slapped free, and her vision blurred from the force of her arousal.

"Now." He dragged her down the bed and to him, and she clung to his neck and looped her legs around him. Her breathing became more ragged, ricocheting off the room's walls, as their hands began fondling.

She clawed at his bronzed chest, licked his nipples, caressed his engorged cock. She wanted to climb him like a tree, to ride him so thoroughly he'd not be able to climb his horse tomorrow. More than that, she ached to be taken. "Lie back with your arms over your head," he commanded.

She fell back on the mattress and lifted her arms above her head. Claymore surveyed the globe of her exposed breast with black, half-open eyes. "That's nice."

He yanked the fabric low to expose the other lush curve and dove and sucked on a stiffened nipple. She gasped, sensations tumbling through her. Her hands flew to hold on to something, and his shoulders felt like rocks under her fingers as she gripped him.

"You're such a wicked girl, Margaret," he said, and sucked.

"Yes."

One of his hands trailed along her sides. "You crave being under a man."

"Yes."

And still, he sucked. He squeezed her rump, and she yelped. He growled, "Lie still now."

He flipped her around and fondled her ass cheeks, pushed them up and sideways with his hands, and his wild tongue came at her skin, licking over and over, torturing the fissure between them with each pass.

She'd never met a hungrier man, not even such a hungry animal.

"Lift your pussy to me." She did by raising her buttocks at an angle, and he buried his face between the soft mounds.

His mouth clamped onto her clit. He sucked so hard, her chest lifted from the bed, the suckles filling her pussy with spasms; then he was sticking his fingers into her swamped cunt, telling her to take them as he skimmed his lips over her clit.

She was undone by him, *undone*. She rolled her hips in ecstasy, whimpering as her movements created the most delicious friction with his impaling fingers and his lashing tongue.

His guttural words caressed her burning pussy. "So wanton . . . so creamy and so very dirty at heart . . ."

Her throat tightened with desire; it was painful to speak. When he urged her onto her back and lifted his head, his face was utterly inscrutable. Captivating in its mystery.

He pushed his fingers into her again. His eyes flashed as she cried out, coming already, the one meant to plea-sure the customer being pleasured instead. She closed her eyes as he played her, mewling deep in her throat when he eased one, two long fingers into her rippling sheath. Her breath hissed through her teeth. She felt such amazing pressure as he screwed a third finger in. His breaths were harsh, the muscles of his face taut with arousal. "You want to be fucked?"

"By you, yes!"

His breath exploded from his lungs as he tore away and rose to his knees, running one deft hand over himself. "Stroke my cock, then, and if you do it well, we'll see how hard you'll get fucked."

He knelt between her legs and she reveled at the sight of him, cock jutting toward her body, muscles damp with sweat, glistening in the filtered moonlight. The sac of his testicles was heavy, drawn tight, and terribly tempting to her fingers.

She sat up and reached out immediately, securing his manhood between both her hands. Never had she held something so scalding or delectable as Claymore. Her mouth watered; she wanted to take him in her mouth again and drain him of every drop.

Instead she rubbed her cheek against the distended head and fondled him gently with her fingers. He hissed, bucking. She tightened her hold and put her lips on his abdomen, up to his throat, his shoulder. His hips started to swivel, and her thumb encountered a silky wetness at the tip of his staff.

He ducked, taking her shoulder with his mouth, pressing his thumb into her heatedly. "Your cunt." He touched her sex with four more of his fingers, the other hand splayed on her ass. "Lie back and show it to me."

"I—" She scrambled to do his bidding and quickly sprawled back to be observed. "Like this? Do you like—"

He groaned as he bent over her and licked her ear.

He was frenzied, out of control, his voice demanding and utterly sexy. "Part your thighs. I'd like to view your cunt fully. How swollen and moist it is."

"Please."

He forced her thighs apart and sprawled authoritatively on top of her, pushing the soft mounds of her breasts together and massaging them between his hands.

Then he peered down at what she displayed between her parted legs.

His eyes, tangible as a touch, probed deeply, took in every detail of the glistening sex peeking amid her moist curls.

He stroked her wet cunt with his fingers. Her eyes rolled back as sensations stormed through her. She felt taken and discovered, owned and commanded. She had never realized what a freeing, beautiful feeling it would be. She didn't even try to hide it.

Claymore moaned as if her abandon pained him, and she groaned without control. He made pumping motions with his hips as her body took those long fingers. He used one finger, then two; then he plunged in three. Swallowing back a cry, she buried her face in the neck that smelled of man and opened her legs more as he twisted in his fingers.

Her breasts were hot and heavy and crushed against his chest, her legs scissored wide open. When she lifted her head, she saw him positioning himself to mount her.

She tensed as he grabbed her hips and aligned their bodies. For three seconds, he only rubbed against her, and they moaned in unison as his shaft glided across the slick folds of her sex. Then in a blinding second, he rammed his hips against hers and impaled. Stars exploded in her eyes as a wrenching relief tore through her. His head fell back as though unhinged, his face twisted in agony, his muscles rippling and flexing as he began to move.

Margaret closed her eyes, pulled into a frenzy of need, delighting to each slide of the steel rod inside her. The way he stretched her brought with each thrust a sweet pain, special somehow, welcomed. Like a dark secret between them, a balance. He enjoyed taking her. She enjoyed giving to him.

He pulled back and drew her up to her knees, yanking her against his cock. He hissed, "Take my cock. All of it—take it deep!"

She mewled as he rammed into her.

"More, Margaret, more!"

She sobbed in pleasure. Her sex opened as more inches entered, then closed tighter around his swelled member and squeezed. He growled, grinding his hips against hers.

"Christ, when you take all of me like this, I could go mad!"

He desperately sought his pleasure, and Margaret

thought that now, unguarded as he rutted, he looked exposed. Overpowered. Vulnerable.

He stopped moving, his thick cock inside her, their eyes locked in a storm of passion. Then only his hands moved as they tweaked her nipples between two fingers. He said one word: *"Come."*

She came with such intensity, Gavin gritted his teeth at the feel of the soft milk of her pussy against him. He flipped her around as she was still shaking and flattened her on her stomach. As she trembled with aftershocks, he spread her thighs wide and aligned his cock into her swollen entry.

Her skin was dewy with sweat, tendrils of hair clinging to her temples. Fleetingly, he glimpsed her rosy ass cheeks, heard her moaning as he nudged his cock between her pussy lips. He gave a bark of pleasure when he was balls deep in the tight passage. And still he pinned her hands at her sides, extended his arms for leverage, and watched her undulate under him as he rocked his hips back and forth and, blinded with ecstasy, took her.

Her hands fisted on the mattress. Pleasure jolted through him.

He didn't know why with every mighty thrust, he felt powerless. This wrenching lust and wanting inside of him had been there, ever present, for years. Every ounce of this wildness was hers, every suck of air, every plunge into her body was one he'd never been able to give anyone. Now he was ready to come in her, to lose himself inside her warmth.

He bent and dragged his lips to her temple, plunged his tongue into her ear, and breathlessly murmured, "What is my name, little one?"

"My lord Claymore."

He turned his mouth to hers, groaning as he pumped. Bliss surged through him, pulsing, hot, pulling him taut. "Margaret."

"Claymore."

"I wish you to call my name when you find pleasure. Say Gavin."

"Gavin."

"Yessss. Say *Gavin!*"

"Oh, god, Gavin!"

He yelled out as her pussy started milking him. His plunging cock jerked inside her, so hard it broke a cry from her lips. When she cried his name, no power in this world could have stopped it.

He came so violently his cum seemed shot out of a pistol, hot as it splashed into her womb, warm and welcome. He took a deliciously long time in spending himself; Margaret's own climax followed his, so that their bodies rocked and spasmed together for what seemed like forever.

She had never experienced this. She felt free, far away from this place and from herself, her past, what she'd seen in France in the slums, on the deathbeds of her parents. She wept, trying to suck back her tears, but they rolled down her cheeks.

She was sobbing uncontrollably when he went still and extracted himself. His seed swirled down the inside of her thigh. She wanted to take it with her finger and push it back inside her, taste it with her mouth.

Up on his arms, he gazed into her face, and her lips quivered. A weeping whore; he must think her comical. But there was no distaste in his eyes, only a flash of disturbance. He raised his hands as though to wipe her tears, then halted, seemed to think better of it, and disengaged himself.

She wiped her face furiously, trying to get back in control as he rose to get dressed.

From the next room, Nuri's voice rose. "Oh, you're a beast, an animal! Oh, Mr. Schmidt, I've been waiting years and years to feel like a woman again."

His head jerked up. Their eyes met, and inexplicably, deliciously, his lips quirked. "You toyed with me, little Margaret."

She would have been mortified if not for the glimmer of amusement in his eyes, and she felt a laugh bubble up her throat. "A girl must rely on her memory when she is at a loss for words," she said.

He buttoned up his shirt and waistcoat, and then came over, holding her face in one large, wide hand. He whispered tenderly, moving his thumb. "Thank you, little one." And kissed her lips.

But when he searched inside his pocket for the money, she did the unthinkable. She curled her hand around his, closing his fist. "No." Startled, his eyes flew to hers, and a sudden warmth crawled up her cheeks. "Keep it."

It was the best she could do not to say *thank you*, as well. *I adore you. You are wonderful.*

One did not say these things to these men.

He seemed to soften for an unguarded moment; then he turned his hand and pressed the money into her palm. "Your heart does not belong . . . with what you do." She flushed as his lips softened. "And I don't like to hear you say no to me." He nodded, his gaze strangely stark and forbidden. "Take it. You need it."

She knew a moment of despair as she watched him leave, then gazed down at her hand as Mr. Schmidt's and Nuri's cries of ecstasy echoed.

He'd given her fifty pounds.

A fortune.

A. *Fortune.*

Margaret should be ecstatic, leaping with joy. She was as rich as she'd never been. Instead she curled her body and tucked the pillow to her chest, wishing he were still kissing her breasts.

Chapter Five

~

M-my lord . . . I seek a home, am a sad little pussy in search of company, and—

Gavin slammed the tome shut and tossed it against the bookshelf. Who the devil was Margaret playing pussy with now?

He frowned at the brandy his footman had delivered, sitting untouched on the glossy surface of his desk, and he struggled with a strange desire to meet the simpering idiots she'd played pussy with and crack all their teeth with his fist. Indeed, boxing had its advantages. To let some bastard muck you up in case you ever had the necessity to punch someone.

But it wasn't the desire to maim some unfortunate bastard's face that had been keeping him awake at night.

It was a woman and her silly, childish games, and her hot, receptive body.

Underlying the desire for her was an unguarded possessiveness he didn't understand, let alone want to feel. He should be thinking of how Lady Georgiana Seaton had fluttered her lashes at him and how calm and self-possessed she seemed to be.

Instead he was consumed by a prostitute's generosity. Her passion. Unflinching, unapologetic. He kept envisioning her face as she declined the money. What had she meant to say by this gesture?

And what kind of hellish emotion had he felt the moment she did it?

Awe. Amazement. Respect. He had felt . . . humbled.

He imagined someone touching her this very evening, and felt strangely agitated. He rose to pace, his duties, the stack of papers on his desk, all forgotten, as they had been for days. And he thought the same thought that had been haunting his mind every second since he'd left her.

Give the poor pussy a home.

Margaret gazed across the gloomy park for the sixth night in a row. And no, Claymore wasn't there. But in her mind, he was kissing her, so heatedly her lungs expanded in her chest. His manly scent had permeated her body, lingered on her skin, in her sex, in her nostrils.

Nuri sighed beside her.

"If you plan to be moonin' over 'im, then you're a fool."

Margaret's gaze once again swept across the lawns. And Claymore was still kissing her.

"Not coming back, that one, at least not anytime soon. Margaret, he's a *lord*."

"Yes, I know."

Their heels clapped across the walkway. A breeze rustled, but still the fog closed in on them.

"Leave the daydreaming for the ladies, Margaret. We must be practical."

"Yes, of course."

And Claymore was kissing her.

"Look, those two over there. Fine specimens, they are."

Those two were decent-looking fellows, true. It would do no harm to frig one off or let him spend himself in her mouth. She supposed she could go back to work in the match factory, too, but the memory of what it had done to her mother held her back. No. She would not walk willingly into death.

She was no innocent, had done sinful things, and none of those things seemed to have marred her hope. She had used her body, and some said she had lost her soul—and *still* she hoped. That one day she would be happy. That she would be loved. She believed in it, not in the passing fancy of a gentleman with an erection, but in real, true, momentous love. Sometimes she thought that when she stopped believing in it, in love, she would die. It was all that took her through the day. Thinking that it was not always like this, and that it would not always be like this. That it could be better.

"Evening, gentlemen," Nuri said chirpily, drawing Margaret by her side.

And Claymore was still kissing Margaret, even as the gentlemen hailed a carriage and they headed off toward the house. Margaret let her customer put his hand on her knee, and gazed outside all the time he petted it. She couldn't afford to be a silly fool. She had to make do with what she had, and what she had was a willing customer.

They entered the establishment, but as they did, her stomach began to contract. And there . . . there was Mrs. T.

"Margaret." She crooked her finger, and Margaret excused herself from the gentlemen.

"We'll wait upstairs for you, Margaret," Nuri said.

But Margaret barely listened, for Mrs. T., with her usual stern expression, was handing her a large box and an envelope to go with it.

"This was left for you."

Once, long ago, she had received a gift from her father; that was before he passed and things went on to the worst. She remembered feeling giddy with excitement, her mind rushing to conjure what the box must contain, uncertain whether she wanted to know what was there. Would it exceed the lovely fantasies of her mind? Did she dare open it?

Now, though she felt a stunning curiosity, she left the note for last, because *that* she wanted to pretend was from him.

Finding an uncrowded corner, she opened the package with fingers that moved with difficulty, and pulled out a large fan, the most beautiful in the history of *ever*, with long, satiny white feathers. She stroked the tips and felt an emotion close to pain crowd her heart. For a moment she gathered her breath, and turned the envelope around.

There was a symbol—very elegant—on it. Her heart leapt to her throat, and she broke the seal and pulled out the letter as if it was the last thing she would ever read. But it was not even the first. Clutching the fan, she carried the letter back to Mrs. T. "Can you please tell me what it says?"

She harrumphed, then spread it open and cleared her throat very importantly. "So that together we may fan the flames of our passion. Lord Gavin Claymore."

Margaret clutched the fan tightly to her chest even as her heart seemed to grow its own feathers. "No jest. It is from him?"

"Who else buys such an expensive thing but a lord?"

"Yes, yes, of course."

"Oh, and an addition." Mrs. T. peered down at the letter, reading, "My man will pick you up tomorrow at six of the evening. I should like to see you again."

Tomorrow. At six. She would see Gavin Claymore again.

"Well?" Margaret asked excitedly the next morning as Nuri scrutinized her teacup.

Her friend looked as if she were fiercely concentrating, lines carved into her brow, and Margaret's heart pounded in her throat.

"Tell me," she urged, squirming in her seat.

She wanted to listen to a story like the ones her mother used to tell her, the ones that ended happily and left her smiling. She wanted Nuri to tell her that she—she, Margaret Bigler, a nobody, a fallen woman, a whore—had found true love in this life. She wanted to hear Nuri tell her that this man, Mr. Momentous, would give her that.

She was French, after all. She did not believe so much in marriage. But she believed in love. And her mother had always allowed her to dream of it. Margaret had always hoped, suspected, and prayed that she would experience the wonder of it.

Nuri's eyes widened when they hit the bottom center of the cup. She stared long and hard, then lowered it with a slightly cryptic expression. "Oh."

Margaret's chair seemed to have broken under her. "What?"

Nuri shook her head, and her hand trembled as she smoothed her skirts. "We will do this again later."

"But later I will be with him."

Nuri's gaze seemed to fall everywhere except on Margaret. "The teacup must be dirty."

"Nuri, just *tell me*. My heart is near bursting, Nuri. Please speak. Will he be the one to take me out of here? Will he . . . will he give me romance? Some happiness in my life?"

Romance. Beauty. Yes. The Frenchwoman in her was singing now, stoked by a gift from a beautiful gentleman.

And when finally Nuri's gaze settled on Margaret, the grim expression on her face wasn't what Margaret had hoped for. "He will give you romance," she grudgingly admitted.

Her heart soared at this.

"He will give you love, Margaret."

"Oh, my."

"A love he will never speak of."

Her heart soared higher. Up beyond the room. Beyond the sky.

"He will give you everything . . ." she said, voice dropping, "and in the end, he will have given you nothing."

Margaret froze, then blinked in confusion. The end. Nothing.

She stared for a moment, then frowned. "I suppose

that you suppose that I'm supposed to know what you mean?"

"Just what it is."

Nothing.

The word had the finality of death. Why had Margaret not noticed this before? *Nothing* was such a . . . such a horrid word.

"Well, it's just a silly teacup, isn't it." Margaret sniffled and got up. "He already gave me a fan, and that is not nothing to me." She sniffled again, and an old, stubborn cough threatened to emerge. "I make my own future." She smiled pointedly at her worried friend. "And for one small amount of anything you mention, I would give my life to experience. I would have one happy day for a thousand sad ones I've lived through."

And with that, she left Nuri alone with her teacups.

Chapter Six

*A*t six in the evening, Margaret boarded Claymore's carriage. December was always dismal in London, and yet today the sun could have been up and the sky uncommonly clear, she felt so very exhilarated.

At six twenty, she descended. His townhome stood gray and fine along Picadilly, and Margaret couldn't stop arranging and rearranging her bodice while she waited for the footman to answer the door.

But when the door swung open, it was Claymore, dark and captivating, who appeared, and Margaret went light-headed as he soberly beckoned her inside. Oh, she really was mooning. Over this lord.

He wore fine evening attire, and she didn't know whether he'd dressed so impeccably to see her or whether he was going out or whether he'd been somewhere just before, but she thought no man filled his clothes as regally as Gavin Claymore did.

She surveyed his furniture in awe. Tasteful, it was, with the carpets spreading out splendidly side to side, the ample windows allowing in streaks of the setting sunlight.

As she navigated curiously around the sitting area, she became aware of his eyes, dark like a Gypsy's, and how they gazed at her so intently. His eyebrows were drawn as if he were trying to guess her thoughts, and the fading sunlight from outside picked out gleams in his hair.

Margaret belatedly remembered her manners. She curtsied. "Thank you, my lord. For the gift. The feathers are very soft, and white! Such a pure color. I've never seen a bird with feathers so large."

His eyes roamed her face, slowly, as though storing it in memory. "Indeed," he murmured. "They're peacock feathers. I'm told white peacocks are quite rare."

He had an unbending air about him today, a formal one, and was silent, more silent than that first evening.

He dragged his gaze away with apparent effort, pondering something. To the room in general he murmured, "They're said to be compassionate and sensitive." He regarded her as though she were a peacock herself. Compassionate and sensitive. "It is thought they die of grief when their mates die."

"Oh." She hadn't known. Animals did this? How incredible. "That is quite . . . tragic. Was that what happened to mine?"

He tangled his fingers in his hair, sending a rush of

longing up her center. "I couldn't say. Would you like to think so?"

She thought quite hard. Tragic and romantic. "Yes, I believe that is just what happened to mine." *And now my mate gives it to me.* She did not say this, but she thought it. No. She wished it. That he be her mate.

He approached as she continued standing, his size rendering the blue settee nearby somehow more delicate. His fingers linked with hers and he stroked her palm with his thumb, his eyes glistening with light-hearted mockery. "The bedrooms are upstairs. Forgive me if that is all I seem to think of."

Heart pounding, she followed him down a quiet hall and up the sweeping stairs. Her body was quaking. Her fingers, still in his, were also quaking.

They entered a bedroom so large, one could ride a horse in it. The bed stood at the far end, its carved wooden headboard fit for a . . . well, a future duke.

"My fingers itch to touch you."

Spurred to action, she whirled around and began unfastening her dress. But Claymore caught her hands and drew her to him until her breasts were crushed against his chest. He lifted a hand and caressed her cheek with his fingers.

"No hurry."

He turned off the smile before she could fully enjoy it, and the intensity of his sober expression made something pulse within her—between them.

His fingers trailed over her bodice, soft, like his voice, and unlike his gaze. "Did you enjoy your evening with me, Margaret?"

"Yes," she breathed. Awareness of his desire for her streaked across her skin. A pulse began beating in her womb, down her legs, up her breasts.

He was visibly trying to find words, and all the while, his fingers stroked her. Long moments passed. When he again spoke, his timbre was so deep, she felt it sink into her bones. "Do you know what I most remember of that night?"

She tried for a smile. "The exorbitant fee you paid me, no doubt."

His eyes were afire. He stroked his thumbs across her cheeks roughly, as if she had smudges there, and said thickly, "I remember the way you cried."

She cast her gaze downward, hiding her face.

His lips grazed the top of her head. "Sometimes extreme beauty . . . or extreme pleasure . . . is perceived as pain."

She gazed thoughtfully at the tapestried walls, wishing she hadn't cried, unable to do anything about it, but certainly determined not to cry now. "I found it both beautiful and pleasurable." *And eye-opening and heart wrenching and addicting and . . .*

"Do you enjoy pain, Margaret?"

She blinked, taken aback. "My lord, I do not seek pain, if that is your question."

"I see." Disappointment? Was that what she saw in his eyes? He pulled at his cravat and said, "Undress."

Margaret hadn't predicted that to get out of the dress Nuri had helped her into, she might need the same kind of assistance. Nonetheless, she tried to make do with her own two hands.

"The human mind is extraordinary." He pulled off his jacket and tossed it onto a chair. "Did you know that when we cut ourselves, it takes a moment for it to ache— a moment before the event registers in our brain?"

There it was again. Pain. The talk of pain both excited and frightened her. "No. I did not know."

His garments seemed to be piling up on the chair, while Margaret still struggled to unlace herself.

"It leaves one to speculate on what happens if one's will is stronger than one's mind and dictates another response to the painful occurrence. One that converts it to pleasure. Do you need assistance?"

"I . . ." She gave up her attempts and came over. "I do."

But instead of undressing her, he hauled her up to the bed, plopped her down on the edge, then grabbed her legs and spread her open.

His fingers eased through fabric, revealing her cunt to him. The look in his eyes was worshipful when he spotted her pussy.

"I confess." His features were shadowed, his cheekbones dark and forbidding, and he smelled so utterly male, she worried she'd faint before their climax. "I haven't drunk from a woman's quim before."

"You have not?"

"No." A hoarse, dry rasp as he knelt between her legs. "Has someone's tongue been titillating it?"

His provocative words sent ripples through her bloodstream. "No."

"I would like to use mine to taste." He licked his thumb before he used it to penetrate her. "Tease. Explore." He circled it inside her channel.

Her veins bubbled with lust, her sex muscles clamping over his roving thumb. "W-why have you not tasted a woman before?" Such a worldly man.

"Perhaps because I did not think it would bring me pleasure." He pinned her with an intense look, adding a second finger to her drenched pussy. "But you . . . It brought you pleasure when you took my cock in your mouth. You drank of me and vibrated with need."

Such bold talk she'd never experienced. Such arousal with just talk she had *never* experienced.

"You taste milky and salty and feel . . . hard and powerful in my mouth." Her words sparked a flare of dark lust in his eyes. She added, stroking his silky ebony hair, "Yes, it gave me pleasure."

"You could have reached climax. Drinking me."

"I almost did."

"I wonder . . . if I taste your lovely little quim . . . will I take pleasure from your pleasure?"

He withdrew his thumb. She made a sound; a sharp inhalation of breath.

"Lift your skirts higher, Margaret."

When he disappeared under them, her legs went limpid and her head flew back as she felt a warm, moist flick. Passion coursed through her as he began to kiss her there as if it were her lips, his growling sounds muted under the fabric of her skirts.

She pulled the fabric up to her waist to see the dark crown of his head buried between her thighs. Never had she pictured such a decadently arousing sight. His lashes lifted; he stared into her eyes.

"Spicy," he said, by way of explaining his hunger, and spread her legs farther apart and continued with his investigation. Her thighs looked creamy white next to his tanned hands as they held her open. And his tongue. Goodness, his tongue. Wondrous instrument of pleasure. Her hips rotated up, seeking its expert plunges, ripples going across her body as he dragged it up to the little pearl he had teased to life.

It was on fire under his rolling tongue.

"My lord."

"Gavin." He brought a hand up to insert his thumb into her swelling entry. "I will be a man to you, Margaret. With you. And you will call me *my lord* when I say so. And you will call me *Gavin* when I say so."

"What should I call you now?"

"I said so before. I say it now. Gavin."

"Gavin . . . does tasting me give you pleasure?"

"Immense."

"Immense pleasure."

"My cock is jealous, Margaret, of what my tongue is doing." He licked the wet sex again. "I can feel every clutch of your pussy in my testicles."

She closed her eyes, edged closer to his mouth, draped her legs around his shoulders.

"Yes, that's it. Let me feast." He bent over again, and she could feel the thirst in his plunges increase, the passion in him rise as she leaked and leaked into his mouth, giving him that spiciness he tasted. "Yes. Yes, Margaret, yes."

"Yes."

They said the word in whispers and groans; he said "yes" and licked and lapped, and she said "yes" and moaned for more.

Then she gasped, for he'd moved fast and suddenly slapped her cunt. Her shocked cry ricocheted across the room, not yet fully fading before another came forth.

He'd slapped her once more, with his entire palm. Her whole body jerked from the impact. Pleasure shot up from her extremities to her center.

"My lord!"

He drew back. His shadow loomed above her and his breathtaking eyes shone powerfully in the shadows. The drapes on the window had been left open, and the inky planes and angles of his face were illuminated by the teasing flicker of moonlight.

He wasn't smiling.

"If the hurt is too great, stop me." His voice was coarse, his breathing irregular as he retrieved a glass object from a drawer. As he spoke, the tip of the sleek glass phallus found her center, pressing but not entering. "You may have this, Margaret, but only if you pay the price of desiring it."

The back of Margaret's head furrowed deeper into the pillow as she arched up to the cool, hard object that resembled a man's penis, a man's authoritative erection. Juices trickled along her pussy folds.

She had never been so aroused by an object.

"Could a woman like me afford to pay?" she asked.

What would be the price of wanting Gavin Claymore and his debauched sexual acts? How many lifetimes would a girl be in debt to such astounding fantasies?

Under her palms, his shoulders were hot, rigid, and she sank her nails into him and drew him closer. Just feeling him, feeling the desire that stormed through him like a wind, sent her into a tailspin.

Over her bodice, he grabbed one plump breast, grasping her pointed nipple and pinching it hard.

"Your submission, Margaret. That is all I crave."

"Oh, oh!" she cried as shuddering jolts of pleasure bolted down to her clitoris.

"Your submission to *me*. And to what I can give you."

As he buried deeper between her thighs, his cock

brushed up the side of her knee. His hand brought the tumescent head of the glass phallus to fondle her clit.

Gasping at each upward stroke, she clawed down his arms. Her womb felt heavy and near bursting. This wasn't just desire, but another kind of need cramming her insides in a way that made her want to scream. A need for this man, this stranger. "My lord, please."

She sensed the tension in him, palpable in his body. It was as though he was trying to be slow for her sake, but Margaret didn't want slow. She wanted fast. She wanted all of him, all of that inanimate sexual object he teased her cunt with. Even the pain—good god, even *that* she craved.

She slid her hands down his muscled, bronzed chest and pinched his nipples. He cursed under his breath and groaned, "Margaret, I will hurt you."

The place between her legs felt like a blazing flame, and her chest hurt even more. "If you hurt me," she whimpered, and gripped wads of silky black hair in her fists, "I will relish it."

"Christ, you're a little whore." The word *whore* in the manner he spoke it sounded admiring. As though above a lady or even a virgin, he respected a whore. He whipped her around then, to her stomach, and pulled her up on all fours.

He pressed into her backside with his front and thrust his tongue into her ear, acting as aroused as Margaret had ever seen a gentleman. "You'll get fucked for that." His hand burrowed between her thighs, bringing the glass dildo to fondle her moist folds. "You'll get fucked everywhere, Margaret. You'll get fucked on your tongue, in your pussy. You'll get fucked until morn."

She wanted it desperately, and nodded vigorously as she said, "Please." How she loved to beg! How she loved to feel womanly and frail, and how she trusted this man would give her what she needed.

Gavin withdrew and brought the moistened glass cock to her lips. He teased her parted mouth with its wide head. "Lick." When she helplessly, hungrily, lapped at the moisture, sipping the musky taste of herself, he purred, "Good girl. Like a little slave girl, obeying master." And then he licked the phallus with her. The corners of their tongues brushed. Need tightened and twisted in her womb.

When he lowered it between her legs again, his eyes trapped hers, stormy with lust. "I want us to withhold our climax for a while."

"Pardon?"

"I want us not to come. I want you near bursting."

She stared into Gavin's eyes, the pupils dark and dilated with desire. He forced her chest down, breasts crushed to the bed, and pulled her backside higher up.

"Spread for me."

She spread.

"Wider. Spread wider." He flattened a hand on her upper back and pushed her body lower still.

She gripped the comforter in her fists. "How long are we supposed to . . . withhold?"

"As long as possible."

He thrust the cock into her moist cleft, and to hold back a scream of ecstasy, she tensed and gnawed her lip. "I want you, Gavin." She had to say it; she had to have him.

He twisted the penis back in. "Do you? Do you?"

"Yes!"

"And yet I do not pay you to want me. I pay you to please me."

"I . . ." The magic of that smooth cock continued to work deeper into her channel. Her throat closed with desire, and her forehead rolled on the bed in bliss. She had seen men stick women with objects, but never one as lovely, as similar to a man's organ, as hard and long and thick as this.

"Your pleasure is my pleasure, my lord!" she cried, relishing his dominance, his power over her.

He stopped feeding her pussy with inches and inches of hard glass shaft and instead pressed a thumb into the rosette of her ass. "Stay still while I get in here."

She protested deep in her throat, wanting more of what he'd been doing, but still she enjoyed—*delighted in*—the surprising penetration of her tight ass.

"Cease your whimpering, Margaret. You'll get cock soon. You might even get it here."

"I want it now—"

He moved like a lightning bolt. One second she was urging him on; the next he whipped her around, captured her wrists, and held them trapped in one hand high above her head, submitting her to him in that dominant pose. "Wicked girl."

"I'm sorry, my lord. I . . . I'm so impatient."

His eyes were like moonless nights. Stark and black and utterly shadowy. He reached for his own shaft and guided it to her slit, using the coating of juice to moisten himself. "Now you'll have to take it."

"Yes."

He nudged her with his hips and her knees fell sideways so that his shaft and balls couched against the cradle of her thighs. "Jesus, yes. Take all of it! Take it like you took the toy!"

He spread an aperture at the top of her dress and pulled out her breasts, the creamy white globes enhanced by the thrusting nipples.

"What a feast."

His lips settled on her risen nipples, suckling them so forcefully that she felt turned inside out. And when she moaned, he ground his penis against her, slapping his bollocks against her bottom. *Yes, oh, oh.* She gripped the muscles of his buttocks and pulled him deeper, wanting him inside her, and twisted up and offered her mouth, moaning in delirium. He seized her mouth instantly, his tongue foraying steadily inside; then her own tongue was drawn into his mouth with a strong, succulent suckle.

He spread her lips open and watched his cock emerge, coated with her desire and with his own. "From now on, this pink little entry is mine. Perhaps you would like to own my cock for the evening?"

Her vision faded as he once again eased into her. She raked her hands down his back, hauling him closer, biting at his shoulder. "Yes, it is mine. I want it."

"Where do you want it? In your hot, wet little quim, Margaret?"

He had such a wicked, laughing look, she could not resist. Her stockinged legs clamped around him, her thighs tightening as he plunged inside.

She screamed in ecstasy.

"Margaret." His hands tightened on her waist and the intense pressure of his grasp didn't cease, as though he was silently demanding she look at him.

She pressed into him, conforming her body to his as her palms opened on his back. She chanted, out of her mind with desire, "Don't stop, don't stop, don't stop. Please don't stop."

He growled something like *fuck* before he went into a frenzy of movement and thrust up higher, harder, notably too undone to talk now, just grunting, growling, rubbing his face up her neck. The muscles on his back vibrated under her hands as he plunged and rammed and stabbed.

In scantly understandable murmurs, he groaned things into her ear. Exquisite words. Heart wrenching. She could comprehend only a few, like *pretty pussy* and *fucking mad* and *spend inside you*, but they stirred every tiny inch of her body.

Sweating and panting and pounding her, he seized her ankles and pulled her legs up, folding them around his shoulders, adjusting his position so that when he fucked, he fucked all the way to her heart.

It was painful and it was naughty and it was wonderful. Margaret was fully open with her legs draped around his shoulders, and when he inserted a finger into her anus, she wanted to die.

"My lord!" she shrieked, tensing to climax.

His kiss was brutal, rough, holding no finesse, only hunger and need and passion. His tongue swept up to the roof of her mouth, then down, quickly retreating before it stabbed in again.

When he stopped kissing her, he drew back slightly and their gazes met. Some dense, fierce emotion flickered in his, but she couldn't understand its meaning. It felt as though he wanted to say something with his eyes, but what?

Nothing she'd ever seen in anyone's eyes when they'd looked at her before.

Then those eyes fell shut as he lodged his cock deep inside her and snarled as he started shuddering. The feel of his hard body coiling and flexing as he spasmed completely undid her. She climaxed with a gasp and clung to him as her orgasm crashed like a cataclysm across her body, shaking her.

It felt as though they shook and trembled forever before she even realized they were like lifeless puppets on the bed. His body pinned her down on the mattress, and though it was hard to breathe, she didn't care.

When he shifted to her side, he didn't say a word, only held her against him. It took a long time for Margaret's drumming heart to regain its usual rhythm.

"Christ, you've no notion of the things I'd like to do to you."

She stirred at his words, and when she caught him watching her, she couldn't control the impulse to reach up. Three of her fingers ventured to his jaw and felt the rasp of his rougher skin, the tautness of his bone. She loved his debauchedness—she loved how it brought out hers, and gave her permission, without judgment, to be who she was. "Whisper your fantasy to me," she said. "I will grant it."

He halted her hand.

"You." A thoughtful silence, then more of his powerful stare. "You are my fantasy."

Those were the most beautiful words ever spoken to her. No surprise that her heart soared so high, Margaret thought she'd never catch it.

She sat up, attempting to regain her thoughts. "I don't understand."

He stacked his arms behind his head and gazed up at the domed ceiling. "My friends are having a wager." He shrugged to himself. "Sir March has a wagging tongue, you see."

"What has it been wagging about?"

He did not look at her, his gaze fixed on the ceiling.

Then his lips curved, wickedly, absolutely. "He seems to believe I am taken with you."

She tripped on her own words, laughing as she spoke them. "Nuri seems to think that I am taken with *you*!"

His gaze met hers. They both smiled. "Are you?"

Yes, yes, yes! Softly, trying to regain herself, she admitted, "I cannot afford to be."

"And if you could?"

She stared, entranced by the stark darkness in his eyes. There was so much need there. So much solitude.

"If I dress you up and set you up in a house and promise you will not want for anything—" He stroked her hair, his hand heavy. "You would do everything you do at this time, but you would do it only with me. Would you submit to me? Belong to me?"

Momentous, Margaret. Momentous.

"Forgive me for my stupidity, but could you elaborate on this . . . proposal?"

He touched her face, tenderly, as though it were precious. "I've tortured myself all day, wondering who is touching you. The thought of you playing pussy with another man is wreaking havoc with my mind."

She rose to tidy herself. "Oh, nonsense. I've only had but three men today."

His arms bulged as he pushed himself up to sit. The expression on his face was positively sober. "Do you shatter for them like you did for me?"

She smiled. "I am fooling, my lord."

He swung his legs off the bed. "Do not. Fool with me, Margaret." But his face lit, like a sun warming the daisies, and she ached to make it light up again and again.

She'd never had this with a man, this unique feeling of closeness and oneness. Could they have this in there lives?

He came to her, and the air she inhaled was warmed by his breath. "What would you say, Margaret?"

He was so ludicrously sexy, made her feel so positively divine, she did not even hesitate. "I would say yes, Claymore."

The ripple of heat that vibrated through him seared her to her soul. "And if you knew I intended to hurt you?" he asked then.

"Like tonight?"

"Indeed. Like tonight." He gazed at her breasts and pinched one so hard, she cried out in shock. "When I look at you . . . I wish to give you pain, Margaret. It excites me. Can you understand that?"

A kernel of fear settled in the pit of her stomach. She swallowed, striving to put space between them.

He spoke from somewhere atop her head, while she . . . she couldn't breathe as the words registered. "I dream of you screaming with pain and climaxing with it."

She swallowed again, but the lump in her throat had grown tenfold and it was nearly impossible to dislodge it. Why was it that the notion of pain, coming from his hand, aroused her body? She hadn't realized that she was pacing until she found herself by the window.

"Margaret." He sighed. "My mood today. I apologize." He rubbed his face and began to dress.

Margaret spun to face him. "Yes!"

He froze, his hands still over his shirt buttons.

"Yes," she fumbled, nodding and nodding, every passing second wanting it more. "It will give me pleasure to . . . take the pain. Greater pain."

Had his face not tightened and contorted, she'd have guessed he hadn't heard her, for he was holding his breath and it seemed to take minutes until he expelled it. He stalked over and kissed her mouth, a kiss of possession and somehow of gratitude. Their lips opened simultaneously and his tongue stroked over hers. "You will be mine and mine alone. I do not share what is mine."

"Nor I," she said, grinning. His lips twitched in amusement, as though the thought that she owned him was preposterous. But she was to be his mistress, wasn't she? She would be his mistress and she would tend to him, she would pleasure him, she would cherish and devote herself to him, and she would . . . not . . . share.

Chapter Seven

~

Gavin set her up on Jeremy Street, near his gentleman's lodgings and in a spacious town house he arranged to have furnished fashionably for her. From there, Margaret could roam London freely, though many times, he caught her gazing out at the hoop-jumping children and strolling ladies from the window seat. The acclaimed portraitist Lawrence painted her miniature for him. Gavin had to have it, for some reason. When the Duke and Duchess of Hartfield went away to their country estate in Norfolk, he took his mistress to their box at Covent Garden. He bought her armloads of gowns— and that was after purchasing her the loveliest mare at Tattersall's.

And Margaret—she smiled. And smiled. And laughed. And he was so addicted to giving her pleasure, he worried about the day she'd take that smile from him.

He was beginning to fear that smile, how effortlessly

it manipulated him. Her face moved him to cherish her, to protect her, to bring all kinds of light to it. She was like a butterfly, fluttering around him, her wings touching his cheek, his nose, every part of his body.

Whenever he scolded her, she gave him a look of kittenish appeal that always left him undone. Frequently, he found himself sitting like a man in a trance, watching her, sipping his drink as she moved around in all her glory.

Mistresses weren't so common anymore, not under Queen Victoria, but within the fortnight, Gavin could not imagine living without his.

Margaret did not so much enjoy strolling the city as Gavin thought she did. True, she delighted scavenging the stalls of the Soho Bazaar for pretty items, and the theater never failed to please. But still, the difference between his station and hers seemed all the more stark in daylight. It all got worse during the season, when his friends were in town.

On certain evenings, his acquaintances entertained their paramours, and Gavin was unfailingly invited. Those nights, Margaret resented not being alone with him.

The smoke of their cigars brought on Margaret's cough, and Margaret frequently got the gentlemen's names mixed up. Too, the men were fond of discussing Whigs and Tories, which Margaret didn't give a farthing about. Of course, sometimes they discussed women. Once they even discussed *her.*

"I have observed your eyes to be quite restless this evening," Lord Phillips said.

Gavin grunted behind his cards. "They go where they like to go."

And Phillips, blond with a flat nose, fingered his cards. "I see that. I see that."

Sir March reclined in his seat with an air of mystery. "Your mistress has you tied around her little finger, Claymore," he said.

Gavin seemed unperturbed, and, oh, how Margaret admired and loved this nonchalance about him. "Perhaps I enjoy it," he said dryly.

"You still have duties as an earl and future duke."

"A matter of which I am aware."

Margaret spied all this from outside on the terrace. At this point, she was beginning to feel a fit coming on.

"You can dress her in all the finery you like; this will still not change where you found her. Hell, how many men, gentlemen or otherwise, can you guess have ventured there, as well?"

Gavin's tone sent warning bells chiming all over Margaret's head. "Ventured where, pray?"

"Claymore, we all know you're her benefactor. Margaret is charming, I admit, but she's nothing but a common—"

A chair scraped across the floor. Margaret's hand clamped over her mouth to cover her gasp.

The inside of a tomb was merry in comparison to the quiet that settled over the room. Margaret waited expectantly, a silly, whimsical part of her wishing to hear the sound of Gavin's knuckles meeting with the other lord's flapping jaw. Obviously, it needed serious quieting.

But the silence stretched, so long and unbearable that Margaret feared whatever broke the silence might not be what she hoped to hear. Quietly, she tiptoed around the trellis and back into the sitting room, where the women giggled and exchanged intimate details about the men.

The evening was the longest of her life.

She sat quietly on their ride back to her house, watching the other carriages while pretending she was not also watching Gavin watch her.

When he'd boarded, something tumultuous had come with him, charging the air with tension.

Margaret could not seem to look into his eyes; she felt inexplicably, utterly blue.

Because for the first time, she realized that just maybe Claymore thought a little bit like the rest of his peers did.

Margaret was no good for him.

"This evening finished a bit early, wouldn't you say?" she said at last, and went to the vanity and ran the comb through her hair, hard enough to pull out the roots.

"The conversation left much to be desired."

That was all he said, in a tone that warned, *Do not inquire further,* as he removed his coat.

Margaret watched him head out of the room, and she pushed aside her wounded pride. She lived a wonderful life. She enjoyed the use of his horses, carriage, and house. They'd spent a handful of incredibly lovely evenings at Thomas's Hotel. Gavin slept with his hand under her pillow, and he laughed at Margaret's anecdotes about Minnie and the other prostitutes. He'd asked her to purchase a gown for the Cyprian's Ball—that scandalous soiree, full of all the demireps and their protectors. He gave her a hundred kisses before he left for the House of Lords. She lived only in his sight, had been made for his love. She lived in a lovely house all her own, with a housekeeper and footmen, and surely, surely, surely Gavin felt something for her.

And yet . . .

You can dress her in all the finery you like; this will still not change where you found her. How many men can you guess have ventured there, as well?

Dozens.

Dozens over dozens had ventured into her body.

The security she'd blissfully blanketed herself in for weeks had disintegrated with a simple phrase.

And with this emotional stab came a great craving

for more pain. Chastisement for being who she was and for what she'd done.

She craved Gavin's discipline like she craved his love.

Her need for it was so profound, so deep-seated, that nothing would ever convince her she did not deserve his sensual punishments.

Nothing could absolve her but that.

So when Gavin returned with a glass of wine and fell into a chair and wearily rubbed his face with his hands, Margaret knew what they had to do. If he'd wanted to be alone, he'd have sought out his own company tonight.

But he'd remained here.

With her—his whore.

Who ached to please him, and at the same time ached to anger him so he would sanction her once and for all. The thought of being punished for taking all those other men, of perhaps being forced to walk around the house naked while the servants watched, of sitting at his feet by the fire like a dog waiting for him to pet her, made her pussy grip with tight heat.

After a slow sip, Gavin set aside his wine. He jerked on a button and rolled the cuffs of his shirt up to his elbows. "Come here, Margaret."

Margaret approached.

Her mind spun in a thousand directions, while a lick of anticipation swirled up her spine.

She'd done nothing intentionally to hurt him, but

Margaret had clearly dishonored, humiliated, and embarrassed him, and she savored the penance she would have to do to make amends. Suck him. Kiss him. Please him. Anything for his pardon and forgiveness.

"It appears that all I do is regard you," Claymore said, without inflection. "As many men have before me."

He set his glass aside, and her heart quivered in her breast when he reached toward her. He undid the front clasp of her bodice and displayed her breasts, pressed upward by her corset and pushing out greedily toward his heavy-lidded gaze.

He reclined in the upholstered chair, leaving her achy and standing before him as he scrutinized the puckered pink areolas with the spiked tips.

"Perhaps I should look my fill at what they did."

His voice dropped to a rasp as he did just that; looked until the bulge between his thighs grew so large, his britches seemed ready to pop open.

Margaret remained motionless, allowing him to see her breasts and excite himself, allowing him to make her blush with his unabashed gaze and excite *her*.

"Turn around," came his thick whisper, and he twirled his finger in the air.

She turned around, her legs liquid as an ache for his touch began to spread from her breasts to her stomach to her sex.

He unhooked and unlaced her corset and tossed it

aside, then parted her dress until her skirts pooled at her feet in a puddle of silk and taffeta.

His fingers slid down her legs as he removed her stockings.

She began to pant.

She felt his gaze on her bare bottom, caressing the curves like palms and fingers; then, as he fingered the fissure between the cheeks and made a pass of his thumb over her anus, he at last rumbled, "Bring me the scarves."

Heart galloping full speed, Margaret walked, naked but for her jewels, to a small chest by the window and pulled out two silk scarves.

Imagining all the ways Claymore could tie her with them, she moved toward him, her steps flowing and seductive as she trapped his gaze, her hands graceful as she trailed the scarves over her breasts and hips.

Gypsies did this. . . . Nuri had taught Margaret.

And Margaret had never been so aware of how erotic the fabric felt over her skin until Claymore's eyes were watching it flutter. Perhaps being a whore had its advantages, after all.

He'd gone still in his seat, but his chest rose and fell fast. The muscles in his face pulled and tightened at her unexpected show.

Slowly, Margaret approached, mentally daring herself to trail the scarf between his legs and over his balls, across his face and lips and chest.

He caught the scarves in each hand before she could,

but rather than prying them away from her, he wrapped them around her nude waist, trapping her breasts above them, and hauled her in between his splayed thighs.

His tightening grip excited her as much as did the famished look he gave her dimpled areolas.

A need spread through her breasts and caused a painful tingle. To suckle Gavin from her breast . . . to suckle her lover . . . then his child.

He regarded her for a dark moment.

"There are penalties," he said, gazing at the breasts she inconspicuously inched closer to his face, "for brazen women who dance and arouse men, wantonly displaying their breasts."

"Penalties." Live, excited little things burst in her stomach.

"Many, Margaret. Penalties."

His fingers closed around one pointed pink pearl, twirling and squeezing, igniting a firestorm in her body that she could not control.

The scarves fluttered down the back of her legs to the floor. Her head fell back as she gave out a strangled exclamation, a combination of "Yes!" and "Please!"

His eyes sparkled with purely wicked intent, and the corners of his lips curved into a satisfied smile. "I can smell your wetness from here. You feel titillated at the thought of being punished? For being such a cock tease?"

His filthy talk was the sweetest, most excruciating

torment of her life, stirring her desire to great new heights. "I'm sorry, my lord."

He plucked the tip of her tortured breast, making it redden. "Sorry for what?"

She ached to speak dirty, too, and blurted, "For being a cock tease and a whore and for having sold my pussy."

He captured her nape in the cup of his hand, his face a mask of arousal. "Being sorry is not enough, Margaret."

He leaned over and drew her nipple into his mouth and suctioned so hard, her toes curled into the rug.

She caught his head to hers and trapped him there as his tongue swiped, maddening her with its promise of pleasure.

The sound he made, so low and animal, made her blood boil in her veins.

She peered down at him from beneath her eyelashes, and found his smoldering stare rising to meet hers as his tongue traced a circle around her wet nipple.

Then his mouth drew from her once again—hard.

Her womb contracted, her gaze trapped by his dark one as his mouth worked. She had never witnessed anything as beautiful and sinful and erotic as Claymore looking into her eyes as he lipped her breast.

He inched back for a moment and blew air across her moistened skin. "You are truly lovely."

The praise made her vision waver.

Claymore knew her darkest secrets, her every depraved pleasure. He knew her past, and sometimes it was a marvel that—still—his body wanted hers.

He stood up in silence, the warmth of his body singeing hers.

For a prolonged moment, he set their foreheads together and breathed her breath, his mouth open over hers. Her breasts prickled against his shirt-clad chest.

Then he turned his head slightly and nibbled at the corner of her lips. "I have something special in mind for you tonight, Margaret."

She caressed his broad back and undulated against him, reveling in the strength of his long, hard body. "Your desire is mine, my lord. Your need is mine. Your hunger is . . . mine."

Her soft moans seemed to provoke his urgency.

He spun her around and pinned her back against the wall, his eyes flashing pure heat.

"I do hunger, so much I cannot get enough of you, your lips, your moans." He groaned and shook his head, then released her and stepped back, as though he loathed having admitted this.

He motioned toward the bed, his voice gaining its usual strength. "I hunger to watch you touch yourself—and you will satisfy me now. On the bed."

She cupped her breasts and kneaded them for him as she strode across the room to where he wanted her.

He shook his head, dragging the chair closer to the bed. "Slowly," he crooned, folding into his seat.

Fevered already and trembling inside, she climbed into bed.

When she lay back against the pillows, she let her mind wander to when they were together and how he looked when he came. So positively wicked and undone. Her head fell back as she relaxed, her hand trailing a path down her abdomen.

His eyes flashed. "Touch it."

She shivered.

Then her finger slid between the folds. As he watched, Gavin's face was hauntingly erotic and virile and dark with desire.

She let out a groan and rubbed her fingers more insistently over the lips of her sex.

"Put one inside you, the longest."

She used her fingers to part her pussy lips, inserting the middle one inside. Pleasure pulsed through her as a groan tore from Gavin's lips.

"Put another one in."

She closed her eyes, impaling herself with a second finger. His face hovered in the back of her mind as she'd last seen him—in that chair, straining in his pants, his face ravaged with desire, his eyes hot.

She shuddered on the verge of her climax, tugged and pulled at her clit, pumping her fingers into herself.

Her eyes fluttered open when she heard footsteps. She found him looming by the side of the bed, his elegant fingers gradually undoing his britches. "Keep going."

Heart racing, she inched back to lean against the headboard, and started to twirl her clit with her thumb. She watched him pull out his swollen member. "Good girl . . . that's how I like it . . ." he crooned, heavily petting her hair with his free hand. "Good, good girl you are . . . a good, wet girl, Margaret . . ." He stroked his cock slowly up and down. Heat laced through her stomach to her womb as she penetrated her sex with two fingers, all the while staring at his firm, strong cock gliding inside his fist. "Now, if you want me to give you this, you will pull out those fingers."

A storm of desire raged inside her, clawing for release, but she withdrew her moist fingers.

Then he urged her onto her stomach, and Margaret obeyed.

When he tied her arms to the bed and spread-eagled her legs, Margaret moaned.

He mounted her from behind and began pushing his cock into a new, tight entry, and she screamed in agony and pleasure as the channel opened.

Fire streaked through her.

"Some pussies like to be taken like this, don't they, Margaret?" He rolled his hips and possessed her fully, as long and wide as she'd ever felt him. It was like being penetrated by a tree.

Margaret buried her sob in the sheets, the pleasure great enough to bring tears to her eyes. "Yes, Gavin."

"Are you my pussy, then, to fuck as I please?"

"Yes."

"If you ever leave me, pussy, I'll be very displeased."

"Never."

"If you even think about another place, another man, I will be very displeased. Very displeased!"

"Never. I vow it. Never!"

He groaned and bit her earlobe, devouring her like something adored, and Margaret was so aroused she humped her hips against him, desperate for her release.

When she climaxed, she screamed his name. And Claymore yelled out hers.

He did not return for days. Two weeks, in fact.

Whether he was trying to prove something to his loathsome friends or to himself or to Margaret, she didn't know, but this evening was no different. The footman rapped on her door, and he peered in to announce, "Lord Claymore will not be joining you this evening. I'm afraid there is a pressing engagement at the Morrisons' he must attend."

She was sure she would become accustomed to this disappointment. But she was wrong. A pang struck her midsection, and rose to her stupid, lonely heart.

For a moment, a beautiful moment, she delighted
in a private vision of rising to her feet and proudly de-
claring, "You may tell His Lordship, if he comes calling, that I am indisposed to see him, tonight or any
night."

The vision was followed by another, less stellar one,
in which Margaret imagined herself being put out on
the street without a farthing.

Why?

Why was he treating her like this?

Because he'd been reminded that she was a common
whore? Or because this whore made him yell passion-
ately in ways a lord would be reluctant to?

Margaret didn't know how long she lay on the bed,
drowning in a sea of anxiety, tormented by images of
returning to her old life, when the slamming of the front
door rattled the window casings.

She flew upright.

Footsteps echoed out in the hall, loud and purposeful.

Her heart stopped when she saw him, his clothes
conforming to his magnificent body. Lord almighty, but
the sight of him *hurt*.

Margaret smiled (how well she did this), but Gavin
merely stood there, not quite in the room but not quite
out of it. He didn't smile back. His dress was impeccable,
reminding her of his status.

Her heart thundered in her chest as he tugged on his cravat with single-minded purpose. And her body began to burn. Two weeks. Remembering his touch, his words, his scent clinging to the sheets like the memories of his loving clung to every thought.

Her skin became a hunger, her nerves like pins and needles, and her lungs . . . her lungs closed every time she saw him, as if being suffocated by her expanding heart.

With as much dignity as she could muster, Margaret rose to her feet and pulled the robe around her waist, thrusting her chin out. "I heard you would be at the Morrisons'," she said, using every ounce of strength in her to appear calm.

His eyes, straightforward in a way that alarmed her, settled on her bosom. "The Morrisons was a bore."

He shut the door behind him, his eyes never straying from her bosom. She watched his fingers move; deft, elegant. No, she would not remember how good they felt, how they'd touched her.

"So what brings you here at this late hour?" she asked, crossing her arms over her chest to hide precisely those mounds that he seemed anxious to see.

He cocked a brow and began to advance, yanking open his snowy white shirt. "I cannot come to my mistress?"

I am his mistress, she thought. *He pays me to fuck him, and that is all. Do not forget, Margaret Bigler, who you are.*

"What brings me here," he continued, and caught her arms and yanked her brutally to him, "is me . . . wanting to fuck you."

She wanted to refuse. In the pit of her, she wanted to deny him. But his eyes; she felt their gaze like the burn of hot black ice. His scent, dear god, was heavenly to her starved senses.

When he lowered his head, her eyes drifted shut, her lips parted of their own volition, and her need overpowered her. She gasped; she felt his tongue on her lips, sliding between them and inside her. He groaned and tightened his hold on her arms.

"You're angry," he rasped, nibbling her lower lip.

She tore free and avoided his penetrating gaze. He undid his trousers and tossed them aside. Somehow sensing he was at the edge of his control, Margaret scooted back on the bed until she lay on a tower of plush pillows. There were circles under his eyes, faint lines across his forehead, and the testament to his misery was like a salve to her wounded female pride.

He took a step. "You're angry you wait for this all day, never knowing when I'll show up, if I'll show up."

She scoffed. "Oh, I *know* you'll show up!"

"You're angry you need this inside you." He grabbed his erect shaft, yanking it as if out of his body. "You're angry you'd die for it."

"I would not die for anything, my lord. Not even for you."

But her cleft wept between her warming thighs. Her nipples pricked in anticipation of his decadent torture.

His anger seemed to escalate as he laughed with heart-stopping menace. "Yes, you would. You'd do anything I say."

He ripped open the nightdress, and an overwhelming desire swam through her. She melted in his arms.

"My lord."

He groaned, dropping his voice as he touched his lips to her shoulder. "Aye, Margaret." He licked her ear. "Your lord." He cupped her face, stuck his tongue in her mouth. "Your one. And only. Lord."

Pleasure bloomed inside her at his possessiveness, and she felt herself go lax as he began to search between her legs. He hit the spot—oh yes. That very spot, and a white-hot pleasure fluttered through her entire being.

After two weeks of loneliness, two weeks brainsick of solitude, of waiting, waiting for Gavin, her body sang with joy.

He sprawled on top of her, pushing the soft mounds of her breasts together and massaging his cock between them.

Fiery sensations licked the insides of her body. Her cunt squeezed so tight, she wondered if there was space enough left for him to fill it. She purred low and deep as he worked himself up and down, his expression one of splendid concentration. It was as if he did not want anything to intrude on his thoughts, deep and dark as they were. Her womanhood rippled with wanting as he pushed her breasts tighter against his cock and closed his eyes, shooting his milk across her skin and pumping as he did.

He opened his eyes, and it was like staring into a fire. "Lick the milk."

Margaret, frantic to please and claim him entirely once more, began to lick and lick all of him as he dragged his cock down her belly, past the fluffy mount of her quim, then stroked against the entry. He was still so erect. She bit back a sound of pleasure as he tantalized and teased her with the bloated crown . . . and then he was sliding farther down. His head, that glorious virile face, drew level with her very center.

"I have seen my share of wet little cunts." He pushed a finger into the pouting lips of her cunt, watching her white, swollen breasts jerk as she bucked. "Never one as wet as this."

She arched her body with a hoarse scream. He inserted one finger inside her, then two, and positioned his thumb over the little bud of pleasure above. He flicked it, moving his fingers inside her, and the pleasure became absolute.

"Oh, god—"

He withdrew his hand. "I gave you no leave to speak, mistress."

She nodded, biting back an effusive "Yes."

"Those other men. Did they take the time to pet you here?" His eyes blazed with jealousy as he rolled her clitoris under his thumb. "It is hard with desire. Like a little pearl."

Unlike the tautness in his face, his touch was light and masterful. Magic.

"But so . . . sensitive," he said, "when I do this." He pinched. Margaret bit her lower lip to halt the scream at her throat as she galloped toward the peak of ecstasy.

He took her hand within his large, warm one. "This is where I am most sensitive." He guided it over his cock and his pupils seemed to dilate further, his eyes all black now. He curled her fingers around him. So *big*. "Here," he said in a guttural voice. "Here my heart pulses. The center of my being focuses when it throbs. I become single-minded, owned by my prick. . . ." He licked her ear. "I like it when my mistress is owned by this prick, too." He licked behind her ear. "When her need is so great she could sob for it, kill for it, die for it." He licked *inside* her ear, and whispered against the shell of her ear, "For me."

The man overwhelmed her with his sensuality. He was so lazy and comfortable with the sex, it seemed unfair. Margaret—the one who should know better—was panting in agony. He did not seem possessed, but like a man who indulged in this all day, enjoyed it like he did his port or sherry or wine; a man so confident he felt no anxiety that he might not get what he craved.

While he stroked her weeping cunny, she writhed with fevered desire and held her breath, afraid that she would spend all over his fingers.

"Already there, my pet? On the brink? Hmm." He plunged his tongue into her mouth. She savored, hungrily suckling what he gave her. "When I come to you, I expect you to be like this. Obedient. Submissive."

Her tongue curled and twined with his. "I will be obedient, my lord. I will be submissive, but please do not punish me with your absence."

He pushed his juiced fingers into her mouth and watched her eagerly taste herself. "I'm lord and master here, Margaret," he said, his voice both heat and ice. "I do what I please, when I please. But you . . ." He weighed her breasts in his hands, testing their fullness before he gave each peak a quick lick. "Your desires are mine. Your breasts are mine. Your cunt is mine." As he spoke the last, he shoved his fingers back in, twisting his wrist to bury them deep.

"Oh, my lord, I . . ."

"Hush." His jaw hardened with determination. "You will not speak a word until I say so—and then all you will let me know is what you want."

Her senses swam, the art of his black seduction irresistible. Women like her weren't seduced. They need not be. But she always felt seduced by his touch and by his words and by the bobbing cock and heavy testicles she caught glimpses of here and there. He was erect and perspiring slightly, and his breathing gave him away, even if outwardly he appeared calm.

He liked control. Was a man to be obeyed, in command.

What he wanted, he asked for. She did not need to guess what he liked or did not like. A feeling stronger than need speared through her every time she heard his softly spoken commands. He was riveting—his body, his manner and speech, his mouth and his face.

"Touch me, Margaret," he said then, stretching his body over hers and shuddering when their sexes brushed. "Damn you, touch me."

They touched for hours, so that it was torture, the *wanting* him. She felt like his personal toy, like an instrument he played, and she liked it. She gloried in it. She had missed and needed it. Now she felt possessed and controlled, and she let go of all her restrictions and restraints. His tongue flicked every part of her. Her tongue flicked every part of him.

Their bodies rolled on the bed until he was mounting her.

"Did you fuck yourself while I was away?" The light in his eyes was swallowed by the darkness of his pupils. The darkness of his lust.

He was finally pushing his cock inside her, causing her to cry out in relief. She moaned, "Yes."

"You stroke your pussy while you think of me?" Claymore demanded.

"Yes!"

"Now you may make noise for me. Just for me. Here in my ear. Like you do when you fondle yourself."

She did. Lord, did she. She made so much noise, he seemed to think it prudent to silence her, and brought his mouth to hers. He murmured, "So good."

His tongue plowed deep and sure into the depths of her, and she moaned as his intoxicating flavor invaded her. Utopia, paradise—he was all that and more.

Their tongues began to mimic what their bodies did.

He didn't seem so lordly or in command now. He lifted her legs up and draped the back of her knees around his shoulders, penetrating her more deeply. She cried into his mouth. He sucked on her tongue like he was famished, pushed and pushed so that the creaks of the bed resounded in the room.

Soon the simmering passion became an erotic frenzy, and he was whispering the words they all said, all the men, but *these* words she clutched to her heart. His lashes rested against his cheekbones as he grimaced in pleasure. "Darling . . . Christ, Margaret, you drive me mad. . . ."

He flung back his head as he spent himself, his orgasm shaking his enormous body fiercely as he roared. She felt the hot splash of his cum flood her, saw the look on his face and tucked it into her mind so as never to forget it, and she shattered with him.

For long moments they lay there, together, but Margaret had never felt so apart. Her body delighted in their games and yet inside . . . inside came a craving so powerful, so potent, it was pulling her apart.

Respect.

Perhaps she would not have it from society, but every fiber in her being demanded she have it of the man to whom she showed all of herself.

She would not, would not, be punished with silence. She could bear anything except that.

Gathering her courage, Margaret sat up and said, "Claymore, do not leave me like this again. Or I shall leave you."

Gavin lifted his head. It was the force of her words, coupled with the wild, fierce look in her eyes, that rendered him mute. His mistress had proven a complex creature, blazing with passion and with a coy virgin's smile, and now she looked on him with the determination of a petulant child who wanted something beyond reason and would not be denied.

And even as the grip of lust squeezed around him with all its might, he felt a wild moment of wanting to dangle that toy she desired out of her reach, to bait her, goad her, so she kept coming for it, until she begged for it, for him.

"You will not have me leave?" he asked, half amused and half vexed by her nerve.

"No."

He chuckled—he couldn't help it. Jesus Christ, he had missed her. He had never had such dreary days as these he'd spent away from her. "How am I to conduct business then, mistress? Naked and in your bed?"

"That is quite the thought, my lord, but no. All I ask is that when you leave, you must promise you will always, always return to me. And if you leave for long, then a note would be appreciated."

He gazed into her luminous blue eyes, his chest cramping at the thought of leaving her, not returning to her. Would he ever manage to stop wanting her? Would he ever, even with wife, children, another life, not crave to spend every minute of his day with Margaret?

He'd stayed away for long, wretched evenings—determined to break his habit of her, his addiction. No wife desired a husband who kept another woman, but of Margaret, Gavin could not cure himself.

Nothing he did removed her from him. Her scent lingered in his skin, the image of her eyes altered his every sight. Her words, her unspoken thoughts, her giving nature haunted him morning and night.

Margaret was more real to him than any being he'd ever known. The darkness in her wanton desires appeased and admitted the beastly tendencies in Gavin. Like an embrace between shadows, they were overlapping and entwined.

And this evening, rather than escorting Lady Georgiana, the proper, well-spoken woman his parents expected him to marry, he'd broken down and had ridden fast and hard to come bury himself in his mistress.

Perhaps he relished controlling Margaret's passion in a way he could not control his crumbling world.

Or perhaps he merely needed more of the strength she gave him for what needed to be done.

Maybe after a dose of Margaret's surrender he could bear bending his knee, and praising eyes that weren't blue, and asking for a hand that wasn't hers, and pledging his heart to a woman who wasn't Margaret.

But who would have to do.

Chapter Eight

꧁

$\mathcal{T}$hey fell, willingly or not, into a new game. A tug-of-war; Gavin thought of it that way. Margaret seemed to want proof of his desire for her—and she submitted to him only after she made him long for her.

And long for her he did.

Her moods, her unpredictability, excited him—a ploy, true, but effective in pricking his interest. Sometimes, his temper, too.

Frowning this morning, he leaned back in his chair as Margaret paced the breakfast room in a dishabille; she was so utterly tempting. "Come and have breakfast with me," he said.

She sniffled, harrumphed, and ignored him. She muttered something about not being able to find an earring.

The jiggle of her breasts was visible through her camisole, and he could outline the dewy pink of her areoles. He set down his tea and leaned back to watch her. Perhaps she craved more discipline?

Highly likely; it had been weeks since he'd taken a hand to her. His father had fallen sick again, and Gavin had been riding to Norfolk, something his little mistress never liked.

His cock stirred like an animal waking from slumber. "I said, 'Come and have breakfast with me.'" When she ignored him, he added on a warning note, "When I issue an order, I expect it to be obeyed."

She tossed him a look, her eyes like gimlets. "And if I don't want to obey?"

With an emphatic shake of his head, he shoved back his chair. "You will obey, or you will suffer the consequences." His cock jerked against his britches at her rebelliousness.

She pivoted to leave, but he pounced and caught her, then dragged her to him by force. "You're wicked, Margaret. You're a wicked mistress. Do you know what I do to wicked mistresses?" He ignored her futile struggles and cupped her breast. "I take my hand to their rear. And I leave my mark on it."

The footman stood quietly in the corner, and when she froze and her eyes darted to him, Gavin slapped her rear so hard, she winced. "Is he the lord here, or am I?" he demanded.

She was breathing fast. He slammed his palm into her buttocks again, and this time his middle finger dug in between the cheeks before he pulled back. "I asked you a question, Margaret."

"You are."

He nuzzled her scented hair, forgot about spanking her, and pressed her tighter against him, fondling her breast as he kissed her neck, enjoying the contact of their bodies. "I am what?"

"My lord."

He was playing with her, like a cat with a mouse. He let go of her, crossed the room, and produced a birch rod from within a small chest.

Streaks of fire raged through him at the swish of the rod against his thigh.

"Perhaps you need disciplining."

Her eyes sparked with lustful violence. "Perhaps."

He gestured toward the dining table. "Please. Get comfortable."

His balls felt laden with cum, drawn tight against his shaft, which pressed painfully into his britches. After a moment's hesitation, she spread over the table. With a single look and a simple command to go draw his mistress a bath, Gavin sent the footman scurrying up the stairs.

"There, now. Where were we? Ahh, yes, your punishment."

She was incredibly quiet as he gathered her skirts at her waist. She was naked under them—entirely naked. His balls ached at the sight of her exposed cunt.

He smacked her lightly once. Then twice. Harder. Impressing her cheeks with pink.

"Sweet cunny," he whispered. "It puckers up for me with one mere slap and lubricates for penetration."

He swished the birch rod over the luscious globes of her ass. Already his vision dissipated with desire and heat, like a foggy night when you cannot see the ground where you step. He smacked again. *Whack.*

She whimpered.

"Who does this rear belong to, Margaret?"

"You."

Whack.

"Who do you belong to?"

"You."

Whack.

"What do you want more than anything?"

"You."

"My cock," he gritted.

"Yes."

"Say the word. It's a filthy word, not supposed to be uttered. Even roosters stopped being cocks. But this." He ground said instrument against her exposed buttocks. "This will always be a cock. And you want it, don't you?"

"I want your cock. Please."

Securing her gown well up on her hips, he eased apart the plump half-moons of her buttocks and pulled out his erection, pressing it to the tip of her rosette. He nudged her.

Whack.

"Please!" she cried.

He slid his cock lower, to the wet slit that peeked under the flesh of her bottom—still bright red from the pass of the birch rod. He touched the little rosette of her ass with his thumb. "You liked it when I fucked you here. You want me to do it again."

"Oh yes, please, my lord."

"Hush," he commanded, strengthening his hoarsened voice through sheer will and effort. "Sit on that chair, Margaret. Your cheeks will smart. Your quim will hurt. And you will sit there and eat what I feed you. If you're a good girl, then you will spend yourself in my mouth. And if not . . ."

"No, please."

"Do it, Margaret."

Trembling, she sat on the chair he'd instructed. He hauled his own to sit next to her, his eyes glimmering dangerously as he plucked up a biscuit.

"Eat, darling."

Her buttocks ached, he supposed. Her pussy was burning; he was sure of this. Her eyes glistened with tears of desire. She opened her mouth, nearly sobbing with need, and ate, the biscuit disintegrating in her mouth.

"Buttery? Warm?" he asked.

"Yes."

Next a plum followed, which she munched obediently.

"Good girl."

"Please, my lord."

"I told you to eat what I feed you."

"Feed me your cock."

"Lift your skirts first. Over your waist. Spread your legs open. Expose your sex to me."

She lifted her skirts, parting her slim, creamy white legs wide enough so that the dark valley of her curls greeted him.

Her lips were swollen, ready. He rose and unfastened his trousers. She remained on the chair, shivering, parting her lips in anticipation.

His fingers tangled in her hair and he gave her his cock. "Finish it. All of it."

While she ate him, he seized the birch rod and trailed it along her exposed sex so she felt the feathery stroke of the rod along her slit. She whimpered.

"Shh. Sit still, Margaret." He ducked to press a kiss to the top of her head. "And drink my pleasure."

He spent himself almost immediately, and Margaret drank him up as the rod continued stroking gently along her clit.

She was shuddering violently when he extracted himself from her mouth, knelt at her feet, and buried his tongue in her warmth.

She began to whimper. "Thank you, thank you . . ."

Her flavor invaded him—trailed down his throat, swamped his mouth, his heart, his entire body. Her gratitude, her submission, touched him so deeply that his legs felt weak when he came to a stand.

Margaret wept.

Because she felt helpless, felt possessed, and did not know if she was mentally ill or only sinful for wanting this so much.

"Shh. Why do you cry, my love?" Gavin asked.

Margaret cried harder. Because she felt like a puppet she had once seen, tangled in its own strings.

"Do you not like our games, Margaret? Do you realize how hard you reach your peak this way?"

"Yes, I do. I'm . . . I'm a whore."

"Hush. You are my mistress, my every fantasy, my every desire. *Why are you weeping?*"

"Because I cannot think of myself when I am with you. I only care to give you pleasure."

"Do I not take care to please you, as well? Have I not shown you a pleasure in the extreme, the pleasure that lies beyond the normal limits?"

"Yes! And it has made me your slave! You are not helpless, as I am." She wiped furiously at her tears.

"Sometimes I feel I am." He gathered her up, pressing her cheek to his chest as he carried her upstairs. "I'm tied by obligations, possessed by my own title. I cannot go where I like, do what I like—"

"Nor can I! I wait all day for you. I think only of you. I crave your love *and* your punishment! If the devil possessed me, I do not think he would take so much of me."

"And you equate me to the devil?"

She sniffled.

"When I am gone, I think of you, too." He grazed her soft, pliant mouth with his. "I reach for your warmth in the night, and want to pound something when I don't find you. I ride distances, and you're in every mile. I see your face and your smile, and think of my mistress." Trying to be gentle, he carried her to the warm bath that awaited her. He was hard again, he wanted her again, he was obsessed with her body, and he felt like a bastard for thinking of sex while she wept like this. "I see jewels and I want each and every diamond for you. I see gowns and imagine them on your body. I see night and think of my times with you, and I see day and wonder what you do."

He ducked his head and undressed her with care, then set her inside the tub, leaving her in the warm water, so that she dipped her head and let it wash away the tears. As he exited, he added something he wasn't sure she could hear.

"And when I give you pain, I want to *die*."

Inside his study, the side table crashed to the floor and the glass vases shattered. Gavin fisted his hands, breathing hard as he surveyed his doing. He'd hurt her. He was base; what he wanted was wrong, even for a woman of the night. Perhaps he was the devil. He wanted to go to her and say, *I need you to ease me again. I need you to take me and ease me again.*

He'd hurt her, and he was still throbbing, excited, aroused. He pulled his cock out and began yanking with a vengeance. . . . Her smarting little buttocks . . . that little rosette he wanted to take . . . her cries of pleasure . . . even as she cried, the things she'd said . . . titillated him. Excited and aroused and tormented him.

"Margaret." He bucked into his hand, closing his eyes, fucking his fist as he wanted to fuck her sweet, smarting little ass. "Margaret!"

He left the next morning.

Margaret cursed herself over breakfast. She'd needed too much, she'd asked for too much, and weeping women were not what a man like Gavin wanted.

Every day she donned a beautiful dress, hoping that this day, this day Gavin would walk through the doors.

He didn't.

Finally one morning, a package arrived. And a letter. Margaret jumped to see both. One contained the most mesmerizing diamond necklace, with a pear-shaped ruby pendant the bright color of which she'd never seen the like.

She rushed to the oval mirror across the sitting area and slipped it on, then tucked the letter away. She could not ask anyone to read it to her, for what if it said something intimate?

That evening he appeared.

"Thank you for the necklace," she said, feeling strangely shy and vulnerable. He'd sent a letter, as she'd requested. And she had missed him terribly. She wasn't even angry anymore, only lonely and excited by his presence.

He handed his hat to the footman, followed by his coat. "You received the note as well?"

"Yes." She smiled. "Thank you."

He clasped his hands behind him and leaned back on his heels, as if waiting for more. Something in his expression alarmed her; it was as though someone had died.

Margaret waited for the footman to be out of hearing. She considered saying, *I would love it even more if I could read it*. But her embarrassment was too great. So she said, "I love your penmanship. It is very fine, my lord."

His expression altered from somber to surprised. "That is all you have to say to me?" he asked, brows raised.

Puzzled, she nodded.

What could the letter possibly say? His reasons for leaving so abruptly? That he loved her? Could Claymore even love someone like her?

Gavin kept regarding her as if expecting an answer, his gaze gaining such intensity, she could hardly bear it. He loomed in the room, dark and commanding, and how these rooms and these eyes and these lips had missed him.

"I have been waiting," she finally whispered under her breath. "For you to come take your pleasure from me."

For a prolonged moment, he didn't make a move to touch her, and every part of her screamed for him to. Then she felt the heaviness of his hand on her hair as he inclined his head to her ear. "And here I am."

Not possible. No tantrum? No word of protest?

Gavin warred between incredulity and lingering desire as he soaked inside his bath, rivulets of water swirling down his neck and chest as Margaret pressed the sponge against his throat.

Her skin was flaming from their recent exertion, and her hair tumbled down her bare shoulders in a waterfall of silk.

"Would you care to join me?"

He signaled at his lap, his limp cock gradually fattening up again at her gentle ministrations, but she smiled to herself and continued gently scrubbing.

They had taken each other hard, and once done, Gavin had made her stride around naked for his perverse pleasure. He could not get his fill of her curved body, her skin. He loved to get a glimpse of her pussy as she bent or moved.

Christ, he'd missed her!

As she ran the sponge along his chest, she circled his nipple until he arched reflexively and caught her wrist.

They shared a smile over her mischief.

And Gavin's grin widened when he thought of his prim-and-proper wife ever learning of this. Of him. His carnality. His Margaret.

Fully erect now, he slowly stood in the tub, dripping wet as Margaret scrubbed his buttocks, his testicles, his swollen member. His lustful eyes tracked her efficient movements. His mistress seemed lost in thought, unaware of Gavin's growing desire.

He watched her push back her hair and change the sponge to her other hand; then she passed it between his legs again. He clamped his teeth as an arrow of pleasure shot through him. He could order her to bathe with him, true, but today he didn't want her to do what he told her to, or do something merely to please him.

Today he ached to know what was in that mysterious mind of hers.

As she bent to scrape his thighs, he curled a lock of hair behind her ear, a drop of water sliding down his finger to her ear. "You're quiet this evening, hmm?"

No mistress enjoyed learning her benefactor was taking a wife. How could Margaret be different? He'd loathed having to write to her about it, fearing her jealousy, but now he loathed her lack of it.

"I'm wondering," she said at last, dropping the sponge into the tub.

"Wondering. What does my mistress wonder about, *I* wonder?"

"What your letter said."

He wasn't aware that he chuckled until he heard his own laugh resonate in the room. "Ahh, at last we come to the topic." He stepped out of the water and seized the towel she held out.

A crimson blush spread across her cheeks, and in that instant, Gavin realized what she'd meant. "You do not know how to read?" he asked.

Casting her face toward the floor, she bit her lip and nodded. "I should like to."

Restless, he walked around her, briskly toweling dry. Why had he expected that she would? Her parents had been factory workers, poor immigrants from France. Her origins were low. Why in the world had he expected her to know how to read, like a lady?

Because I'd give anything for her to be a real one. One I could marry.

Christ, so she has not read the letter.

The thought blasted into his brain and spread an unexpected wealth of gratitude inside of him. She had not read the letter; she did not know of his upcoming marriage. Maybe it was a sign. Maybe he needn't tell her, at least for some time.

Unless she insisted on learning.

"And you'd like to learn?" he queried, partly willing her to deny him.

Beaming at him, she nodded, then rushed out to the hall.

Gavin dressed in silence, the tension easing from his body as he realized she did not know yet.

And she did not have to know for a while.

He retired to his study, and she found him there, pacing.

"You'd teach me, my lord?"

His stomach constricted when she crossed the room and handed him the letter. He'd read it a thousand times, had written several versions, finding all the words lacking in what he'd wanted to express.

> *Margaret—*
> *I shall come to you tonight, but first I must*
> *tell you of an important change in my*
> *circumstances. The time has come for me to*
> *take a wife. . . .*

And just like that, he crumpled both page and envelope in his hand and tossed them into the fire.

"Forget this. Let us tackle something infinitely more interesting." Ignoring her startled look, he pulled a book from the bookshelves, settled down on his leather chair, and patted his lap. "Frankenstein. Shall we?"

Chapter Nine

⁓

The best part about learning to read was the manner in which Claymore taught her. Margaret didn't care so much about the subject, sometimes, as Gavin was fond of strange books. And yet . . . Margaret relished the sound of his voice rumbling close to her ear in the evenings.

Five months later, on a Sunday, Margaret attempted what she prayed would not prove impossible. She took out a book, brought it to the light of an oil lamp, and tried to read for the first time ever without assistance.

Words popped into her head at once.

She stopped reading immediately, waited for her heartbeat to settle down, and then continued. She read aloud this time.

"I am no bird; and no net ensnares me; I am a free human being with an independent will; which I now exert to leave you."

The words lingered in the air as she fell quiet, shocked in hearing her own voice reading to herself.

She'd selected a random page, a random sentence, and somehow it spoke to her as if it had been written for Margaret alone.

Making a note to read the entire Charlotte Brontë book later, she stepped out of the room, spotted the housekeeper busily polishing the brass frame of a landscape on the wall, and quietly slipped into the study.

Claymore calmly sipped his tea as she strolled inside, the book she had just *read* from clutched open to her chest. His head lifted, and awareness lit up his eyes for an unguarded moment, showing the depths of his feelings. Slowly, he lowered the cup.

"My lord," she said, softly, meaningfully. A cozy fire flickered in the hearth, and it could pale to the flush creeping up his taut face.

"Ahh," he said, "you're reading. *Jane Eyre?*"

"I am."

He seized the book in his big hand, skimmed the pages, then lowered it. "A fine book for a woman, I suppose."

She fairly flung herself at him, caught instantly in his embrace. "You are a grand teacher and a grand man!"

He made a gruff sound as he rubbed his lips against her temple, squeezing her. "Nothing about me is grand, except my fortune, Margaret."

He was surly as a bear, and though she couldn't understand why, she loved him, wanted to hold and love him forever. She held him so tight she had no space to breathe. "Gavin, I love you."

After a fraught moment, he held her at arm's length, a muscle ticking in his jaw as an emotion much like pain crossed his eyes. "Margaret, sometimes I think if you leave me . . . if you look at another man the way you look at me . . . I could kill you."

She laughed. "But why would I look at another when there is you, Claymore?"

Kneeling at his feet, she kissed each of his hands, rubbing her cheek against his thigh, humbling herself without shame, letting her love spill in a deluge.

If he loved her, she didn't care that he governed her.

If he loved her, she didn't care but to make him love her even more.

And he must love her. He must.

"My lord, I pray that if you love me, you will tell me."

He knelt down with her and pulled her up against him. "Nay, I do not know how to love." He kissed her lips softly, tenderly, but his hold was almost violent, as though someone were tearing her away from him and he were holding fast. "But you, Margaret," he said, almost in a hiss. "Your love is so sweet, so absolute. There is no shame in it, no selfishness." He rocked her against him, dragging his lips across her forehead. "It is my most prized possession—you. Your heart, your love."

Her heart felt ready to burst.

Nuri had been wrong.

He hadn't given her nothing. He'd just given her the world.

And Margaret wanted to be in the cocoon of his arms, drowning in that melted velvet of his eyes, wanted the last words she ever said in her life to be his name.

Gavin Claymore.

Gavin Claymore felt like a condemned man.

A liar.

As dirty as a bastard, and more.

His innocent mistress believed he was grand and marvelous, gazed at him as though he had hung the stars, and every day in his mind Gavin heard the seconds tick.

Tick, tick, tick.

Closer to the moment when he'd have to unveil her eyes and show himself to her.

There was no hiding from her adoring gaze.

Not while he slept, not while awake, not while he watched and watched and watched her. With her, he was obsessed. Without her, he was obsessed. Every moment of his day—at gambling tables, at a soiree, at the House of Lords, even parading Lady Georgiana about town—Gavin wrestled with an infuriating sense of possessiveness, jealousy, and wanting. When those eyes met his, there was such trust in them, he felt it like a blow in the crotch, the heart, the soul. He loved her. Completely. He'd fallen in love with his mistress.

And he had to inform her, without delay, that he was about to marry.

If Margaret's happiness increased even a tad, she was certain she would explode from it.

Claymore had been in London for weeks now, and the man's thirst for her was as unquenched as ever.

She sat in the grand study, near the cozy fire, glancing at the clock; she expected him any minute.

But the man who appeared in the doorway made her blood run cold.

Gavin looked like a man hanging by a thread off the edge of a cliff, and Margaret's horror was so great her copy of *Jane Eyre* crashed to the carpet.

A bleeding slash cut vertically through the center of his forehead, as though he'd banged his head into a lamppost—on purpose.

Gavin kicked off his Hessians, his lips the thinnest, grimmest line she'd ever seen.

A sensation of dread and foreboding made her think her legs would splinter as she rose. Her anxiety brought on a wild burst of coughing, and she gripped her midsection tight in an effort to still it. She surveyed him.

"My lord?"

He fell into a chair and spread his legs out, slapping his gloves aside. "Expecting someone else?"

Frowning at his ill humor, she picked up her book and set it on the bookshelf. "Perhaps another one of my lovers; one never knows when they feel like coming," she said with a shrug.

He caught her wrist and his face twisted into a wolfish snarl; his teeth had never looked so shiny. So white. "Do not toy with me this evening."

Laughter escaped her, nervous laughter. "What ails you, my lord? Whatever it is, I shall make it better."

A fierce sheen of possessiveness glazed his eyes, and Margaret couldn't help but smile. She would see him through whatever distressed him.

"I wonder if you'll be smiling so when I tell you I am to take a wife on the morrow."

The tone he used struck her first, the leering way his lips formed the words. He tossed a miniature at her feet, and for a bemused moment, Margaret gazed down into the oval face of a young blond-haired woman.

Understanding smacked her like a thunderbolt.

I am to take a wife on the morrow.

For a moment, she looked up and blinked, suspended in disbelief, staring into his grim face, sure that it would break into a smile. He loved Margaret. Margaret loved him. Surely this wouldn't happen. Surely.

When the smile did not appear, Margaret fell back on her heels, feeling her face harden as if turned to stone.

So *this* is what it felt like to be on the bad end of a cannon blast.

She found no voice to give to the pain hacking through her. The one she heard, so dead, could not be hers. "A wife."

"You don't read the papers?" He scoffed. "What good does it do a man to teach you to read if you do not read the papers, Margaret?"

He sighed drearily, but even that sound could not shield his predatory gaze. "My father's dying wish. I am to marry Lady Georgiana Seaton. She accepted my suit months ago, but then, who would not? Can you think of someone who would not want to be a countess? A duchess, in time!"

Margaret's stomach churned with such force, she thought she would vomit. Her eyes flooded, distorting his large, once-perfect figure into a black blur, and Margaret knew that when the tears eventually spilled and her vision cleared, all she would see before her was a stranger.

"She's not at all unpleasing to the eye. Maybe I can even stomach taking her to my bed."

She sucked in a breath, anger pummeling her chest with every harsh hammer of her heartbeat. Utter and complete wretchedness robbed her of their every good moment together—every smile, every loving caress and word—until she could not remember anything but the sensation of being guillotined.

How can I move? she marveled. Like puppets moved, doing what had to be done. She fetched water, a rag, and began to soak his cut.

His chest jerked violently with each breath. Her eyes burned. She could barely see what she was doing, but miraculously, the tears did not fall. The gash continued to bleed, and she felt a perverse pleasure seeing it, felt cruel and inhuman to relish this little thing that made him mortal.

Gavin caught her shoulders in a crushing grip, glaring at her as if she'd done something to hurt him, as if *she* were the one with a saber in hand. "Have you not heard a word I said? I am to take a wife!"

"I heard every word you said. I am not deaf. I am not *deaf, you bastard!*" She sucked back her tears. What could she do?

He would *touch* another woman. Take another woman. Kiss another woman with his *lips*. He would give another woman a lovely black-haired child. And his noble name. And Margaret . . .

"Leave that be. Disrobe now."

She started. "What?"

"I said, 'Disrobe.'"

She stared at him, at the calm, collected monster he'd become. A monster trapped in the cage of his upbringing and his duty. The black of his pupils swallowed his irises, and he was bleeding contempt as much as he was oozing blood. Rage rippled along his sneering lips, trembled in the muscles of his jaw. "Did you not hear me, madam?"

Savagely, his hands closed around her shoulders and he crushed her to his sitting form, closing his mouth over hers brutally. He kissed her unmoving lips with an agonized sound before he put her from him—no more a gentleman; hardly even a man.

"That is what you do, Margaret. You are my mistress. You are good for a fuck. That's all you are and all you will ever be." His merciless words bludgeoned her senses. He was goading her. Inviting her to lash at him, claw the emotionless mask across his face, do violence to him.

Margaret wanted to find a knife and drive it deep into his skin, and then she wanted to drive it through her own. She stood. Oh, good. She could do this.

Claymore caught her elbow in a manacle. "What do you have to say to me, little Margaret? What vile words do you know that can describe me, hmm? Gentleman? Because that is what I do out there, that is who I am. What am I here? Am I still the devil? Perhaps I am worse than that." He used his free hand to yank up her skirts, his face twisted in pain. "And you will still beg me to take you, won't you? You are the moth caught in the flame. You know I will hurt you. I warned you, and you still *like* it."

She imagined slapping his face. She imagined ruining it with her nails, sinking them in as deep as the gash on his forehead so he would never, ever, be looked upon with desire again.

She felt her lips tremble. No. She would not let her temper clash with his, would *not* give him the satisfaction, would not let him see a single tear.

On his feet now, a tower of terror over her, he pinned her hands at her sides and crushed her mouth, pillaging it with his tongue. She bit his lip, drawing blood, making him growl.

"Good. Very good, Margaret. Now tell me what you feel. Tell me you hate me, how despicable I am."

She wanted to. Oh, but his kiss—so passionate, so desperate—only made her grief complete.

"Well, Margaret?" he asked in the voice, as powerful as morphine, that was her addiction. "Did you think I'd marry you? Hmm? Did you? Did you think because my cock doesn't know or want anything but you that my family would allow me to marry you? Shout at me, damn it. Say something!"

A winged shadow of raw, pure hatred spread inside her, tainting all her love.

She had given everything. She would not give him any more quarter.

Instead she jerked free and walked woodenly upstairs. To the bedroom, to the bed. His footsteps followed closely, so closely.

She lay facedown on the very bed where they had loved and played, and said tonelessly, "Take your fuck. My lord."

A chill jangled through his body as lust roared

through him like a living, breathing carnivore. He wrestled with his cries of anger, curses to the world, and merely wanted to hold Margaret. But he was angry at her, too, angry for being who she was, not who he needed her to be, not someone he could freely, proudly love. Damn her. What did she expect of him? Did she not *know* who she was?

Gavin grabbed her up and kissed her with hot impatience, but her wooden lips bit into the rawest of his nerves. "Margaret," he commanded, his kiss demanding a response, his hands tangling around her hair until there was little chance one could untangle them—she'd have to chop off his hand, take the rest of his virility, take his pride, everything that was noble in him. "I will give you everything, Margaret. I will make you as happy as you make me. I will make you forget I have a wife; you have my word."

Her voice was cold and pelted him like a hailstorm. "The word of a man who will promise to God and church to love another woman while he—"

He shook her. "Yes! Yes, whatever I've done, I will not lie to you. I can lie to the world, but not to you."

He grabbed the top of her gown and yanked it to her waist, until he could see her breasts. Those breasts. Gavin's breasts. Tenderly he cupped them and blew air across her nipples, sucked and blew, but nothing could excite her desire for him. His hand plunged between her legs and she wasn't wet, wasn't wanting him. She was limp as a doll.

But a mighty cyclone of need pushed him onward. He freed his cock and pushed her down, spreading her arms, her thighs open any way he could.

He stopped when he caught the look in her eyes, stone cold, no longer shining with worship.

"No," he said, stepping back. "You will *forget* this," he vowed. "And you will forgive me. And you will understand that I have responsibilities. You will forget this and you will love me again, Margaret."

But Margaret was gone from him—he could see it. Her body did not respond to his. She shook not with arousal but with rage, and Gavin was so horrified, he began backing away. He trembled with a need to fuck her like a man let loose from hell. But he was shackled by his pride, starving in anguish. "You will love me," he said again, reaching the door. "You will."

He had *not* betrayed her. He had promised nothing but what he'd given. His name was not his to give her, *damn her.*

"I will not," she said, softly. She sat up and arranged herself with the calm of a maid folding clothes. "Never again."

And Gavin Claymore loathed how that soft vow trailed behind him as he left.

Chapter Ten

"How much for this?"

The pawnbroker eyed the fan Margaret held out. Nuri stood at her side, pulling out more of Margaret's once-precious articles.

"These dresses are all silk, and some haven't even seen the light of day."

There was panic in her thoughts, making them tumble one against another, but there was one that she was able to embrace.

Leave.

Leave Gavin Claymore.

Margaret's chest felt so tight, she could not breathe. The man—elderly, stoic, and well dressed—surveyed her fan from behind the counter and said, "Five pounds."

"Only five?" Margaret whispered.

Give up that fan for five pounds?

"She'll take it!" Nuri said, elbowing her sourly. "You're not in a position to negotiate, Margaret. 'Tis the truth."

"Wait!" Margaret's frantic word halted the man before he could tuck away her fan.

She bit back a cough as she reached for it, the poignant beauty of all that whiteness spreading feelings of black inside her.

She had never known such misery could live in one human heart. She was helpless in the brutal grip of her love for him, could not *stay* and ever feel even a kernel of happiness again.

But in leaving the mantle of his protection, she could not aspire to live comfortably, to stay out of the streets, for long. She had to plan for herself, try to build a happy future without . . . him.

The thought sent her into a fit of coughing so great, she spit up blood.

"Margaret!" Nuri caught her, steadied her, and Margaret blindly reached for the handkerchief the pawnbroker shoved out.

"I'm all right—merely tired and ill slept." *And heartbroken. And lost.*

Nuri's tanned face had, remarkably, drained of all color, and her usual merriment had all but fled.

Swallowing and wiping the moistened corners of her lips, Margaret turned on her heels abruptly, faced the owner of the establishment with a measure of dignity, and went back to business. "May I keep one feather?"

The servants' chatter clipped and died at once as Gavin entered. As he stormed through the house in search of her, they all disappeared into the kitchen.

He found her facing the hearth, her hands folded on her lap as she watched the books he'd recently given her burn to ashes.

His heart felt the blow as though she had tossed it, too, into that fire.

She must have sensed him, for she turned. A shadow stirred behind her eyes, stealing their gleam.

He stiffened, expecting a blow. Softly, she said, "I understand what your duties are. What you feel you must do. So I hope you understand what I must do."

Devil take him, but this was not what Gavin had imagined for a life. He had imagined his noble name, his wealth, would spare him much heartache and drama. Instead, his noble name and his wealth had taken the one thing he desired.

Now he walked in misery, talked in misery, slept in utter and complete misery.

He sat on a chair and stared sullenly into the flames. "Why do you burn them?"

"Because you gave them to me."

He was too overwhelmed by her actions to notice how gaunt her face looked, how tired she appeared.

He said, "So that is how we are to play this, then?"

"You set the stage."

"You would destroy what we've given each other?"

She cocked a brow. "Think of your wife, my lord. You have responsibilities."

"Nothing has to change between us, Margaret! Damn it, in this house we can go on as before. You will hardly notice a difference."

Silence. Broken by the crackling sounds of the fire.

He sighed. "If I were to do something . . ." He stared at her rigid back, considering. "If I were to drag my name to the gutter and leave . . ." He laughed, shaking himself. "See? You're manipulating me. You're sullen and angry, and you want me to bend to your will and do as you want me to."

"You're wrong."

"I am right! By god, if I don't know my own mistress!"

Margaret stormed out of the room with a great bang of the door, and though he swore to himself he would not follow her, to teach her who was master here, he was quick to trace her angry footsteps.

Margaret lay in bed, under the covers.

And he was not ready to take nay for an answer.

Shaking from the force of his arousal, he flung the

coverlet aside, seized her knees, and pulled them apart, hungrily eyeing the little rosette of her anus and the swollen lips of her labia under her sleeping gown.

"You still belong to me, and you'll still give me what I need every night that I come for it."

She didn't stop him as he brushed his thumb down the fissure and plunged two fingers into her pussy, screwing them in with such force, she gave a strangled sob. "My lord," she moaned, visibly fighting her arousal.

"Say you love me."

She didn't deny it; didn't admit it. But Lord, she was so angry, she trembled. And she was also incredibly wet. Stroking the outer rim of her anus with his thumb, he brought his mouth to her buttocks and smoothed his tongue across the white flesh of her cheek. "Declare your love to me, Margaret."

She lifted her face from the pillow, and a sound tore from her chest as he spread her cheeks apart and gave a deep, satiny lick of his tongue at the very seam of her pussy lips.

"Oh, god!"

"Declare it." He carefully inserted his digit into her ass and tested her tightness, watching her juices stream like a river to her pussy lips. She cried out in fury and frustration even while rocking her hips to his finger and tongue. Then he went to his knees and teased her with the tip of his member.

"Who's your lord, Margaret, your master? Whom

do you belong to?" He held her hips and pushed his erection into her scorching sex, swiftly gliding through the warm nectar of her juices.

"Call your lord. Ask him to make you come. Beg him to love you!"

She cried, weeping in her desire, her pain.

Gavin hadn't predicted how maddening, how exhilarating, how shattering her orgasm would be, but when it hit, he needed to taste it. He dove between her legs and greedily suckled her nectar. A pool of her heat gushed down his throat, and he lost control.

"Oh, darling." Thrusting his tongue into her, he began pumping against the mattress, and he yelled gutturally into her pussy as a mind-blowing orgasm began to mount in him; it took every ounce of power in him to hold it.

Margaret convulsed, bucked, writhed, and he was licking her, kissing her, eating her. He shuddered in pain, pleasure, agony, and steeled himself against the ripples around his fingers. *My mistress. My woman. Mine, mine, mine!*

When she became still, he rose and pulled her arms above her head. Their chests heaved, his aching cock nestled in the cradle of her thighs.

Seizing her lips in a rapacious kiss, he rubbed up along the moistened slit of her pussy, kneading the softness of her breasts in his hands. Her arms remained above her head, her eyes glazed.

A tear trickled out of the corner of her eye.

He bent his head and licked it, then sank his teeth into her lips, and bit her some more.

"I've dreamed of giving you so much pain you'd scream and climax with it." He dragged his tongue down her chin, her neck, until he was sucking a breast tip. "Now I ache to make it better," he murmured. "I ache, Margaret, because this pain isn't giving us any pleasure. It's eating me up inside."

"I cannot bear it. Let go," she murmured.

The pain of her rejection was like the pleasure she'd given him: all consuming. He thought his heart exploded in his chest and the shards were cutting him on the inside.

She rolled to her side and started coughing, violently now.

Gavin's heart stopped beating altogether.

A drop of blood emerged from between her lips. He peered over her shoulder. "Your cough persists even with the medicine the physician gave you?"

She coughed still, and Gavin's stomach knotted at the sight of more blood. "It's getting worse."

Fear unlike any he'd known spun like a whirlwind within him. He tried to gather her against him, but her arms weakly held him back. "No. Don't touch me. Just let me rest."

She curled up, coughing still, and Gavin's entire being seemed to shrink in size, until he knew only one word, one thought, and it would slowly, surely, murder him.

Consumption.

"How long?" he demanded. "How long has this been worse?"

She shook her head, damp tresses clinging to her neck. "Days," she said. "Weeks. I don't know."

"And you didn't think to tell me? You didn't see fit to *inform* me?"

Silence.

Grinding his teeth, Gavin crossed the room with single-minded purpose, flung the door open, and barked into the darkness, "Get me a physician. I need a doctor—now!"

He slammed the door behind him and charged back to her.

"I do not want a doctor. Not want . . . your help," she said lifelessly. "Not . . . want . . . anything from you."

His eyes burned as he watched her eyes drift shut, the color leave her face—and he dove for her. Gritting his teeth, he crushed her to his chest, heart pounding, rocking her.

"No. No, you will not leave me. I will not allow it—do you hear? You will stay with me. You will remain right here with me, damn you. Are you listening to me!"

"I . . . hate you." She cried, and coughed, and clung to him with deteriorating force.

"If you leave me— Margaret! Open your eyes. Listen. If you leave me now, Margaret, I will hate you, too, *forever*—do you hear me? I will follow you wherever you go, and you shall never know peace. Do you understand me?"

Shudders wracked her body, and the metallic scent of blood began to seep out of her pores. "Those peacocks," she croaked, using every ounce of strength in her frail bones. "They are wise to die when their mates die."

"No, they are not. They are not! They're imbecilic little animals with brains the size of a pea!"

"You are dead to me, Gavin."

And the sorrow the words gave him was so profound, he could not summon a response for it.

They are wise to die when their mates die. . . . You are dead to me.

But Gavin . . .

Gavin's curse was to live.

Chapter Eleven

*M*eredith choked back her tears, gasping for air.

"Meredith!"

"S-stop shaking me!" She flailed out, catching James in the jaw. He reared back, relaxing his grip on her upper arms. The muscles of his face remained bunched up, however.

He peered down at her with a frown. "Ouch," he said, rubbing.

"She's coming to."

A slim, petite woman stood next to the bed, her face strikingly familiar. She tucked a stethoscope back into her leather bag, moving with slow, methodical precision.

Meredith realized in a flash that she was naked under the sheets, and a bubble of panic rose within her.

"Meredith?" James's eyes brimmed with concern. But she was blind to his face, deaf to his words, aware only of a rising hysteria clawing inside her and of the presence of that blond stranger in the room. The stranger whose face more and more began to resemble the miniature.

"Cordelia," the woman offered, eyeing Meredith with that smile doctors give some patients. "Myers."

Meredith stared, bewildered, as this little tidbit sank in. James's ex-girlfriend. Lady Georgiana—Gavin's wife!

Meredith had never in her life been so slow to react. A fog cloaked her thoughts, while the frantic pounding of her heart wouldn't cease for anything. "You're a doctor," she said.

Cordelia's pink-glossed lips quirked and she glanced at James with a she'll-probably-be-all-right-tomorrow look. "Orthopedist."

Anger whipped through Meredith, mingled with despair and disbelief and all kinds of feelings she didn't want to examine. Why, of all the doctors in the city, did he call her? *Her?* An orthopedist!

Hands quivering, Meredith wiped the moistness from her cheeks, nodded, then somehow managed to stand. She struggled to keep the sheets wrapped around her as she searched the bedroom for her clothes, and when she found her coat—her only clothing, because she'd been stupid and reckless and fantasizing about driving a particular imbecile crazy—she briskly put it on.

James's murmurs reached her across the room. *Be all right . . . I'm concerned I may have been rough on her. . . .*

Feeling windless, airless, and ready to disappear, Meredith slipped on her shoes and didn't bother to fasten the straps. "I'd better go," she said quietly.

He looked at her strangely and held up a finger. "Give me a minute."

But no. Meredith didn't give him a minute. She couldn't see him, couldn't, couldn't, couldn't see James.

Unable to button her coat, she let go of the sheet and used both hands, then straightened with a huff. "I really have to go." She wobbled across the room, trying not to trip on her shoe straps.

At the elevator, James caught her elbow. "We're not through, Meredith."

There was such authority in his words, the same authority she had always admired and the same she was beginning to loathe.

She punched the button with force. "I said I'd come tonight, and I did. Now I'm leaving."

Couldn't, couldn't see James.

"Who's Gavin?"

She blinked. "Gavin."

His gray eyes had darkened like storm clouds that were a drop away from spilling out the thunder. "Yeah," he said flatly. "Gavin."

Her heart thudded alarmingly. *Gavin,* she thought, the name wrenching a new, god-awful pain inside her.

She shrugged off James's touch, her stomach sick with tension, but James caught her once more, his grip becoming a manacle. "Who the hell is he, Meredith?"

His eyes bored into her like daggers. Meredith felt weak.

She'd remembered another life. . . .

Another life with *him*.

And now he wanted to know. Who Gavin was.

A schism spread between them as they faced off in brutal silence. Meredith could feel it growing, growing, growing. Anger. Jealousy. Distrust. It was all there, standing in the five inches between them. And Meredith was sure that if she answered him, James would not hear or understand or begin to comprehend who Gavin was to her. How could he?

Even now, a part of her still fought against what she'd seen. Remembered. *Lived.*

Struggling to keep her roiling emotions in check, she punched the down arrow again, about ten times, until the chime came and she was finally able to board the elevator. She spun around to face a somber James. "Good-bye," she said.

But the elevator didn't move.

Stretching those long arms to each side, he held the doors open, and the calm, cementlike set of his face didn't fool her one bit. His eyes were positively wild. He'd been with her the entire time she'd been out, and she sensed that the horror he'd lived through needed an

outlet. "You lied, Meredith," he said, his voice deceptively even.

"What?"

"You said there had been no one serious." The slow
manner in which he crossed the elevator and planted his
hands on either side of her face entirely contradicted the
coiled force vibrating from his body. "Who's Gavin?"

The doors slid shut behind him, and Meredith felt a
slight lurch as the elevator began to drop. His jealousy
was such a live, beating thing, it seemed to drain the
area of air. She felt desperate. Desperate to leave, to
scream, to weep, or just to flat-out hit him. Her lungs
were near bursting for just a little bit of *oxygen*.

Growling, James closed the space between their bodies and ground himself against her, making her gasp at
the hardness she felt, at her body's instantaneous, unwelcome reaction. "Does Gavin give you that? Does he?"

Every breath she dragged into her lungs took effort.
Lust surged with a vengeance, fed by his possessiveness,
his jealousy of himself. The idiot! She hated him, hated
wanting him, hated knowing him, hated that throughout the years, she had always been his and yet had never
really been cared for. Never really trusted. Never really
loved.

He had given her . . . nothing.

Nothing!

"I want to know who he is," James purred in her ear,
fitting his body to hers, flattening her back against the

mirror so she had no choice but mold to him, feel his need, tremble in response to it. "And why you cried for him."

She squirmed against him, but it only brought their bodies into more heated contact. "Stop it," she panted. "Go back upstairs to your . . . your . . ."

"Friend."

"Yes!"

"No, Meredith. What I want to know is, Why don't you come upstairs with me?" he asked calmly, stroking his thumbs up the inside of her arms.

She thrust her chin up. "I'm not into threesomes, thank you."

His hands tightened around her wrists. "I'm not suggesting a threesome. I'm suggesting you go upstairs and fucking *talk* to me. What *in the hell* just happened?" he exploded.

The elevator wrenched to a halt. Meredith darted through the doors the second they rolled open.

James cursed loudly behind her, but just like another man, in another time and another place, he was too proud to follow.

Storming through his penthouse, James thrust open the double doors of his office and slammed them shut behind him.

His home office. A sanctuary. Where he evaluated his losses and plotted his comebacks. Where he'd spent countless hours staring off into space, thinking of a red-haired temptress with striking blue eyes.

The one thing he'd wanted in life and couldn't manage to have.

The wall at the far end of the room was an entire floor-to-ceiling window, the city skyline a perfect backdrop to his massive leather-topped oak desk.

A half dozen plasma TV screens on the right-hand wall, which usually enlivened the place with noise and light, were currently off, and lent a gloom to the area that James found quite the match to his mood.

What the hell happened?

He'd never imagined Meredith passing out in the midst of their lovemaking.

James had dreamed of Meredith sleeping in his bed like a contented kitten, her lips dewy soft and her lashes long against her cheekbones, her shiny red curls fanning behind her over the stark white pillows.

He'd never dreamed she'd call another man's name.

He'd never dreamed she'd black out the way she had.

He'd been desperate to get her help, frantic at the sounds of fear and pain she made. And her calls for that man. Gavin.

He gritted his teeth, wishing Gavin was dead. A tight, constricted feeling slammed him in the chest at the memory of her crying as she lay naked and sweaty in his bed.

She was funny and sexy and spirited. She was sweet and responsive. Addictive.

And James had hurt her. His lust, his need for her, had *hurt* her.

Clamping his jaw, he made his way to a sleek, wood-covered wall and pressed a panel, which slid to the side to reveal a mirrored bar. He scanned the bottles and considered. Whiskey? No. Something stronger. It had to be bourbon.

He twisted off the cap and filled up a glass when he heard the door open. He went cold. Setting down the bottle, he snatched up his drink and slowly turned . . . to find Cordelia.

"Oh, Christ, I forgot you were here."

Cordelia assessed him with caution, and stepped into the room as if crossing enemy lines. "I thought you didn't drink, James."

"Now I do." He smiled thinly. "I apologize for dragging you out of dinner."

"Oh, pooh. Anything is better than those dinners." Her eyes sailed over James's attire—if it could be called attire. He wore only slacks, not even fully buttoned. "You look like crap, James."

With a grim smile, James raised his glass to her in a mocking salute and took a long drink.

"I feel like crap."

"So." She fiddled with the collar of her prim, white button-down shirt. "Tell me about her."

James swiped the back of his free hand across his

mouth and then sat behind his desk. "There's nothing to tell."

"She's that lawyer Dad has been mentioning, isn't she?"

A green and sticky feeling slithered up James's throat at the thought. The mere possibility. Of Myers discussing Meredith with his daughter. "Care to share what he said?"

Cordelia laughed, taking the chair across his desk. "I'll keep that to myself for now. What I want to know is, What are you doing sleeping with her?"

He gazed into the depths of his drink and drew in a slow breath. "I'm entitled to a private life."

"Not when so much is on the line. Definitely not when you know what she doesn't: that she'll soon be out of a job."

"I'm not out for her job."

"You've been at Inctel for thirteen years, James." She made a face. "You could have owned it if you'd agreed to his proposal."

James narrowed his eyes. Funny people, the Myerses were. He tossed back his bourbon and rose to pour himself some more. "We gave it a shot, you and I."

She shrugged in indifference. Once, he'd thought they could make quite a match. Cordelia was cold. Calculating. Precise. Very much like James. Very unlike Meredith.

"I'm willing to forget her," she said, casually flicking the lapel of her shirt. "If you're willing."

James caught the tightening reflex of his hand around the bourbon bottle as those two words blasted through him: *forget her.*

Such easy words, and such an impossible task.

How could he forget her?

At the mere mention of her, a surge of possessiveness rampaged through him, a primal, animal urge only Meredith Sinclair stirred in him.

He was out of his mind for her.

It had been too much of her for too many days. Hours and days and weeks. Every graze of hands, every word, every look she tossed his way and that he had returned caused James's desire to build until it felt like insanity.

Maybe it was.

But James could not sit back and watch her go. Could not let Myers—anyone—hurt Meredith.

Damn it, had he—James—hurt her?

Had he hurt her, frightened her, with his sexual games?

He felt twisted. Cheap and dirty and unscrupulous. And yet . . . she'd wanted him. Could she be that good an actress to fake such hot, shattering pleasure? Was he blinded because he wanted her so much? He should resign. It would give him immense pleasure to resign. But wouldn't that cause Meredith a slow, painful death, by bequeathing her a job that would drain her of her passion? She'd be under the old man's boot, and James would not be there to shield her.

James tried relaxing his strained, overstimulated body, and said, with the sureness of one who lives by his legal contracts, "Make no mistake, Cordelia. Your old man will deliver what he promised."

"You're a fool if you think he's really going to give you E-Doll, much less a percentage of Inctel," she said bitterly. "He promised me a seat on the board, too, and I clearly remember you finding his way out of that contract."

James wheeled around to face her. "I'm sorry about that. Truly. I'll make sure the seat is yours at the new company—if you're interested."

"How?!"

James raked his fingers through his hair. "I'll handle it; don't worry." He was not in the mood for Cordelia's tantrums, not today of all days, and not after Meredith.

"Marriage, James. It's the only solution."

"Of course." James leaned back in his chair. "Marriage. That's your suggestion."

"It's the only way to bend the man. Together."

James studied her, so small and so bloodthirsty, as he carefully kept his face impassive, a thought forming in the back of his mind.

Seconds passed.

"I have a better proposition for you," he finally said.

A spark of interest lit up in her eyes, and in that same instant, James knew he had her.

"What kind of proposition?"

James linked his hands behind his head and smiled his most winning smile. "The kind you like."

Things were about to get bloody.

"I want details—juicy details. And stop stalling, or I'll find a way to yank them out of you, Mer. Come out of that bathroom, will you?"

Wrapped in a cushy bathrobe, Meredith plopped down on her friend's frilly white bed and smeared cream up her legs and arms. "Thanks for letting me stay over. I couldn't be by myself tonight."

Sprawled over the coverlet like a blond, curvy diva in jeans and a T-shirt that molded to her perfect B-cups, Cherry watched her, narrow eyed. Waiting. Frowning, because she, of all people, must already know what was wrong.

Everything.

"You were right." Meredith waved a hand dejectedly. "It's no good. Him and me."

She should've listened to caution, to Cherry, to common sense.

She was still trembling from the effect of those memories and was still close to tears. She'd thought her life was empty before, but enter James Hamilton, and *smack!* It was a mess. Her emotions were a mess. *That feather!* Why had she followed the impulse to send it to him tonight? Why had she gone to him tonight? He was bad for her—he was plain bad for her.

To think she had once, long ago, trusted the man. Made love to him. Said yes and yes and given and given and given to him. To think of how he'd betrayed her.

He was her soul mate. She'd known this, felt this in every pore of her body the instant she'd laid eyes on him.

Maybe he knew it, too.

He was her soul mate.

And he had betrayed her.

Heartbroken and soul sick by what she'd just re-called, Meredith stared off into space.

Cherry brought over a cup and saucer. "Here. Drink this."

"What is it?"

"Rosemary tea. It's relaxing."

For a moment, Meredith sipped thoughtfully. Star-crossed lovers. They never got it right, did they? No matter how many chances they had. This time would be no different. This time, James Hamilton would be the end of Meredith Sinclair. "Do you remember the feather I had framed?" she blurted out.

"How could I not? The frame cost more than the feather."

Meredith smiled a smile lacking all humor and

glanced past her shoulder, out the window. It was rain-
ing again in Manhattan. "I took it out," she told her
friend, curling her legs under her body. "I gave it to
him."

She couldn't meet Cherry's intent gaze—she had the
oddest eyes; one gray and one blue, and they always
seemed to follow her—so Meredith instead sniffed the
tea. The fresh, sweet aroma permeated her nostrils.
"How do you do it, Cherry? I can't, for the life of me,
see him tomorrow. I can't separate sex from feeling, and
now that there's feeling, I can't separate work from it,
either."

Cherry snorted, peeling open a Snickers bar. "You'd
have feelings for that man even without the sex, Meredith. You were half in love with him before you even
knew him."

Sighing, Meredith went to the cushioned vanity seat
and tried several ways of tying back her hair. Her hands
trembled. Her night with James. Her *last* night with
James. Disaster.

"Leave it up," Cherry said behind her. "Show him
your neck tomorrow morning. Maybe he'll take a bite
out of it."

Cherry grinned at her own joke, but Meredith was
too preoccupied to join her.

Once, she'd thought she knew what love was. A feeling of well-being and stability—*nothing* compared to the
blatantly wild, overwhelming emotion she felt for James.

She knew the feeling as surely as she knew she'd felt it before. For a man named Gavin. Setting down the brush, she spun around to face her friend. "I'm completely in love with him."

Cherry lifted her gaze from her nails. Perfectly pink, manicured nails. "I know, friend."

Meredith covered her face in her hands and groaned. "And I hate him, too."

"Stay away, Mer."

"It's impossible now—I have to look into his stupid, ugly, infuriating face tomorrow."

"Here, give me that." Cherry pushed herself up, a sly, naughty smile on her lips as she seized Meredith's teacup.

Nuri.

Meredith blinked, but in that moment, she saw Nuri so clearly in her friend that she felt dizzy.

A sensation of dread plummeted into her stomach. Meredith swung out her arm. "Stop that. I don't want you to read my future."

Cherry jumped aside. "Maybe it's nice."

Meredith dove for the cup once more. "I know for a fact it's not."

Cherry twirled and skipped across the room. "Coward."

Meredith rolled her eyes. "I'm not one to embrace pain."

"No. You're not. And I'm not going to say *I told you so.* I'll just do this. . . ." She lifted her eyebrows for three long, pointed seconds. Then she sighed. "As for pain, if you hate it so much, you should've listened to me, dammit."

Nuri. She had been a lady of pleasure, too. But in this life, she sought the sex, embraced and welcomed it, while Meredith had been hiding from it. Maybe she had been hiding from James.

How to face him in the office and pretend nothing happened? How to look into his eyes and not want to die all over again? Damn him.

She felt tired, tired of even trying, tired of all the passion inside her, unleashed by one damned stupid man.

With that same long-legged walk that Nuri had expertly employed, Cherry approached the chair and handed back the cup. "Look in there."

Meredith gazed into the cup and saw only white. Not wedding white, but hospital white. Nothing white. There was that word again: *nothing*.

"I saw our pasts, Cherry," she said, softly. "As clearly as yesterday." She sounded crazy. She was a lawyer, for god's sake, talking about . . .

But she felt oddly . . . different. Like someone else. A woman old beyond her years.

"Yeah? Well, your future isn't too good, either." Cherry snatched the cup and glared down at the thing as if chastising it. "He has to give up something to be with you. He doesn't like giving up anything. And neither will you."

Meredith stepped up to the windowpane and followed a raindrop with one fingertip. "Do you think it's possible to . . . remember? Your past life?"

Cherry laughed. "Of course, silly. Why do you think I play with my tarot cards? Knowledge! Of the dark and dirty kind. Robbie over there will reincarnate as a Great Dane or something—he's such a good pooch."

Cherry's Boston terrier perked up from under a chair, ears pricked at the sound of his name, then settled back down.

Meredith sighed. "I was a whore, you know."

Cherry slapped her thighs. "No!"

Meredith frowned. "You were a whore, too."

She squealed with laughter. "Nooo!"

"And Gavin was my . . ." *Lover? Owner? Master?* God, old times had *sucked*.

"Whoa, wait. *Un momento, por favor.*" Cherry held out her hand. "You lost me. Who the hell is Gavin?"

With a frustrated sound, Meredith flung her arms up high. "Gavin is *James*."

Chapter Twelve

~⁓~

*J*ames watched Meredith as she skimmed through the revisions, pacing around the boardroom table as she flipped pages.

"I'm not happy yet with clause fifty-five A." She tapped the pen to the pages after this announcement.

It was the first time she'd spoken in long, endless minutes, and he got the message. *I'm not happy.* He disregarded it.

"It's what you requested," he said, setting down his coffee. Black. As his mood.

"We'll need a change," she said matter-of-factly. "Julian won't like this."

James watched her move. She'd been carefully avoiding his eyes, and now surveyed the freshly sliced cantaloupe and kiwi set out on the credenza.

"So, where's your team?" she asked offhandedly.

"Not here. Obviously."

"Why?"

James leaned back and crossed his arms, just as non-chalant. "Because I wanted to talk to you."

"I have a busy day." She began jotting down changes. "Did you want to talk about anything in particular?"

I want to know why you won't look at me. Why you act as though I'm garbage. I want to know why you want me and then you don't, and I want to know if you moan for Gavin the way you do for me.

"You know, I also feel two B needs some further clarification."

He pushed himself to his feet. "Meredith."

Blue eyes rose to his for a second before her lashes dropped. She fingered the filigreed edge of the port-folio. "I trust you'll make it clear this time." She set down the contract, then stepped over to the fruit on the credenza.

James walked around the table, trailing all five knuck-les around the polished edge. It took every ounce of will-power to keep from lashing back at her. She was spoiling for a fight, and James was spoiling to give her one. He felt unmanned. Why did she make him feel that way? He couldn't forget her face, how she looked when she came. Haunting. So damned haunting. Being sheathed inside her tight, pink little sex.

He paused an inch behind her, sensed her stiffen. He could smell her shampoo, wanted to plunge all ten fin-gers into her shiny, restless red hair, turn her around, and kiss her lips again. Softly this time, so he could savor her breath, go searching deep in her mouth.

He raised a hand to lightly touch her hair. "Was I too rough with you?" Her hair was soft under his fingers, tempting him to delve in.

She laughed dryly. "Fishing for compliments, I see."

"I'm not." He studied the graceful curve of her shoulder, the sleek strap that held up her dress curving enticingly around it. "I want to make it up to you." He fingered the strap, his finger of its own volition shifting to her skin to discover it was soft and warm. "We've been dancing around the subject, and I think we need to discuss it. You're a submissive."

She shrugged off his hand and stepped over to the danish, plucking one without preamble. "And you're a dominant jerk. So?"

"Ahhh, Christ." He scraped a hand down his face. "Dominant, yes. Jerk, no, Meredith."

"I'm not into those clubs, and I don't crave the whole lifestyle, so forgive me if I've broken some little rule all good submissives go by. I like to be taken, James, without permission or apology. That's it. That's *all*!"

His cock lengthened at that alone. Tensing as he fought his arousal, he followed her with his eyes as she headed to the table. She was lovely. Her dress embraced her like a second skin. Her long, shapely legs had been around him, and he ached for more.

Rising, he snatched up his coffee and drained it, too restless to sit down. "I want my night."

How could she have been so wild about him and now act so *indifferent*?

Flashes of the moment she fainted poisoned him. The helplessness he'd felt, the rage, had built for an entire day, triggering emotions he'd never in his life had to deal with. "Have you fainted before?" he asked.

"No."

A sudden devastation spread through him like some sort of merciless, sweeping natural disaster. So it *was* his fault. "Meredith," he said, his voice soft, but his eyes were not. Not his face. Not his tightening hands. "Christ, forgive me."

James saw in her gaze the glimmer of knowledge, that satisfaction of having torn James out of his body, of having done what for a decade no one had. Cracked through the barriers, the ice, the composure.

Wildly striving to recover it, James leaned back on his heels, his jaw tight. "I keep reliving it, over and over, trying to know what went wrong."

Meredith folded her arms, her smile lifeless. "Try forgetting; it's so much simpler."

"I'll take it slower, Meredith. I'll set a different pace, one you're comfortable with."

"I don't want comfort."

"Dammit, listen to me. I'm asking for another chance, one to make things right. I'm going crazy here!"

He didn't realize he'd uttered the last aloud until her head lifted and those blue eyes leveled on him. "James . . . You like whips and ropes and power. You like it when I'm . . . helpless. How can that be right?"

His smile was mirthless, and after letting her see it, he shrugged. "Helplessness is power—isn't it? It's power over me."

Her hands fidgeted on her lap. He wanted her to touch him with them. To feel her hands under his shirt, on his skin. He wanted her so damned much.

He unfolded one arm and turned his wrist inside out, where a thick purple vein throbbed and disappeared under his shirt. "I have a bite from you," he informed her.

Her eyes flashed ice. "Are you sure it's mine?"

He frowned. Even pissed, she was beautiful. Breathtakingly, soul-shatteringly beautiful. And she wasn't giving him a quarter.

He fingered the vein, and her eyes watched, warming his blood. "It's yours," he said softly.

When she glanced up, the chilling spark had left her eyes, replaced by a warmer, more inviting glow. "I'm sorry," she said in a dusky, mellow voice. "If I hurt you, I mean."

"I don't want your apology. I want you to do it again," he whispered back.

Their smiles faded.

They stared at each other's lips.

He reached out to her lap, quickly capturing her

hand as she attempted to pull it back. He held her lightly in his fingers and pushed his thumb into the center of her palm with a slow, intense stroke, aware of her sharp, audible intake of breath.

"I need to see you."

She struggled to put space between them, but he followed. "No, James. Other than here at the office, you won't be seeing me again, period."

"James, Meredith, good morning."

James's head fell forward as he cursed under his breath. *Damn, damn, damn.* He didn't let it show, the emotion that swept through him, but it made his arms tremble. She was out of reach, as mysterious as ever, and he wanted to howl at the injustice.

"Good morning, Gregory," Meredith said. She regarded the newcomer with sparkling eyes.

James gaped, incredulous. What the hell was that look? As Gregory returned her smile, her eyes skimmed his face with womanly awareness. *What in the hell!* Jealous. Out-of-his-mind jealous.

"Meredith, may I speak with you a moment?"

Her smile faded. She looked down at her file. "You'll need to work on the revisions—"

He seized her chin and turned her head to him, and she gasped at the intimate contact, so on display.

"I need to see you tonight."

Her lips parted slightly. Her breath was sweet and fresh and distinctly her. "I don't—"

Gently, he silenced her with a finger to her lips. *"Tonight."*

She tugged on her hoop earrings, glanced at Gregory, and smiled. "If you're done with the revisions."

"I'll be done. What time?"

Her smile was flat. "When you're done, I suppose."

Midnight.

Meredith had known he wouldn't be done until *midnight.*

Goddammit.

At twelve twenty-eight, he was hammering on her building's front door.

"Meredith!"

The brownstone stood quiet and dark, a looming shadow above him, closed to him. James pounded the iron door hard, three times, with his palm.

"Meredith, open up!"

Through the intercom, he heard a snakelike hiss. "Are you insane?"

He glanced up in search of a light, but when he saw none, he pressed the intercom button. "Good. You're awake, then."

"You woke up half the building! What are you doing here? Are you drunk?"

"Open up."

"You're drunk, aren't you?"

"Open."

"Shhhh!"

Impatience coursed through him like poison, making him grit his teeth. "Meredith Sinclair, I'll stand out here all night if you don't open the hell—"

The lock buzzed. James pushed open the door and climbed the stairs to the fifth floor. She stood in the open doorway of her apartment. Wearing a T-shirt and a scowl, her hair falling in disarray past her shoulders. Her breasts stuck out attractively when she crossed her arms over her chest, and he couldn't help but notice. "You're priceless, James. Do you know that?"

He took the last steps toward her. "You're a coward."

Her glare deepened. "If that's all you came here to say, you could've called." She stepped behind the door and pushed it closed.

He caught it before it shut, then followed her inside like a deadly tornado. "What gives?"

Meredith stepped backward, the color draining from her face. "If you don't leave right this second, I'll—"

"What'll you do, huh? I'm not someone you want to play games with, Sinclair, or you will *lose.*"

Her lips thinned. It seemed her entire *face* thinned with disapproval. "I said leave, James."

He nodded toward the kitchen. Two glasses and two napkins occupied the counter, and the stools were positioned farther away, as though recently vacated. "Who the hell was here tonight? Gregory?"

"Arrgh. Cherry just left. You're impossible!" Meredith's hands flew to the sides of her head as though she wanted to drive him out of her brain. James hauled in a deep breath, her nearness intoxicating him, driving him mad. He wanted to pull at his hair. He wanted to pull at hers and drag her to him.

Meredith carefully stepped around the living room couch, then strolled toward the kitchen. He waited, his eyes tracking her slow movements as she cleaned up, his shoulders aching.

"Talk to me, Meredith! I can see I hurt you the other night, but honest to god, I don't know what I did!"

She jerked around with the force of a slap, facing him and growing paler by the second. "You . . ." She fought for words, seemed hard-pressed to hold his gaze. "That night made me realize how impossible you and I would be."

"It felt right to me."

Again, the laugh that made a man want to reach out and throttle her. "Yeah, well, it's not."

She stopped by the window, her profile to him as she took a deep breath. And the truth was, he wanted to hold her. His heart pounded in his head, his chest, his cock, the insides of his wrists. She'd run away from him faster than *to* him. It rankled and tormented him worse than Myers ever had.

"Tell me about it. About the feather."

"What about it?" She didn't manage to conceal the wariness in her tone.

"You sent it to me, didn't you?"

Her laugh was mirthless. "Why would I?"

"Tell me."

Her hand trembled as she shoved it through her hair. He wished she'd look at him. He wished he could see her eyes when she explained this—whatever this hell was—to him. "I bought it in SoHo."

"When?"

"Years ago. It was in the display window, over a book. It wasn't even for sale, but I"—she walked and walked every time he reached her and moved to touch her, but she shrugged as though it mattered little—"I asked the shop owner to please name her price."

"Why, Meredith?"

"Why? Why else? Because I wanted it."

Wanted.

She'd wanted it, just as she'd wanted to give it to him. Just as she wanted to hurt him now. Just as she wanted to drive him insane. He couldn't hold back the words, hold back his hand from reaching for her and stroking her arm. She smelled fresh, ready for bed, and felt warm. "You want me, too, so why do you resist me? Why fight what comes naturally to us? It's okay, Meredith, to take pleasure between us. It's not perverted or unnatural; it's damned special to find someone to share this with."

He'd never spoken like this to a woman. So frankly. So not-bullshit-like.

She pried her hand free and stared at the camel-colored walls for so long, he wondered where her mind had wandered off to. He wanted to follow. To be invited there. "Please leave."

James ground his molars, so damned rankled by her volatility that he considered it. Walking out the door. And forgetting. Not forgiving this cock tease, this *puppeteer* who had him upside down. Just *forgetting*. But instead he took a step to her, aching to make her see that whatever was happening to her, he could help. "It's all right . . . you can be submissive with me. Whatever happened at my place won't happen again. I forbid it. Do you understand? I *forbid* it!"

Meredith wanted to scream.

He didn't leave, but stood there, glorious, beautiful, and dominant, looking at her with those goddamned eyes. "What part of *please leave* don't you understand?" she asked.

The sudden squeeze of his hands on her waist made her heart jump to her throat. He yanked her forward. His lips grazed her temple, tickling her ear with his breath. "Lift your shirt. Fold over the desk."

Her pussy squeezed at the unexpected command, and she had to suppress the urge to rush and do as she was told.

She was a submissive. It was impossible to deny. It

was like asking her not to breathe, not to listen to him, to obey him.

Sexual desire crackled in the air, sudden, forbidden, debilitating.

"No," she breathed, but even as she did, she began to quake, quake inside out, with desire. He would spank her. He would punish her. She would *like* it. Oh, god, what was wrong with her? She was a modern woman!

Did she need this? Hadn't she had enough of this? Her eyes stung, and she pulled her shirt up to her waist and bent over her small living room desk, her breasts crushing the piles of papers as she flattened against the wooden surface. "Who do you think you are?" she said through gritted teeth. *Your love. Your soul mate. Your hell and your heaven, your angel and your devil.*

"Good girl, Meredith. I knew you'd come to your senses." Roughly, his voice coated with arousal, he said, "Pull down your panties."

A tornado of emotions seized her. "If you think you can manipulate me with sex . . . nothing will get me off except hitting you."

"Pull them down."

She made an odd little sound of embarrassment as she peeled the silky scrap off one long leg, then the other.

His nostrils flared as he picked them up and sniffed them. Then his tongue—oh, god, his tongue—snaked out and licked the wetness. She'd soaked herself.

He tucked the panties into his pocket and came

behind her. With one tanned hand on the small of her back, pressing her hard against the desk, the other reached out. And slapped.

Thwack.

She stiffened. Her womb threatened to burst, her nipples beaded. A stinging spread across her flesh. Meredith tucked her face into her arms, her cheeks burning as hot as her buttocks. He could see she loved it—how could he not? Was it instinctive? Repeating the past . . .

It felt too good, too bad, too *familiar*.

One tear escaped as he brushed her pussy with his thumb, went down to her clit, then raised his hand.

Whack.

She screamed in pleasure, and his voice was alien, distant, as if from long ago, but close in her ear as he rubbed his body against hers. "Christ, this turns you on. This turns you on as much as it does me. You want to be punished as badly as I want to punish you. You crave pain so bad, you're making up your own little drama to get off on."

Whack.

Her eyes stung even more, and she was close to sobbing from the unexpected pleasure this gave her. Margaret. All over again. Margaret. Giving and giving and giving. No. She would not give everything. He'd all but *killed* her, goddamn him. "Bastard," she spat.

Whack.

"That's not a nice thing to say. Say 'thank you' when I slap you."

"I . . . hate you, you son of a bitch."

"Say 'Thank you, James. Spank me some more.'"

Whack.

He plunged two fingers into her wet pussy. "When you want to come," he said, twisting his fingers inside until she moaned, "you'll show me your appreciation."

She crumpled a paper in her hands, her eyes closed, writhing on the desk to his hands, and cried out, "Thank you, James. Spank me some more!"

Whack.

"Thank you, James. Spank me some more!"

Whack. Whack. "I'd rather fuck you. But you'll have to ask nicely."

She tossed her head back, hearing the desire in his voice, recognizing the need in him, wanting to punish and humiliate him. "James . . ."

Whack. "Say 'please.'"

"*Please*, James."

"What, baby?" he cooed, softening at her acquiescence.

"Please fuck me."

Her voice was breathy and soft, and it was meant to charm him. She had to stop this insanity, take all that he'd taken from her.

His arms came around; one hand slipped under her T-shirt, and the other delved between her legs to cradle her pussy. And he slammed her against him and began to tongue her ear. Meredith's body ached for more, but instead she shoved him off her. "Not like this . . . Take your clothes off." When he growled, she added, "You said I have power over you—so show me."

She was playing with fire. She was playing with her lover, her murderer, and her betrayer.

He *deserved* to be played.

She might not have felt so betrayed if she hadn't loved him . . . loved him as if her life depended on it. . . . And she might not be so angry if she hadn't found Cordelia standing between them. . . . And maybe she might not have felt so afraid if he hadn't already broken her once. . . .

He was pulling off his shoes, his pants. Clearly, he had no idea of the grim direction her thoughts had taken when he stroked his cock in offering and said, "Thatta girl. This is what you need, isn't it? This is what's got you all worked up. You need this dick in you. . . ." He trailed off when she curled her fingers around the hot, hard length of his cock.

His pulse jumped in his throat. "You want that. Say that you want that in you."

A bubble of hysteria rose up to her throat. Lust and fury churned in her belly. It took every effort to keep her arms from shaking. "I want this." She squeezed. "In my pussy."

The air was charged with tension and passion and something violent.

"Take it, then."

"Not until you get naked."

He yanked off his shirt, his muscles trapping her gaze for a moment. He was the most beautiful creature she'd ever seen. "Show me your hands," she said huskily.

Slowly he lifted his hands as she edged closer. The hunger glimmering in his eyes completely belied his docile posture. "Are you going to tie me up?" he asked with a lazy smile.

Though she tried to hold on to her anger, something in her responded to the silky invitation in his voice. A deep and fierce ache made her legs tremble.

"Yes."

His eyes crinkled at the corners. "Wouldn't it be more fun if I tied *you* up?"

She shook her head. "We've done that already."

"Take your shirt off, Meredith. I want to see you."

"No. Right now we're playing *my* game." She jerked her head toward the dining table, her breathing already choppy. "Sit down."

He didn't.

"Sit."

His smile was all sexy. "All right. I'll play." He pulled a chair out and sat. He would've appeared bored if it weren't for the calculating awareness in his eyes.

"Put your hands behind the chair."

His shoulders flexed as he put his hands behind his back. She pulled a scarf out of a drawer, but as she tied his hands behind the chair, she felt his heat, his hunger, pulling at her like a void, something dark and tempting.

His scent infiltrated her lungs, and she had to swallow.

He watched her, gauging her as if she were some strange creature from another planet. She touched his throat, his face. The sight of him tied up and exposed to her made her stomach clench.

His eyes fell to her lips. The muted gray around the pupils intensified to a silver. "I'm so hard for you—"

She dove for his lips. Impulsively, recklessly. He opened up and took her tongue immediately, and Meredith poured every ounce of confusion, of frustration, of self-loathing, of pent-up wanting, into his mouth. He struggled with his bonds, kissing her with searing force. Stunned at how helpless she felt even though he was tied, she drew back. "This may not be such a good idea."

He leaned toward her, seeking the contact. "Christ, don't stop! You're turning me on so bad."

She seized his hard jaw and crushed his mouth in another furious, hungry kiss. He struggled against his binds as he kissed her ravenously, and she thought *Yes*; she would do this, because she was crazy, because she wanted him like she'd never wanted anything in her life. Because if he'd used her, she would use him, too. Because if he'd thought to hurt her, she would hurt him, too. She bit at his lip and he bit back, every ounce of strength in him in his mouth, in the savage power of his kiss.

She tore away, panting. For one electrifying moment, their gazes held. Stormy with lust, James yanked so hard to free himself, she thought he'd break the chair.

"Untie me."

"No." She slid her hand down his chest and he sucked in a breath. He was hard and long and he was pulsing. He smelled of sex and wanting. She rocked against him, licked inside his mouth. He bucked in the chair, strained to capture her lips again.

"Untie me."

He snaked his tongue out past her lips. He twirled it heatedly around hers, deepening the pressure, demanding more.

Her cheeks were flaming, her hands flying over his chest, tickling his nipples until he arched reflexively.

His hips started to swivel, that finely muscled body bucking under hers.

"Fucking untie me, Meredith."

She cupped him in her hand, hot and wet already, and he hissed out a breath when she squeezed him.

He struggled, and his nostrils flared when she began to stroke him up and down, his breath making a whistle. She wanted to torture him, but it was torture for her, too. She wanted to sob and climb on to that big, long penis and ride him.

He was furious, his beautiful chest heaving with each breath. Their breath mingled. Desire won the battle over anger, for he licked at her mouth, as though urging her to kiss him again. His voice was a rasp. "Need to touch you."

She pushed her hair back. "Not yet."

He released a sound of male frustration and let his head fall back, his breath shortening even more.

She crushed his mouth again, and he groaned when she straddled his hips. She caught his shoulders in her hands, dug her fingers into his skin, and rocked over him.

"Meredith." The way he growled her name drove her mad with desire. She jammed her hand between their bodies. His slit leaked with substance. He was hot and hard in her hand. She delved deeper, past the heavy, hair-roughened sac, past the soft spot behind his balls, to an entry.

She pressed the tip of her finger inside.

He barked. "Fuck!" And pushed his hips up. "What are you doing . . . ? Oh, god, *fuck*."

"You like it?"

Her finger eased in deeper.

"Christ." His head fell forward on a note of helplessness. His jaw, raspy with a day's growth of beard, scraped against her forehead.

He smelled of Dial soap and of man, and the scent proved intoxicating to her rioting senses. Carefully, she stroked his cock, and her finger began a very slow in-out movement into his hot, bucking body.

"Admit that you like it, James Hamilton," she purred against his lips. "Admit that you like me fucking you with my finger."

He growled, rubbing his penis against her, a thin coat of sweat glistening on his skin. "Does this feel like anything but me . . . wanting *the hell* out of you?" He turned his head and nipped at her wrist—the closest body part to him. "Kiss me."

She put her lips within kissing distance, intent on teasing him, but he immediately sucked her upper lip into his mouth. Immense pleasure streaked through her, and Meredith tore away.

He rolled his head side to side, pumping to her body, still taking her finger. He was so warm there, so tight.

He tossed his head forward, avid for her mouth. "Ahh, god, kiss me, Meredith."

"Shh."

His nostrils flared. He dropped his head, forehead to forehead. "Make love with me, Mer."

It was a gruff plea.

He rolled his head against hers.

"Untie me. Let me make love to you." He dragged his mouth along her shoulder. "You owe me a night."

She was feeling scorched and branded. When he touched her like that, she couldn't think. But she was determined to do this. She stood up and said, "No, James."

He panted. "OK, I'll just sit here and be a good boy,

and you, Meredith Sinclair, sit on my lap and fuck me, baby."

She hesitated for three heartbeats. God, how she wanted him one last time. *"No."*

"Yes, Sinclair, you *will.*"

"No, I won't. Never again."

He sucked in a breath and glared at her. His biceps were flexing, still trying to get free.

She laughed loudly. "I did a double knot, James. You won't be able to——" Her courage deserted her when he suddenly broke free and stood. The corners of his mouth kicked up and formed an insulting smile. *"You were saying?"*

She spun around, crashed into a floor lamp, and bolted for her bedroom.

In a split second, his shoulders covered the doorway. "Don't run from me, Meredith." His scent overpowered the bedroom all of a sudden, and she had to swallow. She began to tremble.

"Come here," he said, extending his hand. She shook her head. Her knees wanted to buckle.

There was such *need* etched in every line and dent of his face, burning in his eyes. This man was dying for her. Between his powerful thighs she could see the thick, long column of his flesh, swollen almost beyond belief. His prominent erection pressed boldly up toward the ceiling, and the longing of ages and centuries bloomed inside her like a flower.

She began to back away, her eyes wide. "Hamilton."

"Ahh. So now I'm Hamilton." He smiled a slow, challenging smile. "Fuck me, Sinclair. You can do it, I'm sure. You don't even have to like me."

His eyes boldly slid down her neck to her breasts, and the little points straining through the material of her T-shirt. "All you need is to want me—and you do, don't you? You want me so bad, you had to tie me up and stick your tongue in my mouth."

She backed away, around the bed, and he followed her, stalking her. "It turns you on. Pissing me off. Doesn't it, baby?"

Panting and flushed, she flung her hair behind her shoulder in disgust. "I don't think so. *Baby.*"

To her flippant retort, he answered with a slow, wolfish smile. Easily, he swept up his cock in one wide hand. "Come ride it, Sinclair." He cocked a brow. "Unless you're afraid . . ." He squeezed his own balls, the lust in his glimmering eyes fueling her hunger. "Ahh, you're blushing. You like that. Watching me. But you want more than that. You want to scream. You want to sob with pleasure." He slapped it with his hand, tempting her, but when she remained standing there, marinating in her own desire, a desire so overwhelming her legs would give out any minute, his smile faded. "All right. I'm through with games. If we play, we play *my* way."

He moved for her, seething with energy. Every pore of him screamed *sex, sex, sex.*

When he reached her, she thought of running, but instead sagged.

"Please, James."

Her supplication was a wisp of a whisper. An arm slid around her waist to the small of her back, hauling her to him with surprising gentleness. His eyes smoldered with heat. "'Please *fuck me*, James.'"

"Oh, god." Her arms went around him at the same time his did, and she disintegrated. The only reason she didn't collapse was because his hands slid down to boldly cup her buttocks and draw her brusquely up against him.

"Say *it, Meredith!*"

He ground his massive erection against her. She touched his mouth with one finger to quiet him, and he sucked it into his mouth. Her cry carried need and shock and starvation, fading to a whimper as she pushed up on her toes, clutching at his hair with both hands as his lips slammed against hers and their mouths met in a rapacious kiss. Their heads slanted, their tongues sought, found, fought. She moaned. His fingers bit into her ass as he flattened her against him with a long, agonized groan and a frenzied tangle of tongues.

An overwhelming feeling swept through her, and as she gave up her mouth to his hunger, she didn't know who he was or who she was, but only what he'd been to her. Her heart wanted to explode. She dragged in his scent, unconsciously moving her body against his, seeking his strength, his warmth. She had belonged to him. She had given all her love to this man.

"Baby, if you only knew how wild I am about you."

He pressed her back to the wall, his lean, hard body pressing into hers, and she clutched his jaw and bit at his lips. "Don't."

"Don't what?"

"Don't use your lines on me." She dragged in a breath. "You're a player. You're—"

He seized her chin and narrowed his eyes. "I'm your lover." He turned her around, and she caught her breath when her breasts flattened against the wall. He licked her ear and lifted her T-shirt. "I'm the man who makes you come." Swiftly, precisely, he entered her from behind. She shut her eyes, the relief of his thick flesh sliding into her body making her gasp with joy. "I'm the man you get wet for." He plunged his hands between her and the wall and let his fingers stroke her pussy. "I'm the one who fucks you in your dreams." He rolled her clitoris under the pad of one finger.

Meredith's head thrashed to one side when he rubbed himself between the mounds of her buttocks, right up against the tiny dent of her rosette. "And I'll bet I'm the one you masturbate in the shower for." She cried out softly and creamed on his hand as he finger-fucked her, trembling and trembling and trembling as he teased her with the tip of his cock, the head threatening to tear through her little anus. "I'm the man who's fucking you tonight, all night."

The words swept through her, aphrodisiacs to her heightened senses. Her head hit his shoulder, and he dragged his mouth down her neck. "I'm your man, Meredith."

He gripped her ass and rolled his hips to fuck her deeper, hissing through his teeth, "So tight."

She loved the tight fit, but more than that, she loved his wild abandon.

He pounded her erratically, desperately, mounting her so fiercely, she thought she'd shatter at the next banging thrust.

He made noises. Out-of-control noises. Then he emitted a husky sound that hitched in his throat, and she felt it vibrate in her body as if an electrical surge rising from her core.

She trembled head to toe, powerless against the insistent throbbing in her pussy, stroked to a burn by his invading fingers.

He bucked with a great roar and his cock jerked inside her, three spurts of cream shooting into her. "Ahhh, Christ, yes!"

He convulsed so powerfully, a tremble of her own wracked through her. Meredith moaned feverishly and panted against the sturdy wall, enjoying his caressing fingers as they stroked her to orgasm.

Time passed after the explosion.

Meredith felt the calluses on the heels of his palms as they brushed up the skin of her arms. His musky aroma as he leaned into her ear assailed her senses. Then she heard him take a long, thorough whiff of *her*. "I'm still hungry for you, Meredith."

She smiled but didn't turn; said nothing.

He seized her chin and turned her head, peering into her eyes. "You're so quiet."

Stupid, stupid, stupid, Meredith.

Why could she not stay away from the man? It was just like those smokers who couldn't quit—except James was worse for her.

His lips were fat and juicy looking and wet from all his licking.

Boy, it was blatant. The way he called to her made something thrill inside her, something grow tender and wanting every time she looked at him. She didn't know what it was, but it was soft and feminine, something that made her glory in being a woman to a man.

She closed her eyes, unsure whether to tell him, to admit that he'd not only had his way with her tonight, but he had his deal, too.

"Before you got here, I was on the phone with Julian," she said, avoiding looking directly at him.

"What does Julian say?"

"He's . . . disappointed in me," she admitted, turning around.

James straightened. "Why?"

"He wants to close as is. He's desperate to secure the deal."

"Ahhhhh. And you, of course, explained why he needs to hold out, that you're looking out for the company's best interests, et cetera. Listen, there's something in the wings, and your revisions are actually helping."

"I called Myers to accept the terms," she said, playing with the hem of her T-shirt.

"You accepted." He said this as if she were crazy. "You're accepting Myers's offer as is?"

"Julian is my boss, and the owner of E-Doll, and ultimately it was his decision. He wants the deal. Period."

"But this morning you weren't happy with the terms. Of course Julian asked for your advice. Why in god's name didn't you stick up for your convictions?"

After all they'd been through, at least he deserved the truth. "Because I don't want to see you ever again."

From the corner of her eye, she saw his face—the anger, the outrage—but all he did was turn to go.

"Have a nice life, Meredith."

Chapter Thirteen

$\mathcal{B}$y the time she arrived at E-Doll the next morning, cars were parked fender to fender all the way out to the fringes of the underground garage. As the elevator rose, noise from the lobby drifted to her ears. Laughter. Conversation.

It was the sound of happiness and celebration, and the irony of it pierced her like an ice pick. Her company was being taken over today. *Which means James Hamilton will be top dog, maybe even my new boss.*

And things didn't bode well for Meredith.

Did they?

Gathering her courage, she blended into the swarm of people. All of the Hudsons, including Julian's grandmama, aunts, uncles, and cousins, were there. She spotted Kylie, Gregory.

But no James.

"Ah, and there she is!" Julian announced, spotting her among the crowd.

With a proud smile, he came over and steered her to a finely dressed man who leaned against the wall with his drink against his chest. "Meredith Sinclair, I'd like you to meet J. T. Myers."

Meredith scanned the sea of people for James, caught sight of him ducking his head to listen to something Kylie said, then laughing softly when he straightened, and her stomach caved in on itself. How could he laugh or smile? Of course. He'd won. He'd *won*, and her company would lose its identity, be taken in the grips of a monster. . . .

"James has spoken to me about you," the man said with a flatteringly wide smile.

Surprise made her eyes go round, and it took effort to recover. "How kind of him."

Myers's laughter was boisterous in the extreme. "Kindness—there's a first. Now, I don't know about that, but I do know we'll be sad to see him go."

Meredith did a double take. "Excuse me?"

Myers spoke over the rim of his glass. "He's leaving Inctel."

Impossible. He loves his job.

Julian shot her a this-is-your-chance look and puffed out his chest. "J.T., Meredith here has proved to be . . ."

But Meredith wasn't listening. He quit? James quit? Why?

The memory of James making love to her gripped her tummy. Him, desperate to be inside her. Him, all over her, his hands under her sweater, her panties. *Why? Why, goddammit? He loves his job!*

"Kylie!" Meredith halted her assistant as she passed. "Where did James go?"

"He went home."

"Home," Meredith repeated, completely at a loss.

Kylie lifted a large bowl she'd been cradling in her hands. Something inside it moved, and Meredith's heart flipped when she recognized it. "He said to give you your fish back."

Meredith's smile trembled on her face, her insides moving even faster than the fish did. "Oh."

Carefully, she gazed into the bowl, amazed to discover that little Max had survived James Hamilton.

A half hour later, Meredith was in a cab, tugging nervously at the lace hem of her sweater, staring out the window while she rocked herself.

He would deny it.

She would look at him, and in that same instant, she'd know he hadn't quit. His job meant everything to him. His reputation, his power. He had never risked it before, not even for her, for Margaret. So why . . . ?

Her steps faltered as she crossed the lobby. Cordelia was stepping off the elevator, her golden tresses carefully arranged into a chignon atop her head, her body draped in a killer, sleek green dress the same mesmerizing color as an emerald pendant on her neck. Under the glowing chandeliers, she stood small but proud, drawing all eyes to her.

So eye-catching was her attire that either she was on her way to meet a hot lover . . . or she had just rendez-voused with him.

Like a knife twisting in a wound, that thought gave Meredith a new jolt of pain.

She caught the nearly imperceptible widening of Cordelia's eyes before she gave her a curt nod. "Mere-dith."

Meredith tore her gaze away, said "Good morning, Cordelia," and brushed past her.

In the elevator, the trembling returned. Acid boiled inside her stomach as a fierce, unstoppable jealousy spread. Anger. Sticky and thick. Anger at herself; at James. Anger so great she thought she would get physi-cally sick.

How could she have thought for a second that there could be anything—anything but grief and pain and betrayal—from a man like James? She remembered the things he'd said. Last night . . . *god*! To think of all those lines she'd been tempted to believe. All the pain and torment she'd experienced, torn between wanting to trust him and pushing him away. How could James stand there last night, looking at her the way he did, touching her the way he had, making her *feel* the things he made her feel, and the next day . . .

She seethed. Horribly. Overwhelmingly. The doors slid open to that place—the penthouse. And then, there by the bar, like a slap to the face because of his lethal beauty, stood James in shirt and slacks. He looked up, and across the room, their gazes locked. She sucked in breath after shaky breath as he started for her, moving with that catlike grace, a smile dancing on his lips. Her knees quaked from the force of her rage. The unfairness of it all—him, so gorgeous, so elegant, so tempting. So *cruel*.

History repeated itself all the time.

And now *he* planned to repeat his, and maybe even marry that . . . that . . . ass-faced Barbie!

James took her hand and lifted it to his lips, where he placed a wet, indecent kiss on the back of it. "*Hey,*" he said throatily. "I didn't expect to see you."

She pulled her hand from his with obvious force. Knowing it wouldn't be safe within his reach, she tucked it behind her back, hating that the dewy spot he'd left on her skin tingled. "Hello, James."

His playful smile showed that he hadn't caught the coldness in her eyes, the very rage burning in her cheeks. He studied her, his eyes smoldering, and said, "God, I'm happy you're here." He put a hand to her hair and started to pull her toward him. "Don't you have something for me?" he whispered, all silk and seduction.

"As a matter of fact, I do."

She slapped him. He'd been lowering his mouth to hers, and the quick, unexpected slap whipped his head to the side.

Her heart stopped beating.

Nothing moved except an almost imperceptible flare of his nostrils.

A tiny muscle began to flex at the back of his jaw. Fear mingled with her own rage, making her chest heave, her skin break into a sweat. The feelings built inside her, gathering force, until she had to spit out, "Bastard!"

He halted her wrist when she attempted a second slap, hissing through his teeth. Her arm remained in the manacle of his hand, frozen in the air. "I've been called that many times," he said in a deceptively soft voice. "From you I find it insulting. Apologize."

"Never! You're a sleaze. It's you. *Your* fault I've . . . your fault I never want to . . . !"

"What?" The glimmer in his eyes turned tenebrous. "What have I done to you, Meredith? Tell me."

She jerked her arm free. "You make me sick."

"Do I?"

"Yes!"

He stared at her lips, and she sensed him withdrawing, cautiously putting the wall of his precious control back in place. Lips pursed in distaste, he turned away, raking his hand through his hair. "I'm not fighting with you; I have enough going on right now."

She charged after him. "Really? Because last I heard, you don't have a job!"

He spun around, shocking her with the abrupt clamp of his hands on her shoulders. "I am not. Fighting. With you. Meredith."

"Why? Did your new fuck buddy leave you so spent and tired? Aww, poor James."

He snarled as he snatched her by the waist. As if she weighed no more than a feather, he tossed her over his shoulder like a sack, ignoring her shrieks of protest. "The only *woman I'm interested in fucking* is you!" He stalked down the long hallway, Meredith squirming furiously, pummeling his back.

"Let go of me, you sick, twisted— I saw her! I saw her in the lobby. She looked quite blushy and satisfied, let me add. Tell me, does she like it when you spank her, too?"

He laughed and squeezed her rump with infuriating familiarity. "I assure you, I'm not involved with Cordelia. We're doing business, nothing more. We'd decided to offer for E-Doll under the table—but that was before you went ahead and agreed to Inctel's terms. Now let's stop talking about work and get down to business. There you go, on the bed."

Her body bounced on the mattress before he covered it with his. "I think it's cute that you're jealous, but you have nothing to worry about."

He had the nerve to smile as his lips descended, his eyes feasting on her lips with unmistakable intent.

"No." With an inhuman effort, she grabbed two fistfuls of his hair and pulled back until the veins on his throat seemed ready to pop out. "Don't touch me!" she cried. "Everything about you is a lie. Your entire life is some sick, twisted game. Why did I have to get trapped again? Why did it have to be you, of all the people in this stupid universe?"

"Calm the hell down." He pinned down her shoulders with his hands and said through gritting teeth, "I told you: Cordelia means nothing to me. Nothing."

She thrashed under him, futilely trying to wiggle free, but it only brought their bodies into a heated contact that had her even more breathless and agitated. "I'm not talking about her!" she cried. "I'm talking about . . . why did you quit your job? For her? You know what you want, and you want Inctel. Isn't that right, James? Tell me—I need to know! You always take what you want. You'll do it all over again—do it and do it! You're nothing but a liar and a sadist!"

Finally she stopped squirming and gazed up at his face. All of a sudden, she knew something—something among the awful, hateful things spilling from her lips had landed a hard blow.

"I've never lied to you, and I'm not a sadist. But I must know: what is it you expect me to do *again*?"

She groaned, unprepared for this conversation. "Forget it."

He studied her face with glazed eyes that were far

too tender for a man of his cruelty. As she waited for him to speak, she unwillingly became aware of his body, heavy and hot over hers. Where his hips lay against hers, she could feel his desire, and after their struggle, a strange, damp need pooled between her thighs. His hair looked dark and silken; the elegance of his button-down shirt enhanced the raw magnetism of his masculine face. She closed her eyes, pained just by the sight of him. His face.

"Stop hiding the truth, Meredith. What are you so upset about? Why does it matter if I quit?"

"Because," she said, and trailed off. *Because once, you made me the happiest woman alive.*

Once.

She felt the sensual graze of his fingers as he brushed back a damp tendril that clung to her temple. "Why are you here, Meredith? Because you heard I resigned? So what?"

"Maybe," she murmured, her lashes sweeping up to reveal her eyes, "I came to say good-bye."

For some reason, the way he gazed down at her—without anger, without a single shield in those mesmerizing pools of silver—broke her heart. "Are you ever going to tell me what I did to you?" he asked quietly.

Her chin began to tremble. She wanted to hate him, and still she loved him. When she spoke, she was horrified to discover her voice had deteriorated to a croak. "The night at your apartment . . . I had . . . visions.

Strange visions. When we played with the feather. I saw you and me and I . . ."

Inside the dark circles of his eyes, a livid, positively feral light flashed. "So that's it? This is all because of a *dream*?"

She loathed the way his mere tone accused her of insanity. She said, "You're squishing me."

"You're giving up on us because of a *dream*?"

"It wasn't a dream!"

"Fine. All right. So what happened? In this vision. What? Tell me!"

Groaning from anger and anguish and pain, she planted the heels of her palms on his shoulders and pushed. "It doesn't matter anymore. I just don't want to see that anymore, ever. Not in my past, and not in my future."

"Whatever it is you saw, it's not real here; this is just you. And me. Just you and me and *no one* else."

"Just you and me and Cordelia," she whispered.

James stared at her, stunned.

It took him ages to speak, and in a tone so tender and husky, it only fueled her anger. "Cordelia has nothing to do with us," he murmured, and ran the back of a finger down her jaw.

Pushing away his touch, Meredith laughed cynically—and hated how a regular laugh had morphed into something so sadistic. "You're wasting your breath, James. She's got everything to do with us. Or maybe it's not even her; it's just you and your thirst for money and reputation and power and *dominance*. God, just thinking about it infuriates me. Get off me. Get *off*!"

Twisting his features into a cruel, tortured grimace, he backed off, and when his gaze slid away from hers, Meredith was shattered to find she mourned the loss of those eyes. They had been on her for days and weeks, delivering a torment so excruciating and unsettling, she'd wanted those eyes to never again look at her, for fear of their effect on her. Now they wouldn't return, and she felt bereft.

"Leave, Meredith," he whispered. "And come back when you're willing to reason with me."

She sat up, swiping strands of her hair back into the tie at the nape of her neck. *Leave.* Yes, she would leave, though a part of her wanted to stay and keep on fighting until it wouldn't hurt—until James came up with a thousand ways to convince her he'd never betray her as he had before. To convince her that maybe in this life, he could love her. "I'm not coming back," she said, perhaps to try to hurt him, or perhaps to get that into her head.

Rising in a single, fluid move, James grabbed her arm and lifted her to her feet. "Well, then."

Quietly and with impressive grace, she followed him down the hall, his grip unrelenting on her arm as he pushed the elevator button with his free hand. Laboring to breathe, she lifted her head and gazed at his profile. He wore a chilling expression; the expression of someone who doesn't care anymore. Who couldn't care less if the whole world went to hell. Of someone who was already there.

The soft *ding* came. His hand dropped, but Meredith stood fixedly before the open doors, reluctant to board.

He waited in silence. She waited, too. For an excuse, an explanation, something she could believe.

When she didn't move, James leaned close and hissed in her ear, "What are you waiting for? Get in."

She fisted her hands at her sides.

He grabbed her by the elbow and thrust her into the elevator. Her eyes began to burn, so she remained with her back to him, waiting for the doors to close. This morning, she had wanted to believe James was better in this life. That he was ready to love her. That they were meant to be together.

Meredith felt her throat clog as the doors sealed shut, and only then did she flatten her damp palm on the mirror and cry.

Motionless on the terrace, James stared out at the city. He didn't feel the wind. Or notice it was a clear, starlit night. He didn't feel anything—except on the inside. He felt battered. Devastated. He'd never felt like this before.

He'd never been in love. It was impossible to explain to himself, to anyone, what he felt now. He had not been looking for love, or for this particular woman to arouse it in him, either. But somehow he knew his entire future, his life, hinged on Meredith. He wanted, needed her, with a desperation and intensity that couldn't compare to anything he'd ever experienced in his life.

He wanted it all. He wanted a million nights and double that amount of her smiles. He wanted her in his bed, puttering around his kitchen, his bathroom. He wanted to see her when he woke up and to fight with her and make up with her and do everything a man could possibly do with a woman. With her.

He'd always pursued business with single-minded ruthlessness, convincing himself it was enough. But it wasn't.

She doesn't love me. How can she believe some crazy vision instead of me?

Frustrated, he glanced at the feather in his hand. *She listens to those monsters inside her instead of to me.*

She hates me because of a damned dream!

He crushed the feather in his fist, wishing it would disintegrate, but it didn't break. He opened his hand, extending his fingers, and watched it take form once again.

He lifted the feather to his face, intending to blow it into the wind and never see it again . . . and saw blackness.

Chapter Fourteen

⌒

For decades, war had spread throughout the nations like a plague. Where stone keeps had stood tall and proud, heaps of tumbled rocks remained. Fields and crops had been burned to the ground, rivers poisoned by blood and bodies. Cities had crumbled. While the men fought in the Crusades, only the elders were left to protect the women and children—creating a hunting ground for thieves and robbers. People wondered why God had forsaken them and their families.

Darkness hovered over the skies like a premonition, a messenger of things to come, a promise of bleakness and death. More death.

Yet in the smallest corner of the lands, a few towns remained, shielded from the madness by thick, lush forests and hills, where the sun still shone upon the people's faces as they went about their daily chores.

People still smiled at one another here.

People still dared to dream, dreams of peace, of love, and hope. One of those blessed places was a small village.

At nighttime, old Mahon would sit on the jutting rock outside his cottage to watch the villagers gather in a circle. Kaelin the storyteller would stand by the fire, wearing the same shimmering blue tunic he always did, his scruffy beard reaching past his belly and tied into a braid. His hat, composed of scraps of fabrics in different colors, had been mended plenty, but he refused to change it for a newer one, for he said the hat told him the stories, and there was no other hat like it in the whole country. Kaelin's stories were of romance, of hope, of brighter days to come. But there was one story in particular that was a favorite.

With a voice deep and crackling with drama like the fire, and careful to meet all the listeners' eyes, Kaelin began. "Years ago, there lived a wizard, one of the greatest, most powerful wizards that ever lived. He was no ordinary wizard, I tell you. He was the hand of God on the earth, and his name was Weylin.

"His spells were so strong, his visions so clear, his words so wise, that kings had longed to rule with him by their side. But there was one other, the witch Gitta, who sold her soul to the devil to be as strong as he, and she wished Weylin the Great Wizard dead. Were he to die, there would be two hundred years of war, which would end only with the sacrifice of a sacred white bird in the name of true love.

"As the wizard's power dwindled in his efforts to flee the wrath of the envious witch, his spells of protection broke, and one by one, his family was killed. But his eldest son, Artan, only four winters old, was taken to the forest, where Weylin cast a spell so powerful to protect the child—his one last spell—that he had no power left to defeat the witch Gitta. And the fight between the witch and the wizard endured for weeks, until Weylin, our greatest wizard, was killed.

"The witch thought the boy dead, but he was out there, growing silently like a tree. He is there still, a warrior with the call of magic in his hands. He will obey none but his fate, protected by Weylin until his time comes, the time for him to step forward and fulfill his destiny."

All the children applauded at this familiar ending. "Is he as old as Kollsvein now?" a young girl asked, the question drawing all eyes to the large, muscled figure of a young man who sat at the edge of the circle.

"Most surely," Kaelin said, nodding at Kollsvein.

"Is he as strong as Kollsvein, too?" a little boy asked.

Koll laughed, then stood and ruffled the little boy's hair. "Come a few more years, you'll be as strong as I or more so," he told the child.

Old Mahon smiled to himself, for that was doubtful.

Kollsvein had indeed grown to be a magnificent man. His hair was dark brown with streaks lightened by the sun; his eyes—eyes too wise for his years—light blue. He was more than six feet tall, taller than anyone Mahon had ever known in this or any neighboring town. He'd grown fast, the years flying by so quickly that in the blink of an eye, Mahon himself had started using a cane and blinking to see anything up close.

And the boy was a boy no more.

Old Mahon had found him in the woods, living among foxes, with nary a scratch on his body and no human language.

Still, he was perceptive, for when Mahon offered his hand, the boy took it. It was foolish to believe he was Artan, son of Weylin, as the village children liked to pretend. But Mahon rejoiced that the gods had given him a son, the son he'd always wanted.

Of course, he had Oriana, and he'd grown to be grateful for it. His daughter had a man's courage, a woman's stubbornness, and a pet's devotion.

Her hair was as gold as gold itself, her eyes large and amber. When his wife succumbed one cold winter to a fever, it was only because of Oriana that Mahon didn't die himself. And then he found Kollsvein, and had another reason to live.

It was hard to believe more than a dozen summers had passed since then. Kollsvein was a silent, brooding sort, but his heart was twice his body's considerable size, and he would give the coat on his back for anyone.

Kollsvein had set up watch posts for the people, and

daily he hunted for food. He settled quarrels, brought game to the fire when the crops had failed, and had helped them all strengthen their houses and carve escape routes, as they all knew their peace was fragile. He made swords for the people, and even taught Mahon's daughter how to use one when she wanted to learn.

"When will he come?" one of the children asked all of a sudden, and the storyteller grew thoughtful.

"When the time is right, he will come. Now, shall I tell another story? A new story about a dragon?"

The children squealed, and old Mahon gazed upon his daughter, her complexion glowing by the fire. Oriana was lovely, and if she was a handful, he couldn't really complain, for old Mahon had been mischievous himself in his day. Villagers were used to seeing her wield one of Kollsvein's swords, and they were so accustomed to seeing her tie her tunics between her legs that it had stopped causing scandal some time ago.

Mahon saw her gaze at Kollsvein across the fire, then quickly lower her eyelashes when the boy looked her way. Old Mahon might not see very well now, but some things were clearer than ever. He'd never seen a man look at a woman the way Kollsvein looked at Oriana. His whole face would go taut, strong in its maleness, yet overtaken with emotion.

Most times, Oriana would not notice the look, for she'd be playing with the children, or helping to bring water or logs into the house, but it answered a question that had troubled old Mahon: why a man like Kollsvein had stayed in this little village, in the middle of nowhere important, when he could have gone anywhere, been anything, with his power and youth and intelligence.

He had his answer, and knew it well.

Kollsvein stayed for Oriana.

He knew this even though they had begun to fight like cats and dogs. Villagers had begged Mahon to put a stop to it, for their fights were making them moody and out of sorts. One would sulk while the other disappeared into the forest for days, and it disrupted the village's comfortable routine.

Old Mahon was worried, too, and one evening when he saw Kollsvein heading for the woods, he decided to follow. . . .

Only to discover his daughter had the same idea, for from another direction, she rushed toward Kollsvein and got to him first. Mahon was too far away to hear everything she was saying, but he made out "Big, overbearing oaf!" and "Ugly cur!" before she began pounding Kollsvein's chest with her small hands.

Kollsvein remained very still, allowing her to beat him with her fists. Mahon didn't know why they fought, and he suspected the children didn't know, either. Their bodies were calling to each other, and that, perhaps, was the entire reason why.

Finally, Oriana stopped her assault and, panting, stared up into Kollsvein's face, her hair flapping behind her. Then Kollsvein moved. As fast as a forest animal, and with the strength of the knight he promised to be, he grabbed her face and kissed her.

When Oriana wrapped her arms around him and opened her mouth beneath his, Kollsvein groaned desperately. Mahon knew he had to stop this. He opened his mouth to call to them, but suddenly his vision went black. He was struck with the certainty that he would never in his life see them kiss again.

He'd had visions a few times in his years, but never one as strong as this one. His vision turned from black to red, and he staggered. It was death he saw, and he was frightened for them both.

With great effort, he called his daughter's name, and the lovers jumped from each other, their eyes wide and startled and glowing gold like the setting sun. "Go home, child," he said. And to Kollsvein, "I did not rescue you from the forest to have you behave like an animal."

The next day, the midwife was kind enough to talk to Oriana about the nature of things, but the girl just laughed, saying of course she knew. There was little privacy in the village, and she had observed lovemaking. So Mahon had a talk with Kollsvein. If they stayed apart, he thought, they might yet avoid suffering for a love that every day Mahon became more convinced was doomed.

Kollsvein stared at the ground as Mahon explained that his daughter's honor was linked to her maidenhead, and as he would not allow them to marry, Kollsvein would have to stay away. Kollsvein nodded, his face beet red, and told him, "I will not dishonor her—you have my word."

He had hardly been seen with her since then, and Mahon had felt guilty at the weepy look in Oriana's eyes as Kollsvein passed by.

Oriana woke from her dream with a start. For a few seconds, she gazed blindly at the darkness of her small chamber before dropping back her head and staring up at the ceiling. Tantalizing fragments of her dream came back to her—Kollsvein's warm hands stroking her hair, her face. His thumb tracing the fullness of her lips. Kollsvein's mouth exploring every inch of her skin, while her own hands met the hard, smooth angles of his. Groaning in discomfort, Oriana shifted onto her side, every quivering muscle in her body burning in protest. Her nightdress was damp with sweat, her lungs ached for more air, and an acute pain jabbed her between the legs.

It was all Kollsvein's fault—him and his honor. He slept in the stables, for he couldn't bear to be under the same roof as her. He hardly looked at her anymore.

Oriana had flogged him playfully with a tree branch when he'd said they could not marry—at least not yet. She wasn't the only one who wanted him—but she was sure she wanted him more than anyone else ever could.

This want was torment. Her soul and heart and body; all of it begged for him. Always she had it, this want, unending, ever growing.

At last one night, after ignoring each other for hours, Kollsvein followed her to the river. His blood was pounding in fury at the attention she'd been getting from the other young men at the equinox festival. Sounds from the celebration flittered through the trees in the forest, as Oriana stood on the riverbank, wiping away her tears.

She was as furious as he was. Kollsvein had danced with every woman and child in the village except her.

"Oriana."

Lord, there he was, and there was her heart jumping.

She dare not even turn, for she wanted none of him now.

"Leave me be."

But he grabbed her arm and whirled her around.

"You taunt me on purpose. You talk to all the men because you know it tears me apart!" he hissed.

"I talk to them because you do not talk to me! You do not dance with me! All you do is ignore me!"

"How could we dance when the slightest touch makes me burn for you?" he growled, and as his hands seized her jaw, she saw the torment in his gaze, felt the tremor in his body before his lips captured hers.

She had never known such yearning as this. It was all consuming, her need for him, her desire. From the moment she woke up, he was her first thought, and through the day, no matter what she was doing, she thought of Kollsvein.

She tasted the salt of her tears in his kiss, but more than that, his own craving for her, as desperate as hers. In the way his tongue swiped inside her greedily, the way his breath grew harsh, and the way his hands gripped her face so tightly, she knew he was leaving in the morning.

This undid her.

Oriana clung to him, her arms coiled around his neck, and within seconds her back was pressed down on the dampened earth, his body settling above hers, heavy and hard and male. Instinctively she parted her legs to accommodate him, and as their mouths continued to feast, he began to rock his body against hers.

Though they were fully clothed, their need was so strong that the feel of him pressing his manhood rhythmically at the juncture between her legs sent a fire streaking through her body. War—it was inside Oriana now, and there was only one man who could bring her peace.

The laughter of some passersby broke through their passionate haze.

"Oriana, we must stop." Koll's chest rose and fell with his exerted breaths as he put her at arm's length.

But she squirmed to get closer. "No. Koll, no, don't stop. Kiss me. Please kiss me. I'll do anything if you kiss me."

He seized her shoulders and gently shook her, trying to push her away. "Your father forbade me to marry you—do you understand? He forbade it. We cannot do this."

"No. He cannot forbid it! You and I . . . We can run away."

"No, Oriana." Kollsvein released his grip and then briskly rearranged her hair, plucking away the leaves from the tangled mess. "We must not go against his wishes. But I have a plan. I will do great deeds to prove to your father that I am worthy of you."

Great deeds? What great deeds could possibly be worth the torment of being apart? Her voice quavered. "You won't make love to me until we're wed, will you?" she asked as he helped her to her feet.

He stiffened at the question, his voice fierce when he said, "Nay. But I will find a way for us to marry soon."

She smiled sadly, twining her arms around his neck. "Perhaps I should take you by force."

His eyes dipped to the breasts she so provocatively tried to display. He plucked another leaf from her hair and set her aside with impressive self-restraint. "I cannot bend in this. I cannot," he said, turning away.

She reached out to caress his profile and his body responded to her touch, quivering like an arrow ready to spring from its bow. She rubbed up against his side, and he did not stop her, merely frowned down at the ground under his feet. "I beg you not to do anything foolish," he said, his voice thick. He lifted his head and eyed her lips.

She stepped around, so close to him that his breath fanned her face as she beheld his tortured gaze.

"I do not care for my honor nearly as much as I care for you," she whispered. "If you are leaving just to preserve my honor, then don't."

He stroked his hands up her arms in a persuasive manner. "I must go."

"You're running away from me," she accused. "You're leaving because of me. You're a coward!"

"Shush. Oriana, shush. Understand that I have to make myself worthy," he whispered back as his palms cupped her face. "I have to follow my destiny. Don't you realize who I could be?"

His hands were warm and they felt better than any fur pelt or anything else luxurious Oriana had ever touched. His chest was a massive wall, all hardness, and as her distended nipples brushed against his tunic, she almost wept thinking of not feeling this again.

"You are not Artan, Koll. Stay with me."

"God, you're so beautiful, my eyes are sore looking at you," he said, nuzzling her face with his.

She closed her eyes at the hurt his words caused. "Koll, if you do not claim me, then you mustn't speak so."

"Pray, why not?"

"Because it hurts too much," she breathed. She could almost feel her insides breaking against him. "Your words hurt more than if you'd driven that sword through my heart."

"I do not wish to hurt you." He brushed his lips against her own, and inhaled a sharp breath from the shock of their touch. "I would never hurt you."

"You have already—you always will. I love you so much. I cannot feel what I do and not feel pain."

He growled low in his chest and glanced up at the sky. "I will send you the bird, as God is my witness."

"What bird?"

"The bird that stops the war. The white bird. Artan or no, I will be this man for you. I will hunt it, I will find it, and I will spill its blood for love of you—and I will send you its feathers."

Time passed.

The hours became days. Days became weeks and then months. Had he been here ten lives? Fifteen? Merely a part of one? Kollsvein didn't know. The cell door banged closed, and he stiffened as footsteps approached. His head hung low, and he didn't lift it.

He knew who it was.

Rage consumed him, making his arms tremble, the cords bulging as the manacles bit into his wrists. Oriana. He tried to summon her face in his mind. He saw her laughing amber eyes. Gold hair, gold eyes, gold skin.

He felt her touch as something stroked his chest, and he gritted his teeth. He was hallucinating, hungry, weak. Dying.

"Why do you keep me here?" he ground out.

The boy, his tormenter, said nothing. His jailor. The one Kollsvein had come to . . . loathe with his entire being. The boy had beaten him, shredded his clothes, abused his naked body—stripped him of his pride and his manhood. And yet his cock was hardening already. In anticipation of what this creature would do.

"You have not eaten," the boy crooned, caressing Kollsvein's face, then his shoulder. "'Tis not good for you."

Kollsvein was silent.

The touch left him, and he bit back an oath as his body arched, beseeching for more. "Release me," he croaked.

"Of course. That's why I'm here." The boy chuckled and put a wet rag to Kollsvein's chest, stroking it down his torso. His skin cried out where there were bruises, and yet pleasure streaked to his nipples. And then the boy reached his cock. Kollsvein sealed his eyes shut as arousal stormed through him.

"That's it," the boy said, grasping Kollsvein's shaft. "I will give you the release you crave."

Kollsvein didn't know his name. This fiend who came to the dungeon to discipline him. To show him what happened to thieves who stole from their master's lands. And if Kollsvein lived, he was certain he never would forget this hell. Nor how a foolish act of love had brought him to it.

"It's all right. Call out her name."

Kollsvein panted for air, shook his head, jangled the chains in a burst of fury. "I will cut off your hands if they touch me once more!"

The boy laughed softly and stroked his cock upward, and Kollsvein cried out a mighty curse of pleasure. "Damn you!"

"I think of how much seed you spill when I touch you, and I wonder if it is for the woman or for me."

Oriana. He did not want to think of her as the boy stroked his cock, did not want to imagine her hands fluttering all over his aching shaft. His love for her was pure, and this—this was base. He thrashed against his bonds, rattling the chains as he resisted the boy's fondling. "Stop! Stop this, I say."

"But you don't want me to stop."

The boy knelt before him and rubbed his face against Kollsvein's erection. Koll's eyes rolled back, his mind seeking to escape the prison his body could not. Oriana kissing him. Whispering, as they kissed, *Koll. Koll. Koll.*

His testicles tightened when her lips licked a straight path up his shaft and lapped at the drops of his precum. "Yes," he moaned, rolling his head. "Oriana, my love, do you taste my desire for you? Do you taste my hunger?"

"I taste your cum."

He growled and began to pump into her warm

mouth, his buttocks squeezing tight at each thrust. "Oriana," he moaned.

Abruptly, the warmth around him left, and the boy slapped his hard cock. Koll's body bucked in pain and pleasure as he gave out a yell. "Bastard!"

"You're the thieving bastard."

One more slap on his cock. Another.

Kollsvein roared as he kept climbing toward orgasm, the pain of the boy's slaps making him feverish to come. In his mind he was mounting Oriana, her legs embracing his hips, her cunt so tight it pained his cock with every thrust, but he continued on because he was desperate for it, desperate to spill his seed in Oriana.

"The bird was not yours to take."

Slap, slap, slap.

Panting, dripping semen, Koll rubbed his dick against the boy's thigh. "I told you, I promised it to my betrothed," he growled, his balls straining in their sac as he sought to grind himself against something.

"You promised your betrothed a bird?"

The boy stepped back, and Koll's erection twitched in the cold air. Above his head, he fisted his hands in frustration. It was always like this. The boy was the very devil.

Oriana. How long since he'd left?

Would she take him still, love him, when he returned? A boy had left, and not half a man would return. God, Oriana. Here, in this dungeon, it was hard to think he'd ever had something pure.

But Oriana was waiting. She had to be. He would get out of here, and they would live a full life, with babes. He would have his beloved wife to welcome him home. He would feel her warm flesh around him every night.

A harsh squeeze on the tip of his cock made Kollsvein yell in pain. "Your *betrothed* has taken another," the boy said.

Koll's teeth ached as he squeezed out, "You lie."

"'Tis the truth I speak. I have proof."

"Show it to me, then!" he barked, jerking angrily against his chains.

"Kiss me. Show me you're Lucifer's whore. And I will show it."

Kollsvein cursed as the boy reached up to frame his jaw in his hands. The slow flick of his tongue across the seam of his lips made him stiffen.

"No," Koll gasped, but the boy teased him by taking a quick taste.

Koll couldn't react; imagined biting him, killing him, yet did nothing but stand there. Chained. Cold. Tormented.

The boy began to kiss him.

"No," Koll groaned, and the boy took advantage and tangled his tongue around his. Starved for human contact, for warmth, Koll heard himself moan in pleasure as their tongues rubbed.

Lord almighty, but what he wouldn't give for it to be Oriana's lips against his, driving him mad with desire.

Oriana . . .

He made a choked sound of gratitude as the boy's caresses resumed. Lightly, slim fingers traced a line down the length of his erection; then the boy cupped his testicles in his palm and fondled.

Sensations stormed through him, unwanted, unwelcome. Gritting his teeth, Koll began to pump rhythmically. He thought, *Please. Please give me. Please give me Oriana.*

The boy groaned and lifted his tunic and pressed his swollen cock against Koll's. Helpless to stop himself, Koll rubbed against the boy's hardness, head to head, skin to skin. He leaked moisture, trembled with the pain stemming from his center up to his heart, his feet, his balls.

Rubbing felt good.

"You see, you're a whore and you like it," the boy purred, stroking his chest with slow, callused hands.

"Rot in hell," Koll hissed, but continued rocking his hips, galloping toward that peak, a second of heaven in this hell.

Oriana's face hovered front and center in his mind. Koll pictured her, undulating her slim hips against his, stroking and kissing him, and he rapidly reached an explosive orgasm. He yelled out her name, shuddering as he shot his cum onto the boy's body.

And then, as he panted in exertion, the boy chuckled cruelly and slid out of the cell. When he returned, he produced a single white feather.

Kollsvein's eyes ached at the sight. The feather's whiteness seemed morbid here in this dingy cell, its purity soiled in the boy's long, bronzed fingers. "'Tis from your precious bird," the boy said.

A peacock, white and pure as Oriana herself. Kollsvein had followed it for days, intent on capturing the beauty without harming a single feather on its body—for the blood spilled had to be for love and no other reason. But he'd roamed into the wrong territory.

"What has that to do with Oriana?"

The concern in the boy's face—very akin to pity—made Kollsvein's blood boil in his veins. "She sends it to you. As a farewell gift."

"Liar! Why should I believe you?" he demanded.

Silently, the boy unlocked the chains. Kollsvein's body sagged to the floor like a rock sinking into the pits of the ocean. He struggled to his knees, blinking in the darkness to find the boy and grab the hem of his tunic. "Where is she? What happened to Oriana?"

The boy grasped Kollsvein's hair and pulled. "Why ask me? You think I lie."

"I'm sorry. Please . . . tell me."

Slowly the boy began stroking himself, cock bobbing up and down. "Do you want to get fucked?" he asked.

"No!"

His cock continued to swell large and proud, and Koll wanted to tear his eyes out for staring.

"Do you want to know what happened to her? Then 'tis a fact you want to get fucked."

Koll shut his eyes tight and had no choice but to say, "I want to get fucked."

The boy knelt behind Kollsvein and penetrated him. And to his fury, Kollsvein's dick lifted again, long as a sword. He was harder than hard, his channel burning as the boy thrust into him.

"Damn you!" Koll spat, hating how much he liked it.

He imagined Oriana behind him, curling her fingers around his cock, and he relished the moment the boy reached around to grab him.

Soon he was humping the boy's tight fist.

"Moan for me. Moan, goddamn you!" he shouted, cursing Mahon for keeping him and Oriana apart, cursing himself for his foolish notions of honor, cursing his very own god.

He heard moans behind him. Felt the jerk of the boy's shaft in his body. And to his embarrassment, he came again with another yell. This time, in the boy's hand.

Then, and only then, his humiliation was complete. And as he knelt there, weak and coated with sweat and semen, Koll wished for death. "Now tell me, damn you."

The boy withdrew and righted his clothing. "She is in the keep. We gave her a choice."

His heart thundered in his chest. "And?"

"And she agreed to wed my master in exchange for your freedom. On the condition that you have the bird."

Kollsvein saw nothing but red. He'd saved Oriana's honor, her virginity, only so that she could use it to bargain for his life.

Did she think he would appreciate her noble gesture?

Did she believe he would be grateful that Oriana, the one thing that had kept him alive, would be another's?

He'd rather she killed him instead.

He had nothing left. Not his honor, not his manhood, and not her love.

The boy gave him a rough tunic to wear and led him up out of the dungeon. Kollsvein's eyes burned in the sunlight as the boy presented him with a knife and the white peacock.

Kollsvein dragged his feet toward the massive keep, trailing the peacock behind him. And there, at the gate, he killed the bird and began to toss the feathers in the air. "Your feathers, Oriana! That is all you will ever get from me." And slowly he lifted the dripping knife to his throat.

"No! Please! Koll, don't! I love you!"

Meredith awoke with a start, sweating profusely. Shocked and disoriented, she covered her face with clammy hands, then glanced at the clock to find it was past three a.m.

What happened?

She'd been trying to fall asleep, gazing at the ceiling, feeling totally wretched, and after three hot teas and a dozen muttered curses, she'd thought of James.

She'd visualized him in her mind, remembered how he'd used that silky feather on her, and then she'd dreamed. Not of James. Not of Gavin. But of a man she'd loved with the same passion as the others.

Kollsvein.

Now Meredith groaned when she realized there would be no more peaceful nights for her. And what of James?

She didn't know who he was with or what he was doing tonight, but her nerves quivered at the premonition.

She knew, with a surety that alarmed her, that James had been playing with the feather.

Chapter Fifteen

Twelve days, thirteen hours, and forty minutes later

James Hamilton had been watching her.

For how long? Meredith wondered as she stood with her latte in hand, frozen by the sight of James Hamilton—in all his glory—looking at her through the window of Starbucks.

He looked so good, she wanted to run to him and tell everyone, *He's mine!*

But no. She'd quit him. She'd quit James Hamilton and all this love crap.

Still, her heart sputtered as the epitome of manliness swung open the door and came inside.

He wore jeans and a clingy T-shirt, his pitch-black hair glossy in the sunlight. His jaw was smooth and clean shaven, and she ached to touch it with her fingers.

"Hey there."

She stood a moment drinking in the sight of him while her heart jumped in all kinds of directions. It had been twelve days since she'd last seen him, and they had been the longest of her existence.

Had he been following her?

Please let him have been following me.

Please no.

"Hi," she said, marshalling her thoughts.

The tense silence that followed was shattered by a terrible sound James made. It sounded like a groan mixed with a laugh, but Meredith wasn't sure.

"Could we talk?" He scraped a hand down his face—the ragged face of someone who hadn't slept for long.

Her heart went out to him. "I'm sorry, but I'm on my way to a job interview."

A flush crept up his thick neck, flaming across his lean cheeks. Again, he scraped his hand down his face. "I see. Well." He frowned and eyed the people passing by outside, then said, "I could ride with you. Or walk you there. Where are you going?"

Meredith gestured. "Third and Forty-seventh."

After an awkward moment, she led him out of the store, her coffee forgotten in her hand.

She had never noticed how noisy Manhattan was until her ears were straining to hear him say something to her.

She heard sirens. Car tires screeching. Clicks of high

heels. The slaps of cell phones. And as she walked next to him, a ripple of excitement raced to her extremities. She couldn't even remember why she had to stay away from this man; it felt too good to walk beside him.

"I dreamed about you last night." He gazed ahead, at everything but at Meredith, and plunged his hand into his pocket as he always did when he was tense. "You ran away from me, and I couldn't catch you."

His voice was a flame racing up her legs. Her breasts ached. She found his dream laughable, for she had no doubt that if he ever gave chase, she would not make him chase for long. And suddenly she did not want to talk, did not want anything but to be with him again.

"Meredith . . ."

Without looking at her, as if afraid of seeing rejection or loathing in her eyes, he reached out and stroked the back of a finger up her arm.

The touch made her sizzle through her cashmere sweater, through her skin. *Sizzle*. Meredith closed her eyes for a moment and dragged in a fortifying breath. She glanced down at her watch.

"James," she began, "I can't do this right now."

Unperturbed, he continued walking, his voice whisper soft. "When is it a good time?"

Meredith tried a smile, but it just did not make it. "Sometime when I don't have a job interview."

He laughed—the laugh that brought the butterflies inside her. "E-Doll would have you back in a blink."

She smiled tightly and refrained from saying, *It's not the same without you.* Instead she said, "I don't like Myers."

"Meredith, will you meet me after?"

Her steps didn't falter at his question, but her heartbeat did. She suddenly felt fragile, like anything would shatter her composure, her resolve to focus on herself, her career, once more.

She gazed into his gorgeous eyes while a fist of dread squeezed the breath out of her, and said, "I don't think it's a good idea."

His smile faded, but his eyes warmed with tenderness as he slipped a large, blunt-fingered hand into her hair, cupping the back of her head like he did when he kissed her. "I've had visions, too, Meredith."

"Visions," she repeated.

He cocked a brow, daring her to contradict him, and she grabbed the sleeve of his shirt and dragged him out of the crowd.

James obediently followed; then Meredith released him and stepped away, leaning one hand on the window of a Gap store. The day was mild, with the barest hint of a breeze. "Visions of what?"

"You and me."

Oh, god, he was touching her.

His hands slid into her hair. So familiar. So heart-wrenching. And his breath . . . so warm and soft. "I believe you now." He kissed behind her ear, then his mouth drifted down the slim column of her neck. "I saw you in all your lifetimes, and in all of them, Meredith, every single one, you loved me. Do you love me here?"

She trembled. His eyes glowed on her face with an intensity almost too powerful to endure, and she was swimming in need and sensation. She touched his jaw, stroked his lips with her thumb. "I don't want to love you anymore," she said, tears welling in her eyes.

"Can you choose not to? Because I'd like to know why I seem to be stuck with you. With *wanting* you."

She shivered and allowed him to draw her protectively into the warmth of his body. She gazed blindly out at the crowds passing by. "I don't know. I don't really understand it all. I guess Cherry would know about these things."

"I don't know about *these* things. All I know is . . . Christ, Meredith."

He was kissing her, the feel of his lips unmistakable on the top of her head.

She kept her eyes closed, shivering, feeling his words against her scalp, his breath on her, pretending they were alone somewhere and this wasn't noon on a Monday and she needed to be somewhere in less than ten minutes.

James slid his hands up her back.

"I'll do anything to be with you, Meredith."

His thumb rubbed across the small of her back, both soothing and arousing her.

"There's no one else for me." He grazed her lips with his and she tasted hunger there. Patience, too. "I was never really alive until I met you." Her heart pounded. Heat pooled between her legs. "And neither were you. Admit it."

He knew her.

She knew him.

Somehow, it was as if she'd been born for those hands skimming up her sides, for his breath to burst into her. His body was hot against hers, so warm, and she could feel his muscles against her, divinely familiar.

She put her finger on his lips. "I have to go."

He groaned, and it took a second for his caresses to stop. Another for his hands to leave her.

"Good-bye, James."

It was only when she reached the corner, only when she felt the excruciating pressure in her chest mount to unbearable proportions, only when she realized he was following her, that Cherry's words rang in her mind.

He has to give up something to be with you. He doesn't like giving up anything. And neither will you.

She whirled around, struck by a realization as if by lightning. "I'm the reason you quit Inctel, aren't I?"

He had been following her—but she hadn't expected him to be standing so close.

"Yes."

His admission acted like a magnet; she didn't know

if she flung herself at him or he pulled her against him. But the space between them—infinite before—became nil.

Crushing her mouth beneath his in a quick, desperate kiss, he raised his arm and summoned a cab. Then he shoved her inside, climbed in beside her, and clutched her face almost desperately. His eyes appeared exceptionally brilliant in the shadows. Meredith struggled for breath. "Do you want to be with me?"

She stared.

"You adore me; I adore you. Do you want to be with me? That's all that matters, all we need to make it work."

"Where to?" the cab driver interrupted.

Groaning, James spat out his address, and his head fell forward, against hers.

"Answer me. Jesus, answer me now." The weight of his forehead bore down on hers as his thumbs caressed her cheeks. His fast, warm breaths fanned her face.

And Meredith couldn't remember why she could not be with him, couldn't look at him and not want him fully, wholeheartedly, and completely.

"I'm not going to hurt you again. I'm not. I swear it. I'm a different man—"

She reached for his head and pulled him to her lips. "Just kiss me, James."

Their mouths latched instantly. And James grabbed her to his body and gave her a kiss so passionate, so raw, she could barely step out of the cab when they reached his building.

James urged her into the elevator and slammed her against the mirror. Meredith's moans tumbled free as they wrapped their tongues together and rubbed heatedly against each other, talking dirty. So dirty. All she heard in their haggard voices was *cock* and *fuck* and *cunt*.

They reached his floor. Then his door. Then his living room.

A tight tremble went through his great body as their tongues and arms tangled once more. He followed her down on the couch, deepening the contact of their mouths. "I need to fuck you."

She pulled him close. "I need to be fucked." She craved him, yearned for his touch and taste and smell, throbbed to have any part of him inside her. Right now. Right here.

She'd blown off a job interview—oh, god!

She rammed a hand into his slacks, and he hissed out a breath when she squeezed his erection.

"Meredith."

He licked at her mouth, urging her to kiss him again.

And as he groaned and eased her back, his lean, hard body pressing into hers, she clutched his jaw and bit at his lips. "James."

"You've no idea." He took her mouth hungrily, then slowed down and did it softly. "No idea what you do to me." He was in love with her. She could see it. And her stomach clenched because it was all there, that same look he'd given her before, lifetimes ago.

"If we ever hurt each other again, I want it to be only for pleasure," she said, allowing the truth to shine in her eyes.

He dragged his lips to her forehead. Her nose. Her cheekbone. "I'll make it ache, I promise. And then I'll make it better." He kissed her forehead, her ear, drawing her against him. Hot and strong and wonderful.

He took her earlobe between his lips and gently tugged. His breaths triggered a hot shiver as one hand enclosed the burning ache between her legs and gently squeezed. "I'm here. I'm yours, Meredith."

Instinctively seeking more, her pelvis rolled against the cup of his hand, the pleasure so great she stifled a scream. *Please, oh, please.* Her breath grew choppy. This reality was more amazing than the dreams she'd experienced.

Holding her breath, biting her lips against the tempestuous need coursing through her, she undid two buttons of her shirt with shaky fingers.

She watched him through her lashes, remembering the first time Gavin had made love to her, then she undid three more. James went still, and Meredith tugged down her bra and bared her breast. His eyes devoured her, as though he'd never before seen the mounds, the pink peaks.

When he continued gazing at her offering, she seized his jaw and drew him to her nipple. "Kiss me here."

"Oh, fuck. You've said that to me before, haven't you?"

"You remember."

"I remember everything, Meredith, everything. How I wanted you. How I loved you. How I lost you." Rubbing their bodies together, they were both panting in uncontrollable lust. "You'd let a fucking feather take you away from me, Sinclair?" He rammed his big hand between her legs, under her skirt, tickling the hairs at the apex of her thighs. "No one has ever taken you away from me except yourself."

His finger felt so right inside her pussy; she pushed against his hand to take it all in. "Because you won't give me what I need—the love I deserve."

He answered with a brush of his lips against the wet pearl of her nipple before capturing it again. "I will. I'll spend a lifetime proving my devotion to you."

"I'm still afraid," she breathed.

"The thought of you with another killed me once, Sinclair—I'm the one who should have issues." He nibbled on her lower lip, feeling his way across her mouth with gentle nips and brushes and nibbles. "Remember Kollsvein? Because I remember. I remember how I wanted you to love me, how desperate I was to prove myself worthy of you—and how I punished you in our next life for all the pain I went through. You're my past, my present. My future, Meredith."

His finger went in so deep she spread her thighs wide, wanting more. "Have your way with me, James."

"Oh, baby, I'm on it."

James wrenched his shirt over his head and sucked in a breath when her hands roamed his chest, her lips skimming across his neck, his ear, his jaw. His breath became wild. He was motionless as she undid his belt so that his aching cock could rise freely. He watched her, saying nothing, needing to say nothing at all.

His jaw clamped when she reached his navel.

Her heart was pounding hard, and her body was a mass of quaking. "Can I touch you?" She ached for his approval, his direction, his brand.

"Touch me everywhere."

"Do you want—"

"Get naked; that's what I want." He stood to remove his pants, and pulled his briefs down his long, muscled legs that were dusted with dark, silky hairs. She found it difficult to imagine a bolder, rawer image of masculinity than the one he presented. His body was all sinew, all steel, all hard. *Every*where.

Meredith wiggled out of her skirt, then yanked off her blouse. Her bra went flying.

"Good girl. Now open your legs and show me your pussy," James said silkily, a smile playing at the corner of his lips. The hard cynicism she'd seen in his eyes count-less times before had been replaced by an inexplicable warmth that made him all the more irresistible.

She lay her head back as he crawled over her. His hands clasped her behind the knees and gently spread her thighs apart for him, so he could slip his hips be-tween them as he bent over her.

"*This*," he whispered, "is me making love to you."

She shivered at the emotion in his voice.

"We've fucked before, but this . . ." Setting his weight on one arm, he rested his hand on her ribs and grazed the under curve of her breast with his thumb.

She slid her palms up his arms and those mountain-ous biceps of his, enjoying this once-lost freedom to touch him.

His hand covered her little one on his chest. He pressed it flat against his left pectoral. She had never had more sensory awareness, had never been so profoundly concentrated on what lay beneath her palms as she was now. His heart. Beating as furiously as hers. "I love you," she whispered.

He ducked his head and gave her a long, wet kiss. "I love you, too," he whispered into her mouth.

His words, spoken so tenderly, only fueled the sur-real, sinful beauty of this day. He seemed in no rush as he began kissing her stomach, between her breasts, her neck. His hands were but a feather on her skin, tracing the contour of her waist and hips. Panting, she raised her head in time to see that dark head dip between her thighs. The contact of his tongue with the very heart of her felt like an electric shock to her system, making her arch above the bed, gasping. "James."

"Shh." He kissed his way up again, loving her entire body, showing her with his caresses how truly beautiful he found it. His hands were careful, reverent, making her wonder. How was it possible that his hair could be so dark, his face so rough, his eyes so intense, and his body so powerful, yet he could touch her so gently? Love her, just now, so thoroughly?

He surged up, his hips digging between her thighs. "Hold on to me."

She wrapped her arms and legs around him, anticipation making her tremble.

He kissed her lips with a tenderness that washed over her. "Every night when I come home"—he brought a hand between their bodies and gently caressed the damp spot between her legs—"I want you soft and wet for me. I want you burning. For me."

"I *am* burning for you."

His groan was rough and drawn out as he continued to stroke, preparing her body for him. "Every morning I want you cuddled in my bed."

"Yes."

"Hmm." He licked at the seam of her lips. "And I want a kiss each morning."

Her hands slid around his shoulders, holding him tight. "Aren't two better than one?"

"Two will do." He pressed into her, clutching her hips as he delved his tongue into her mouth. "And I want to work with you, as a team, to set up our own firm together. Say yes now, Meredith. Say yes to me." With that he plunged into her, thrusting so deep and hard, she was sure he could touch all the way to her heart, and she experienced a mesmerizing sensation of oneness, a connection that went beyond the physical.

"Yes, James."

He growled and increased his tempo. "When you're good, I'll fuck you, baby. And when you're bad, I'll punish you," he vowed, licking and biting her chin. "*Then* I'll fuck you."

"Please."

"I expect you to handcuff yourself to the bed once a week—and wait for me with something stuck inside your pussy."

Feeling the start of her tremors, Meredith wildly kissed him as she rocked her hips and met each of his increasingly fast and powerful thrusts. "Oh, god, you're so debauched, James Hamilton."

"Fuck. Fuck me, Meredith. *Fuck me.*"

Her hands found their way to the hard flesh of his buttocks, desperately seeking to drive him in deeper, keep him there, inside her, forever joined.

"Yes," she said. "Yes, yes, yes."

When jolts of electricity zinged through her, she cried his name into his mouth and shuddered uncontrollably. Tensing above her, James rammed his hips one last time and released his own loud, thrumming growl.

Seconds later, James rolled off her, sprawled back more comfortably, and dragged her over his lap. Content to sit there in his arms, Meredith tucked her head under his chin and playfully circled a tiny brown nipple with the tip of one finger. "I wonder," she said, turning to press her lips into his neck, "what we should do with the feather."

His chuckle rumbled in her ear, his hand idly stroking her back. "Keep it under lock and key and away from the children."

Meredith frowned, then cautiously peered up into his face. "Children?"

James nodded somberly. "According to it, you and I are going to have quite a few."